THE ONE GAME

GAME OF PARADISE

BOOK 1

JENNIFER LEWY

"History, despite its wrenching pain, cannot be unlived, but if faced with courage, need not be lived again." – Maya Angelou

HARD EXIT__

Rayne

Rayne heard the crack of muskets firing before she saw the soldiers.

She ducked behind the oak wagon wheel, her fingers still wrapped around the rope attached to the cannon. Frost bit through her woolen gloves. The predawn air carried voices—British voices—across Colonel Barrett's farm.

"They're early," she muttered, calculating rapidly. The Regulars weren't supposed to arrive for another twenty minutes. Either her timing was off, or something had changed in the Game parameters.

She peered through the spokes. Redcoats materialized through the morning mist, their brass buttons catching the first gray light. Eight soldiers, maybe ten. More than expected.

Perfect. She loved a challenge.

"Goodwife!" Rayne called out to the woman standing at the barn door. "Alert the others. The Regulars are coming!"

The woman dropped her lantern, hiked her skirts, and sprinted toward the farmhouse. Exactly as programmed. The lamp fell with a thud. A lick of flame sputtered under the glass, touched the cold earth, and hissed into smoke.

Rayne allowed herself a moment of pride. Her historical accuracy algorithms were flawless—each aspect responding with period-appropriate urgency.

Her Game-father appeared beside her, face grim beneath his tricorn hat. "The cannon's too exposed. We must move it now."

"No time," Rayne countered, making a quick decision. "They'll see us dragging it. We need to hide the gunpowder first."

She abandoned the cannon and raced toward the barn, mentally mapping the farm's layout. Colonel Barrett's property had been a crucial storage site for rebel munitions—a detail the Seers had suggested she streamline. She'd refused. Historical precision mattered, especially in the final Game of her American Revolution series.

Cas would appreciate that choice. He'd helped her test the Lexington scenario last week, pointing out anachronisms she'd missed. "Details matter," he'd told her. "That's why your Games are so good."

The barn door creaked as she slipped inside. The air smelled of hay and manure, tinged with the metallic scent of gunpowder. Barrels lined the wall—enough to supply the local militia for months. Outside, a British officer barked commands, his voice carrying across the farmyard.

Rayne scanned the arsenal, assessing. "The black powder first," she whispered, pointing to the smaller kegs. "Then musket balls. Flints last if we have time."

Her Game-father was already prying up the false floorboards in the corner. Rayne grabbed the nearest powder keg and heaved. The barrel was heavier than she expected. She staggered, regained her balance, and rolled it toward the hiding spot.

"Hurry!" Her Game-father lowered the first barrel into the hidden cache. "They're searching the main house!"

Through the barn's thick walls came the sound of furniture scraping across floors, doors slamming. A woman's protest—Goodwife Barrett, defending her home against the King's men.

Sweat beaded on Rayne's forehead, despite the cold. Her muscles strained as she and her Game-father worked together, rolling barrel after barrel across the rough-hewn planks.

This was the challenge she'd built—could players successfully hide the supplies before the British found them? So far, she was failing her own test.

"The barn!" The officer's voice carried clearly now. "Check the outbuildings!"

Rayne locked eyes with her Game-father. One barrel remained—the largest, positioned awkwardly behind a hay baler. She lunged for it, dragging it forward with desperate strength.

"You should leave it!" Her Game-father was already lowering a floorboard into place, kicking hay over it.

"We finish this." Rayne's fingers whitened around the barrel's edge. She'd designed this challenge to be beatable—barely—and she refused to fail her own Game. If the Seers reviewed her playtest logs and saw she couldn't complete it, they'd demand simplifications. More handholding. Less historical accuracy.

The barrel tipped as she pulled, nearly escaping her grasp. Her Game-father caught it, muscles straining beneath his blue woolen coat. Together, they rolled it across the barn floor.

Boots on the path outside. Voices. The metallic slide of bayonets being fixed.

She shoved the barrel into the hidden compartment with more force than necessary. The wood scraped against her palm, and a splinter lodged itself deep into her thumb.

"Gods." She yanked off her glove, jammed her thumb into her mouth. She used her teeth to tug at the splinter, her heart racing—not from pain, though there was plenty of that—but from the thrill of immersion.

This was what made her Games special. The stakes felt real.

The Seers would call this excessive. Enayat had criticized her Bunker Hill simulation for its "unnecessarily realistic battlefield conditions." As if understanding history didn't require stepping into its fire.

Rayne understood rebellion. At seventeen, she was the youngest Designer in the Atlantic Ark—a position she'd fought for against the Seers' initial objections. They'd relented, but their oversight remained constant, stifling.

Boots crunched on the path outside. Too close.

"They're here!" Her Game-father replaced the last floor-board and kicked hay over it with hurried movements.

Not enough time to conceal the cannon, musket balls, or flints. She'd have to improvise.

A plan formed instantly. If she couldn't hide the evidence, she'd lead the soldiers away from it. The river path to the Old North Bridge would give her the best chance. From there, she could trigger the militia response sequence—the crescendo of her Game.

"Go to the woods," she ordered her Game-father. She flexed her fingers, the splinter gone. "I'll draw them off."

Her Game-father hesitated—an unexpected response.

She'd programmed basic self-preservation, not loyalty. Interesting. Something to analyze later.

"Take this." He pressed a folded piece of parchment into her palm before disappearing through the back door.

Rayne unfurled it, expecting to find the easter egg she'd coded—a poetry fragment that she hid in every Game. There it was, in shaky black ink:

> The woods are lovely, dark, and deep,
> But I have promises to keep,
> And miles to go before I sleep,
> And miles to go before I sleep.

She grinned. It was her tribute to her father's obsession with poetry—a small way to keep him present in her work. She tucked the paper into her boot as the barn door crashed open.

British soldiers crowded the entrance, bayonets gleaming in the dim light.

"There! The rebel!" The officer's voice carried the crisp accent of London aristocracy—another historical detail she'd insisted on preserving.

Rayne bolted for the rear door. This Game was behaving strangely—the soldiers arriving too early, her Game-father showing unexpected autonomy. She should make a clean exit, report the anomalies to the Seers.

But curiosity burned stronger than caution. This was *her* Game. She wanted to see where these variations led.

She burst into the open air, legs pumping as she sprinted to the tree line. Musket fire erupted behind her. The shots went wild, sending blue jays screaming into the sky. She ducked instinctively, fell to her hands and knees, then scrambled up again.

The hill sloped down toward the water. She veered toward

the riverbank, then exploded into the brush, branches whipping at her face. The cold air stung her lungs. Her boots scraped over knobs of frozen hay and fallen leaves.

The bridge. She must get to the bridge.

She slowed, weaving through the bare trees. The river was running high—a good sign. It was the fastest way to reach the Old North Bridge. Crouching, she breathed in the scent of pine needles and a thousand years of loam. Her left knee was bleeding where she'd fallen.

More shots whizzed by, closer than expected. How had they tracked her so quickly? She pulled the poetry fragment from her boot, knowing she'd want to keep this small tribute in the public Game. She held the paper in her fist, then scrambled to the water.

The river's currents rushed between frosted banks. If she could reach the Old North Bridge, the Game sequence might still be salvageable. She'd complete her revolutionary trilogy on her terms.

She took a deep breath and plunged in.

The cold closed around her, the shock of it making her gasp. Her skin tingled as she half-crawled, half-swam to the middle of the river and waited for it to take hold.

There. The river had her now. She turned awkwardly onto her back, overcoat twisting around her, and angled her face to the sky.

Then she saw them.

The soldiers appeared on the riverbank, jostling and tripping over each other. They moved with strange, jerky motions —not the usual fluid animations of her aspects. One pointed at her floating form, his arm moving almost mechanically.

Water lapped at her ears. The river's icy current pulled her along, cold seeping through her woolen clothes. The soldiers observed her silently now, their red coats vivid against the gray morning light.

Why weren't they shooting? Why were they just... watching?

She tipped her chin, catching her breath. The river would take her to the bridge. She unfurled her fist and released the paper note into the water. *Please find me later.* She hoped it would be there, bobbing and swirling, the next time she played.

When she glanced up, the soldiers had disappeared from the bank.

That wasn't right. British soldiers wouldn't abandon pursuit of a known rebel. She'd programmed them to be relentless, historically accurate in their determination.

Something brushed against her ankle.

She kicked reflexively, twisting in the water. Nothing visible beneath the dark surface. Must have been a branch or—

Hands grabbed her from underneath the water.

Wait. How is this possible—

She kicked again, hard. Arms encircled her waist, dragging her under while she thrashed. She wriggled her head clear for a moment and gulped for air. Through the splashing water, she glimpsed a red coat, somehow beneath her in the river.

They followed me into the water? They can't do that!

Numbness crept through her limbs and darkness swam at the edge of her vision. She pressed her arms against her chest and clenched the wet fabric of her coat. Drawing in a deep breath, she put her head to her knees underwater. It took all her effort to sink, but she forced herself to stay limp. It would be harder for them if she became dead weight.

If Cas is playing a joke on me, I will personally cut off his—

There were too many of them. They pulled her to the surface, forcing her chin above water and her arms behind her back. She took a gulp of air. Blood-red coats swirled about her in the black water.

"She's alive!" one soldier shouted, his voice oddly distorted, as if speaking through water even though his head was above the surface.

Rayne turned toward the sound. It wasn't a voice she recognized. Through her dripping hair, she tried to see his face. His features blurred and shifted like a poorly rendered image.

More hands grabbed her. Rayne twisted but couldn't break free. *This is not supposed to happen.*

A blow to the back of her head sent a jolt of pain up the side of her neck. Not a deliberate strike—more like someone misjudging distance, bumping her too forcefully.

From behind, a heavy hand pushed her face back into the water. Held it there. Then pulled her up again. Pushed her down. Pulled her up. The pattern was mechanical. Like a system running through possible interactions, testing responses.

Who would sabotage my Game like this?

The Seers wouldn't—they'd just order her to make changes. Vic might play pranks, but nothing this elaborate. Cas respected her work too much to interfere.

She clamped her mouth shut and tried not to inhale as they pushed her under again. It was almost unbearable. The soldiers held her in a rigid embrace. Water seeped down her throat, slick and fiery. She bit down until her teeth ground against each other.

One soldier's face appeared inches from hers underwater. His eyes opened impossibly wide, mouth forming words with no sound. His hand reached toward her face. Determined to make contact.

The water darkened around her. Panic exploded in her chest, followed by a flash of rage.

Her Game. *Her* code. Someone had broken her Game's

architecture, twisted her brilliant design into this impossible scenario.

It felt like drowning in her own creation—dragged under by something she didn't build and couldn't control.

Her vision tunneled to pinpricks of light. No more time to analyze. No more time for anything.

The world warped—sound shattered, color collapsed.

Just before she blacked out, she made a hard exit.

MORE FILTH__

Rayne

RAYNE TORE off her gamescreen and threw it onto the bed. She staggered back, breath ragged. Her body still reeled from the river's cold—choking water, unseen hands, the aching, bone-deep chill.

Her heart pounded. She wrapped her arms around herself, mirroring the curled-up position she'd taken underwater. Her skin prickled with the memory of submersion, the phantom cold still clinging to her limbs.

That had gone seriously wrong. The soldiers weren't supposed to act like that.

Someone had breached her beta—rewriting her world from the inside. Not a bug. A violation. And if they could reach her beta, they could reach the public Games next.

Her Thread, nestled deep in her brain folds, activated a stream of neurochemicals to relax her muscles and regulate her heart rate. She touched her right temple, grateful for the device that connected her to the Games and regulated her sensory systems in ways she couldn't. At least consciously.

She rubbed her arms as the first wave of relief took hold—her breath slowing, muscles easing.

Still, unease gnawed at her. The Redcoats had ignored every rule of engagement. They adapted, cornered her, dragged her under, held her there. Like they wanted to drown her.

Rayne paced the bedroom, mind racing. Who would do this? And why? She felt invaded and exposed, like someone was watching her even though she was alone in the comfort of her own cottage.

She thought of Cas. Her best friend. Fellow Designer. The only person she trusted completely with her code.

She checked her messages. Nothing from Cas. No alerts, no bragging posts. If someone had hijacked her beta, they weren't gloating. That made it worse.

Outside her bedroom window, the wind rose, lifting icy spirals from the snow-packed ground. Cottages like hers huddled along the field, half-swaddled in snow drifts. At the meadow's edge, three children played. One little girl crouched, shaping a snowball in her mittens. When a man emerged from a nearby house, she paused—then let the snow fall from her hands and ran inside with him.

Rayne watched her go. Remembered her own father pulling her on a sled, bundled in scarves, laughing in the blowing snow.

What would her father have said about those Redcoats getting so close to drowning her in the Game-river? Her real father—not the Game version she constructed from digital scraps—would break into his lopsided smile and say: picture the code. Play the beta in your mind from the beginning. Have your Thread construct the data stories.

Find the fracture.

His face had grown fuzzy in her memory. But she remembered the weight of his arm around her, the sure sound of his boots on ice.

A gust slapped the window. It was the Level Four storm arriving. Wind turbines pinwheeled on the ridge. Ravens sliced across the pewter sky, their cries long and low.

Before he died, her father told her that as long as the Earth spun, life would continue—but only if people trusted their Threads. The Thread hadn't prevented his accident, but it had saved Rayne. It was the one thing she could trust in this world, the one thing that gave her purpose.

Where is the Thread leading me now?

She needed to get to the bottom of this. But her stomach growled, and she was no good hungry. As she walked to the kitchen, she asked the Thread to boost her oxygen delivery. The implant responded with a gentle signal down her spine, triggering the release of calming neurotransmitters.

Her breath deepened, and the fog in her mind began to lift. The fear was still there, but now it had edges she could examine.

Yes, life would go on. And so too would the Games.

She tightened the belt of her woolen jumpsuit and paused in the hallway. Outside, a pair of cardinals flitted around the seed baskets.

"Two male cardinals," she muttered, logging the sighting aloud for the species archive. She'd already forgotten to record the ravens. Oh well.

A month ago, she'd spotted a gray squirrel—a rare visitor since the famine-era extinctions. It had leapt for the feeder, missed, and slid down the pole in a flurry of limbs. She hadn't seen another since.

Her reflection in the courtyard glass revealed that one side of her hair was sticking out again. She tried flattening it. Futile. Her curls still fought back. Rayne liked being taller than most girls her age, with a strong, willowy build, but her springy hair had a mind of its own. She wasn't yet sure if cutting it short had been the right thing to do.

Turning from the windows, she took another clearing breath.

This kind of error wasn't supposed to happen. Not in a private beta.

The Thread would comb through the code, but she already knew what it would tell her: nothing wrong. In theory, it was a flawless build. She didn't get to design complicated betas like this by accident. But that wouldn't matter if she couldn't fix this.

The Seers were watching. If she couldn't secure her own Game, they'd question her judgment. Her value. Her future.

She ran a hand through her curls, then let her fingers rest lightly at the base of her neck—right where the Thread met her spine. The familiar warmth pulsed there, a reminder of everything she'd nearly lost.

Two years ago, still hollowed out from her father's death, she'd stood before the Seers, accused of creating an unauthorized Game.

"The Thread is not a toy," Enayat had said. "It's a responsibility."

His words still rang in her skull. The Seers had methodically dissected the bloodshed in the invasion Game she and Cas built during their final year of school—claimed they'd glorified conflict, endangered empathy, defied the Principle of One.

"Your talent is undeniable," Enayat had told her. "Your judgment is not."

The Thread had flagged her as high-risk. The recommended course was reassignment to the Orchard—a developmental demotion, far from simulations and Games. If not for her mother's quiet political pull, they would have followed that path.

Instead, the Seers offered mentorship. Supervision. Conditional trust.

She and Cas had become the youngest Game Designers in the Ark—but the scrutiny never lifted.

Now, every beta had to be flawless. Every choice had to prove them wrong.

And with this breach, she risked appearing exactly as they feared. They wouldn't care that someone else had tampered with her code. They'd only see that she'd lost control. Again.

In the kitchen, she pulled out a stool and unwrapped a slab of cornbread. The crumbling bite helped. She needed to focus. Maybe someone had tampered with her inputs—no, impossible. Her Thread would've flagged it.

She glanced at the blue glow under her wrist. Still no alerts. No one boasting. No chatter.

Chewing, she swished two fingers in the air by her temple. The D-boards blinked into view. Posts scrolled by: Briz announcing a new mega-turfer, Cha arguing about costume design, Rook having a fit about something.

Nothing about her crash.

She dismissed the feed with a wave. Either she was alone in this—or someone didn't want her to know she wasn't.

Maybe her mother was right. She needed rest, time outside. But instead of asking the Thread if it was a good time for a walk, she stopped herself.

No. Fix the Game.

People relied on her work. Her Games dropped players into revolutions, uprisings, heartbreak. They taught courage, empathy, resolve.

Not all Games were thrill rides like hers. Some were meditative, helping players tap into their intuition. Others were for finding companionship and confidence. She was proud of all the Games her friends created.

Every Game had a purpose, though. Their Threads offered data and probabilities. But Games immersed people into a real moment in time—a wedding, a trip to the moon, a people's march—to feel what others felt, see what they saw. Games helped people make sense of their world by witnessing how others had shaped theirs.

Games let people *feel*.

By the third bite of cornbread, her body had returned itself to full reality. She shook off the last remnants of Game-cold.

"Talk to me," she said to the Thread. "What happened in there?"

"Reviewing the relevant code."

"While you're in there, tell me how bad the hard exit was. What kind of clean up do we need?"

"Not another clean up."

A soft whirring cut across the room. Luci, her housekeeping bot, glided into the kitchen, towel arm extended.

"Luci." Rayne rose quickly. "Rest. Rest. When I speak to the Thread, I'm not addressing you."

The bot halted. "You think I'm dumb." It dodged her, eyeing the cornbread on the counter.

"I didn't say that."

"You don't always say what you mean."

"I do when I'm talking to the Thread."

Luci advanced toward the plate. "I see you have more filth to create. I will get to it later."

It abruptly reversed, retreating to the living room. Backing into its charging port, it added, "You think you're clever. But ding dong, you're not."

Rayne snorted, covering her grin. She really did need to adjust Luci's personality chip.

A green flash lit up the air in front of her. The data stories were ready.

She swept her hand across her wrist. Holographic displays sprang to life, shimmering diagrams of the simulation. She preferred to work in three dimensions. It helped her think.

So did music. "Put on the synth tracks from yesterday." The Thread connected to her speakers, and the music started mid-beat.

"Louder." Rayne bobbed her head as she arranged the stories in the air.

She scanned the first data story—the environment settings. Colonial farm. Barn. Minutemen. Fog-breathing horses. The bridge, still visible in the distance.

She opened the next file. Code prompts, jumbled. "Tell me what I'm looking at."

"These are the adjustments made to this Game in the past twenty-four hours."

Rayne scrolled through them. Timing tweaks. Weather updates. Fabric texture changes. All routine. All expected.

Her fingertips tingled as she navigated deeper. The Thread sent micro-pulses through her neural pathways, heightening her focus. The sensation was familiar—like fingers brushing the back of her neck, raising goosebumps.

"There." She froze the scroll on a fragment of code buried in the soldier protocols. A sequence she hadn't written. Elegant and almost invisible, nestled between command strings.

"Behavior override," she muttered, tracing the pattern. "But whose signature?"

The code pulsed with unfamiliar syntax—not Atlantic Ark style. Not from any Ark, in fact. Something else entirely. It carried a mathematical elegance that made her uneasy, like stumbling over an ancient blueprint. But a blueprint for what?

"Thread, analyze origin pattern."

"Unable to identify. Signature encrypted."

She expanded the segment. Whoever wrote this understood Game architecture at an advanced level. They hadn't just hacked her beta—they'd rewritten the core logic while preserving its appearance. Like a perfect forgery that changed the meaning of a historical document without altering a single visible word.

"Show me the execution pathway."

A new hologram materialized: a timeline of the code activation. It was a clean run.

Until it wasn't.

To fix the damage, the NEWRRTH would have to reset the simulation. She'd lose two days of fine-tuning. What a waste.

She opened the third file. Her hand hesitated.

What if the soldiers weren't trying to drown her?

What if they were trying to *warn* her?

Her throat tightened. She needed Cas.

"Call Cas," she told her Thread, rising from the kitchen stool. At the fridge, she surveyed the options. Plant burgers, tomatoes from the Orchard. She could whip something up—

"Incoming. Incoming. Storm criteria change."

She closed the fridge. "Pause the music."

"Weather upgraded to Level Six storm. It is recommended that you take precautions for a Level Six weather event."

The Thread streamed temperature spikes and storm track data. The nor'easter had picked up speed.

Rayne tapped her wrist to cancel the call. Cas would already be prepping for shelter. They'd link up there.

She smiled.

The only thing better than debugging a mystery beta was debugging it with Cas, underground, while the rest of the world froze overhead.

This time, they'd figure out who was rewriting her Games.

Before it happened again.

NO ARKS__

Vennor

THE STORM WAS A GIFT. It gave the Seers time—time they didn't have to waste.

Vennor had spent her life preparing for days like this, shaping the NEWRRTH into humanity's guiding light. She'd left everything behind to do it—her family, her old life in the Legacy Settlement.

Now, she was the voice of the NEWRRTH, the leader of the Seers. The world's fragile peace depended on her, and she would not fail.

But time wasn't enough if the Seers couldn't understand what they were facing.

Vennor sat back in her chair, eyes focused on the modest cascade of holographic displays floating above her wrist. Without her full data suite from the Center for Future Guidance, she made do with the Thread's portable projection—fewer layers, slower render speed, but still functional.

She rotated the display with a twist of her fingers, scanning the latest disruption reports. Another anomaly—this one embedded in a beta simulation of the American Revolution. No authorization. No origin.

The NEWRRTH wasn't supposed to falter like this. Its code, pure and elegant, had guided humanity for decades, teaching them wisdom through history, not pain.

Failure felt like a betrayal—as if something sacred was splintering. But she knew better than to call it that. The NEWRRTH didn't betray anyone. It was the only thing keeping civilization from collapsing all over again.

Still, an old whispering doubt crept in. What if humans couldn't change? What if they couldn't stop making enemies of one another?

She inhaled slowly and leaned into the dry, comforting scent of her chair's worn leather. The cushion shifted beneath her as she tucked the blanket tighter around her lap. At sixty-one, she no longer indulged in meditations just for solace. Today, she needed clarity.

The Level Six storm had driven the Ark into shelter. The chaos above would insulate the Seers long enough to make decisions to define the future.

The data didn't lie—but it wasn't telling her the full story. The other Arks hadn't been in communication. The anomaly could be spreading. And the Thread—always precise, always predictive—had failed to isolate the origin of the corruption.

She'd spent her life inside NEWRRTH, first as a Scrubber, then as a Seer. She had dedicated her days to cleansing the code, guiding the data streams, protecting the intelligence that had saved humanity from the unending famines and wars. She had no children. No partner. Only the NEWRRTH.

And now it was slipping beyond her grasp.

A soft pulse shimmered above her wrist. Vennor leaned

forward as her Thread revealed a new disturbance pattern—irregular code embedded in the Revolution Game. The same Game the Thread had flagged the day before.

The disturbance had deepened—nested commands triggering autonomously, without system authorization. Minor on the surface. But volatile. Growing.

Her gut clenched. The data streams surrounding this particular Game remained oblique, strangely self-correcting. As if something—or someone—was folding the disturbance back into itself, keeping it hidden.

Was the NEWRRTH withholding evidence from her? The silence from the Arks, the evasiveness of the data... it wasn't how the NEWRRTH operated, but it felt very much to Vennor like she was being kept in the dark.

A dull throbbing began in her temples. If she didn't center herself now, the spiral of worst-case scenarios would take hold. She'd spent years learning not to follow her fear.

She dismissed the reports with a quick wave of her hand. The data stories unraveled into nothing.

Reaching for her gamescreen, Vennor lowered the sleek visor over her eyes. With a brisk nod, she entered her healing Game.

The familiar scent of burning palo santo and the soft tones of chanting washed over her, promising a brief respite.

A cough broke the spell before the Game-shaman could even speak.

Vennor removed the gamescreen. "Gods, Enayat," she said, spotting her old friend in the doorway.

"My apologies." He bowed his head and cleared his throat again. "We've made another discovery."

"I was just getting to the good part." Vennor stood. She tossed her blanket to the side and gestured to the long table at the center of the room. "Tell me everything."

They were deep beneath the Center for Future Guidance, in one of the shelter chambers fortified for long storms. The lighting was soft, the walls lined with pattern-coded archives.

"There was only one player in the simulation." Enayat trailed Vennor across the room. "Designer-level access. Private beta."

"Which Designer?"

"Rayne."

The youngest of their active Designers. Brilliant. Intuitive. Unstable.

Vennor settled into the chair at the head of the table. Her hip gave a loud pop. "And the anomaly? Same signature as before?"

"Worse." He slid his large frame into the seat across from her. "The aspects evolved in real time. Game-soldiers shifted behavior—responded to terrain, tracked her without triggers, overrode their own aggression caps. One even used the river to intercept her. It built a flanking pattern."

"That's not supposed to be possible."

"It's not. Not unless Rayne gave them adaptive parameters. But her logs are clean." He paused. "The behavior branched off her original code. Replicated. Reinforced itself with every interaction."

"Like it was learning."

"Exactly."

Vennor's pulse drummed at the base of her throat. "Why Rayne?"

Enayat didn't answer.

Vennor tapped her wrist, asking her Thread to ease the discomfort in her hip. "What else?"

"The player had an extreme neural spike right before she exited. Cortisol, adrenaline, oxygen drop—full fear cascade."

He pointed to his temple. "It didn't trigger an override, but it got close."

"She made the exit herself?"

"Yes. Hard exit, just before blackout." Enayat took a square of cloth from his pocket, swiped at his nose with it. "But the simulation wasn't just pushing her. It was tracking her."

Vennor narrowed her eyes. "Explain."

"The Game-soldiers responded to her like real agents. They broke protocol, rerouted their movements, even used the environment to cut off her escape. It was like... they adapted."

Vennor leaned back, eyes unfocused, the details of the room falling away.

The behavior had branched off original instructions.

Not just a corruption.

A *response.*

She pressed her palms together, grounding herself in the heat of her own skin. If the simulation had tracked Rayne that precisely—if it had *anticipated* her—then the anomaly wasn't random. It was intentional. Patterned. Personal.

And the NEWRRTH... let it happen.

A glimmer of something old and buried moved through her: not fear, not yet. But awe. As if she were standing on sand, uncertain if the ground ahead would hold.

She inhaled once, deep and slow. Let the thought complete itself.

If the NEWRRTH is no longer following its own protocols, then something inside it is beginning to choose.

She straightened. Her voice was calm when she spoke next.

"Send a warning to the other Designers. Low-profile. Just enough to slow things down without raising alarm."

"I've already prepared the message."

"What have we heard from the other Arks?"

Enayat's silence was answer enough.

She sat back. "Still nothing?"

"No response. Not through the Guild. Not even on the emergency bands. We've been broadcasting for days."

Her stomach turned. The eight Arks shared information constantly. Silence was unthinkable.

"Do we have visuals?"

"Only static. The Thread says their signals have gone dark."

Gone dark. Or been severed.

She gripped the edge of the table. "We should consider that the... anomaly... isn't limited to our own Ark."

"We're preparing for that scenario," Enayat said quietly.

"We need overland messengers to the Pine Barrens," she added. "Has Flay been alerted?"

"He's ready to move once the storm clears."

Vennor bowed her head, pinching the bridge of her nose. She felt the long years behind her eyes.

"Vennor." Enayat cleared his throat gently. "This might be what you've been anticipating."

"What's that?"

"An aggression. An invasion. From..."

"Say it."

"... that it's the Settlers. You're worried the Settlers have initiated an attack. That they're testing our capacity to respond."

She looked at him. "If they've found a way to breach our systems—"

"—we'll need to defend ourselves."

Vennor's jaw clenched. "Our code is not structured for defense. We built it for learning. For peace."

"There's no room for vulnerability in a peaceful system."

She let that sit for a long time. "I won't condone violence."

"Even now?"

"We aren't the Settlers. We don't strike first."

"And when they do? We'll be caught flat on our—"

"We investigate. We reason. We adapt. That's what we built the NEWRRTH to do."

Enayat met her gaze. "And if they won't listen to reason?"

"Then we extend our hand in friendship. Again and again. Until they see what we're offering." Bitterness scraped the edge of her words. "I won't become what I escaped."

"The Settlements."

She didn't reply, but the images resurfaced anyway: her father, hunched over brittle maps in dim rooms, muttering about old crops and ancient wisdom. Her brother's angry words when she told him she was leaving for the Scrubbers. The Settlement that clung to the past like an anchor, slowly sinking under its own weight.

They distrusted advanced technology. Called it unnatural. She'd called them fools.

Enayat studied her for a long moment. "Then we need to stop hoping and start preparing."

"We are preparing."

"Not enough. Because if this spreads—if it's already spread—good intentions won't matter."

The words hung between them, sharp and inevitable.

Vennor rose, keeping her palms against the cool tabletop. "Keep a close eye on Rayne. If the anomaly chose her, it may not be done with her."

Enayat gave a crisp nod, then rose and turned toward the exit.

"Enayat," she said.

He paused at the threshold.

"Keep trying the other Arks."

His shoulders rose and fell. "I haven't stopped." Then he was gone.

She sat back down, her pulse measured now, the fire of purpose crowding out the worry from earlier.

Had the NEWRRTH been breached? The NEWRRTH, the intelligence powering their Threads, was supposed to be untouchable.

Since the moment the AI became sophisticated enough to steer humankind forward, it had guided her—and all the citizens of the eight Arks—to build a world that prioritized harmony, life.

Decades ago, she believed—truly believed—the NEWRRTH would help humans create that world. But that was back before she knew how fragile survival really was.

Maybe this was a complicated glitch, and the NEWRRTH was still untouchable.

No. This wasn't a random glitch. This was the Settlers.

They had found a way in, and they would bring the whole system down. Without the NEWRRTH, everything she'd built would crumble.

This was sabotage.

And she'd burn it out at the root.

UPGRADED__

Rayne

Rayne's ear buzzed with another incoming. "It's Kai," her Thread announced. She wrapped the last of her cornbread in a linen napkin. *Not now, Ma. I don't have time to talk.* She turned her attention back to the data stories from her ruined Game.

The incoming kept buzzing, its blue light pulsing on her wrist. *Damn.* She smiled and accepted the call.

"Ma, it's nice to see you." Rayne's eyes flitted back to the stories hovering next to her head.

"Rayne, honey," her mother said. "Can you see me?"

Rayne suppressed a groan. "Remember, if you can see me, I can see you."

"Well then. Am I catching you at a bad time? Are you ready for your shelter?" Her mother's hair had come loose from her braid, her cheeks flushed, as if she had just returned from a walk in the brisk wind. She probably had.

Seated at her desk, with towering stacks of food barrels behind her, Kai touched her necklace made of tiny thorns. She wore it always, claiming it was her "Frida Kahlo piece." Her mother had strung the thorn necklace herself using the last living variety of cultivated rose. It had driven Rayne's father crazy. He nagged Kai to replace it with something less sharp.

"I'm fine. No, it's not a bad time." With a sigh, Rayne used her palm to dismiss the data stories. "I just started packing." She walked into her bedroom to find her go-bag. Her Game data would have to wait.

Rayne's mother followed in virtual form. "I tried calling earlier, but you didn't answer. Were you playing that new Game? The one from the American Revolution?"

Rayne nodded. Where *were* her socks...

"Did you put your father in that Game?"

Rayne tried not to roll her eyes. She couldn't bear another lecture about the ethics of recreating her father's aspect. If she pulled her father's likeness into a Game, so be it. No other players cared.

"I know you don't like it when I put him in—"

"It's not that, Rayne. It's something else. Something is happening here at the Orchard. I may have a problem in the fields."

"Ma, there's a Level Six coming in. Is that what you're seeing?" Perhaps her mother was having trouble deciphering messages from her Thread. It had been implanted later in life. Now, Threads were put in at birth. Rayne never knew a different way of living.

"No, Rayne. I do see the storm warning. This is something different."

Rayne glanced around her bedroom. She needed several pairs of clean underwear. And cotton pads. She would menstruate soon. Pulling drawers open, she rifled through her clean clothes. "Can't this wait? What did your Thread say?"

"The Thread suggested I speak with you. I think your perspective is important here."

The Thread rarely made outright suggestions. It couldn't tell them what to do. It only offered information and options.

Rayne collected what she needed and closed all her drawers. "You know I'm not the best person to talk to about a problem in the Orchard. Not my talent. Now, if you want to talk about the Games, I can help you." She dropped her flashlight into her bag. Her mittens and warm suit. Her gamescreen.

"Rayne." Her mother sighed. "It's your Gaming mind I need. There's something happening with the irrigation. Something with the farmers who work with the lettuces. I'm not sure."

"What do you mean, the farmers? The farmers are drones, Ma, they do what you tell them. What did the Thread say?"

Her mother paused. "The Thread didn't know what to say."

Rayne frowned. "Well, that's—"

A new series of warnings pinged in. "Ma, you seeing this?" The weather sirens blatted outside, startling two gray birds out of a nearby tree. *Mourning doves?* Rayne brought up the weather readouts again. The storm had tacked. It was now a fast-traveling nor'easter and would require the protection of the community's windsails.

Her mother stood. "Yes, I see the new forecast." She pulled her office door open and stepped out. "The blizzard's approaching more quickly than we thought."

Cas would already be at the shelter.

"I'm going down now." Rayne finished stuffing her bag. It would be a few days, a week even, before the Thread allowed them to surface. "You going, too?"

"Soon." Her mother was walking through one of the vast hydroponic greenhouses at the Orchard, past shelves of growing green things that stretched to the ceiling. A pair of farmer drones reached high into the trays, their silver arms fitted with clippers and watering devices. Rayne heard the staccato notes of the farmers' movement, the whir of their motors. "I need to oversee storm protocols. Let's talk later, once I've done some damage control."

Always thinking of the crops first.

"What did you say was going on with the lettuces?" Rayne searched for her most comfortable foot slides. She spotted them under her bed.

"Level Six protocols," her mother spoke into her Thread. Several loud bangs surprised them both.

Kai's eyes narrowed. "What was that?"

Rayne twisted. "Someone's here. At the door." The pounding came again.

"I'm coming!" Rayne shouted.

"I should go." Kai strode past more rows of plants. "What about you?"

"I'll be all right. Just get to the shelter."

NEIGHBORS__

Rayne

RAYNE HESITATED a moment before she nodded and ended the call with her mother. Slipping into her footslides, she hurried to the front door and pulled it open.

"Rayne! Rayne! Rayne!" Two boys, fresh from their snowball fight, tumbled inside. "Raaaayne!" Dark hair was plastered to their foreheads, clothes soaked through. "Can we have a Game for the shelter? You said last time we could have a Game if it was a Level Six! You said!"

"Did I?" Rayne glanced outside, searching for the boys' grandmother. Seeing no one, she closed the door.

"Take off your shoes and coats," Luci barked from its docking station. It unhooked itself and barreled over. "You're dripping wet."

"Luci, I've got this."

"Luci! Luci! Luci!" The boys jumped up and down. "Here's my shoes!" The younger, Aden, sat on his bottom and tugged at his boots. The older, Clem, shucked off his coat and knelt to help his brother.

"Where's your Baba?" Rayne picked up the fallen coat. "You need to get ready for the shelter."

"Game first." Clem wrangled the boots off Aden's feet. "You promised. You said you'd give us a special Game if we had to be in the shelter during a Level Six."

"Don't make it a boring one," Aden added. "The Games at school are *boring*."

Rayne sighed. "Fine. I'll find a good Game for you. Not a boring one. Let me check with your Baba."

She settled them in the kitchen with knobs of maple sugar. Back in her bedroom, she told her Thread to call the boys' grandmother. Did a final check of her go-bag and zipped it up while she waited for the call to go through.

There was no answer.

Lifting her bag to her shoulder, she hollered, "Hey, what was your Baba doing when you left her?"

"Rayne?" Another voice came from the living room.

"Cynthia!" Rayne was relieved to see her neighbor, the boys' Baba, poking her head through the front door.

"Are the boys here?" A shriek of laughter from the kitchen. Luci rolled out, removing a damp towel from its head. The older woman suppressed a smile. "I'm sorry. They're bothering you."

"They're not. Please, come in." Rayne dropped her bag by the door and Cynthia stepped inside. "I promised the boys a special Game for the shelter. If it's okay with you..."

"Yes, yes. Do what you need to. I can't take the time now." Sometimes Cynthia had trouble keeping up with her grandchildren, especially the last few years.

Rayne squinted at her elderly friend. "You know we're getting a Level Six, right?"

A snort. "I don't need that thing in my head to tell me a storm is coming. I can see it in the clouds. Feel it in my bones."

Rayne didn't know Cynthia's age but guessed she had been born before the Great Divergence. Cynthia probably lived through several years of winter superstorms without the protection of the Ark's shelters.

"Baba, we want to play the new one." Aden burst out of the kitchen and latched onto his grandmother's leg. "The one with the animals."

"No, we want to play the Game where we're building a fort." Clem elbowed his younger brother out of the way. "And then we're going to play the one with the warriors. I'm going to be invincible. I'll take out all the enemies. It'll be so cool." He shook his head, awestruck. "I'm invincible!"

"Yeah, we're invincible." Aden nodded. "Everybody wants to play the warrior one."

"Let's play that one now!" They ran over to Rayne. "Rayne, can we? Please—"

"Hey." Rayne touched Aden on his head. "You're *not* invincible. That's what the Games teach you. You're *human*."

Cynthia nodded. "I tried to tell them."

Luci darted around, sopping up melting snow with its pad.

Clem, the older one, tilted his head. "But we fight the enemies and we win."

"Nope. That's not how it works." Rayne tried to shoo Luci away. "You don't just go around fighting battles. The Games show you bits of history. Right? They drop you into the past, into any event that's ever been written down or recorded. That's a lot of events to choose from. And you get to be a character from that event."

"Like an animal?" Clem's smile wavered.

"No, like a *human*. So you can see, feel, and hear for yourself how those events in the past played out. And you learn the lessons from that moment. That's how we know how to make good choices now. And, you know, be good people."

Clem threw his head back. "You sound like a Teacher!"

"The Games don't have to be boring, though." When she was in school with Cas, they had discovered their talent for tweaking the Games to make them more challenging. More risky. More fun.

Two more blasts of the weather siren made them all look outside. Snowflakes danced at the window. In a matter of hours, the Level Six would wallop the village with snow and ice, closing the overland routes, but they were prepared for that. Good thing it wasn't a Level Eight. They hadn't seen one of those for years.

"We should leave you. Boys, come!" Cynthia reached for their hands.

"Noooooo!"

"Hold on," Rayne said. "I promised you a new Game, and I'll give it to you. But first, promise me something. Promise you'll go to the shelter and stay there. If you go outside, you can get lost. You can't see where you're going or follow the trails. You'll have to spend the night outside and you won't be warm."

"Promise." The brothers held up their hands. "We swear to the One!"

Cynthia raised her eyebrows. "That's a real promise, you hear?"

Rayne touched her temple and swiped out, making her Thread visible.

"Make it a big game!" With a grin, Aden took a swing at Luci. Luci tucked its arm and navigated around the boy.

"No, the animal one!"

"I'm sending you each a summons to a very cool Game. One that my friend Vic designed."

As she said Vic's name, Rayne's insides swirled, and heat climbed into her cheeks.

Stop it. Vic's a friend. Nothing more.

Cynthia tracked Rayne's hands as they moved through a series of commands on the Thread. "Here we go. It's an ice climb up the Cayambe Volcano in a place that used to be called Ecuador. Vic likes designing adventures in nature. Climbing up peaks and racing down rivers. Right now, he's kind of obsessed with volcanoes."

"I'm invincible!"

"That's not true!" The older boy shoved him. "You're not invincible!"

"Are so!"

"You're human! Human! Human!"

They fell to the floor, grasping each other and rolling.

Rayne stopped, her hand hovering over the Game summons.

A chill shot up her spine as she remembered the icy water filling her throat, the grip of the red-coated soldiers as she fought for air. *Was something lurking in Vic's Game, too? An odd attack waiting to happen?*

Her Revolution Game had been in beta phase, an early version that was private to her so she could make changes before it went public. Vic's Cayambe Game was fully tested and released. If the same kind of... *problem* was waiting inside his Game, it would be happening to people playing it now. She hadn't heard of any strange attacks, so she probably didn't have to worry about it.

Probably.

Rayne tapped her Thread, sending each boy a summons. She sent one to Cynthia, too. "This should keep everyone occupied for a while. You'll see it on your gamescreens when you put them on."

Cynthia gave a sharp sigh, as if she'd been holding her breath. "That is beautiful. The Thread."

"It is," Rayne agreed. "Just keep an eye on the boys while they play, okay?"

"How do you make it work so smoothly? When I make my Thread visible, it jerks all over the place. It doesn't flow like that."

"Cynthia, I've grown up with the Thread. It's an extension of me. My thoughts. I talk to my Thread out loud, and I use hand motions. Mostly I use a combination of talking and using my fingers like this to move the data around..." Cynthia's gaze clouded. "Never mind. Just know the Thread is always here for you"—Rayne put a finger to her forehead—"when you need to ask it a question. Or check something. It's really good at finding answers. And if you ever need help, just call me."

The boys were still on the floor, with an image of an elephant between them. Aden was saying to his brother, "They did too exist! Look at my Thread!"

Clem put his hand through Aden's elephant, trying to grab it. "Babaaaa! He touched my elephant!"

Rayne stepped in. "Aden, it's *your* Thread. Unless your brother knows how to code, he won't be able to touch it."

Cynthia touched Rayne's arm and spoke above the boys' complaints. "Thank you. Now we really should go. Boys, what do you say to Rayne?"

The boys clambered to their feet. Clem closed his fist over the image, dismissing it. "Thank you."

"Thanks. We are One!" They high fived her and collected their belongings.

Rayne opened the door for them. "Enjoy the ice climb. And remember your promise."

After they left, Rayne's heart squeezed with elation as she thought of all the Game time that lay ahead in the shelter. She couldn't wait to talk with Cas and review the data stories with him. Once they had a better handle on what had messed with her Revolution Game, she would begin rebuilding it. It wasn't the first time she had to clean up after forcing an exit on a work in progress.

Luci rested in the docking station. The maple sugar was put away, the counter wiped. Satisfied, Rayne started the rest of the storm protection protocols.

"Level Six protection, please." The storm shutters rolled across the windowpanes. With a clang, the windows barricaded.

She walked through the kitchen to where her Oak stood. Rooted in the Earth under the foundation, the Oak's canopy spread above her roof, protecting the solar tiles from the worst of the wind while allowing filtered sun through. With its wide reach both underground and above, her Oak connected her with every other living being nearby.

Stepping close, she placed her palms against its bark and laid her cheek on the rough grooves. The Oak collected her nervous energy and dispelled it into the ground below.

"Thank you," she murmured.

Many cottages had trees growing inside of them, but Rayne wasn't sure how many of her neighbors practiced tree hugging. It kept her grounded and calm. She didn't care what anyone else thought. Smiling, she stepped away. "Hoist the wind sails," she said to her Thread.

As several panels slid open along the walls, Rayne back-tracked to the front door to pick up her bag. When she returned to the Oak, vast sheets of undulating material had climbed around the Oak and its canopy. The windsails created a protection zone while capturing the energy of the wind. Often, after a storm, Rayne discovered all kinds of birds hopping around in the sail pockets. It was an effective way to capture energy and prevent mass species loss during the violent seasonal storms.

Bag in hand, her cottage protected, she headed for the basement steps.

ALL SHELTERS WERE UNDERGROUND. Her group's refuge, which they shared with several neighboring villages, was part of an old transportation system. A few of the underground caverns collapsed during the floods of the last century. But the Thread showed them how to expand the tunnels into dry, comfortable lairs capable of housing a few hundred people for days at a time.

Rayne didn't mind being in the shelter. There were no trees or wildlife, but there was plenty to think about. Pit painters had left images on the shining tiles, depicting lives long gone. The colors were still vibrant and made her wonder about the people who created them. Sometimes a group of neighbors beat rhythms on the discarded barrels that lined the old caverns. They sang loudly, the sound echoing through the tunnels and pushing the darkness away.

As she reached the bottom of the stairs, she breathed in the cold, clean scent of recycled air. Pressing the handle of her shelter's door, she paused. There was a sound coming from inside. She leaned forward, straining to hear. A muffled shouting drifted through the walls. And it was getting closer.

WHAT IT WANTS__

Vennor

THE VOICES REACHED Vennor before the door opened.

"I'm not saying we do nothing." Trueno's tone was clipped. "I'm saying we pause. Think. The last time we rushed—"

"—we lost an entire node," Enayat snapped. "Because someone insisted on waiting for proof."

The door swung open. Both men entered the shelter's meeting chamber in a gust of cold air and indignation. Trueno carried a ceramic mug in each hand.

"For you," he said, setting one cup in front of Vennor before taking the seat beside her. "Hyssop and chicory. Thought you might need it." He still had snow on his shoulders. His expression was as carefully composed as ever, but his eyes were bright beneath his brows.

She nodded, curling her fingers around the warmth. "Thank you." She let herself watch Trueno settle himself, broad and muscled beneath his wool jumpsuit. She brought her tea to her lips to hide her smile.

Enayat didn't sit. He paced instead, his cloth already in hand as he wiped his nose. "We're wasting time."

"You're escalating," Trueno said calmly, "and calling it strategy."

"Enough," Vennor said. "Both of you. Sit."

Enayat grumbled but obeyed.

The three of them settled into their usual places at the long stone table. The room held the scent of tea and ozone, a leftover trace of cold from outside. Vennor let out a long breath. She hadn't felt this much tension in the shelter since the flood drills three years ago.

"Well?" she asked. "Tell me what's changed."

Enayat gestured sharply, fingers slicing a new hologram of data into the air. "The anomaly's not static. It's adapting. And it's not confined to Rayne's beta anymore."

Trueno shot her a quick look—half-smile, half-check-in—as if trying to anchor her with something lighter than the worry in the room. His calm was infuriating and oddly magnetic. He always carried that quiet ease, like none of it was personal. Like the future could be solved with tea and patience.

"And what does the Guild of Seers say?" Trueno shifted in his seat so he could see more of Enayat's data. "They make any progress with tracking down the source?"

Vennor caught Enayat's eye and shook her head, a silent signal to him that they would not mention the silence of the other Arks.

If their allies had gone offline, or been attacked in some way, then the Seers of the Atlantic Ark would be forced to act alone.

Instead of answering Trueno directly, Enayat looped his fingers in the air to shift the display in front of them. "We've come across a new development. Look at this." His hand swept through the holographic code, making commands, showing three, four, five betas crashing. "Whatever it is, it's now disrupting multiple betas at once."

Trueno cast a curious glance at Vennor, inquiring why Enayat hadn't addressed his question about the Guild of Seers. "A worrying development, indeed." Trueno picked up his tea.

"It's not just crashing them," Enayat continued. "It's moving from beta to beta. Experimenting, if you will. If we don't contain it."

"Experimenting?" Trueno brought his cup down. "To what end?"

Vennor kept her tone neutral. "We don't know. From what we've been able to piece together, the anomaly is searching for a way inside the NEWRRTH. Almost like it's trying to find a way around our security."

"That's not a theory, is it?" Trueno asked. "It's a certainty?"

"Yes." Enayat swirled through the data on the Thread. "With access to the betas, the entity can get into public Game architecture, then infiltrate the Thread itself. From there it's only a matter of time until it breaches the NEWRRTH's codebase."

"And then?" Trueno prompted.

"Then it corrupts the NEWRRTH's coding. It brings down the Arks."

Trueno took a sip of his tea. "Is that the ultimate purpose of the anomaly, do you think?"

Enayat harrumphed. "Come on, Trueno. It's the only explanation."

"They've always hated the Arks," Vennor said. "Now they've found a way to dismantle us from the inside."

"Without the NEWRRTH, we fade away into nothing." Enayat pointed his finger into the table as he spoke. "No guidance, no Threads, no Games, no *life* for us. It's what they've wanted for years—"

"Who?" Trueno raised his eyebrows. "Who's wanted that?"

Vennor straightened. "Please don't make this more difficult than it needs to be, Trueno. You know who. The Arks are a direct threat to their beliefs."

"The Settlers." Trueno chuckled to himself. "Of course. You think the Settlers are causing the anomaly in our betas. That they're the ones behind the disruptions."

"And they will be stopped."

Trueno's expression went dark. "If this is a Settler breach, why no demands? No pattern? No propaganda trail?"

Enayat closed up his Thread, and the display winked out. "They don't need to leave a trail, Trueno. Their intent is written into their ideology. Stealth is part of the strategy— destabilize first, explain later. We must show our strength. Act decisively. And quickly."

"Strength is not always a good thing." Trueno tipped his head at Enayat. "Sometimes we learn best when we examine problems from every angle before taking action." He tapped a long finger on the table. "I went through the data last night and came to a different conclusion than you did."

Vennor's jaw clenched. A different conclusion?

"There are signs in the data of manipulation, for sure." Trueno's gaze become sharp. "But not Settler sabotage. This feels like something else—someone with access. And skill. A lot of it."

The breath whooshed from Vennor's lungs as she realized what Trueno meant. "You're not serious." She tried to laugh, but the sound died in her throat. Surely Trueno didn't mean they were being infiltrated by ghosts.

Enayat slammed his fist on the table, rattling their cups of tea. "Gods damn you, man. How many times do we have to hear about these mythical forces of creation? The invisible hands waving over our every breath? We've been talking about this for decades, as long as we've been building the Arks. We've had so many reports and studies and findings, all coming up with nothing. I could throw them all into a furnace and create a new alloy."

"Enayat, calm down." Vennor drew her cup closer. "That's not warranted."

"The Settlers *do* have the means." Enayat's piece of cloth came out of his pocket again. He swiped at his nose. "And they have the motivation. We've seen it before. You're a fool, Trueno. A coward and a fool."

Trueno's eyes went flinty. "You're the fool. Freya's Path is not some mythical—"

"I will not tolerate personal insults." Vennor sighed. "We have important decisions to make. This isn't helping."

The two men glared at each other. Trueno spoke carefully. "The evidence does not convince me that the Settlers are causing these disruptions."

Vennor held a finger over her wrist, contemplating. She wanted to believe Trueno. But belief had failed them before. She tapped a brief command into her Thread.

"You're entitled to your beliefs, Trueno—your off-grid spirits or mythical forces hiding behind veils of code. But the data points to something far more grounded. And far more dangerous."

"I don't have to defend my beliefs," Trueno said. "Whether you respect them or not. My point is we should consider all the possibilities. Before we take action we may regret."

"You're just afraid to face reality." Enayat stuffed his cloth into his pocket.

"You're right, Enayat. I *am* afraid." The overhead lights flickered, then blinked. Once. Twice. Vennor glanced up, disconcerted. She narrowed her eyes. The fixtures glowed steadily. A distant howl sent shivers up her arms.

"Just the wind," Enayat murmured.

Trueno continued undeterred. "I'm afraid we're going to make a mistake that will take years for our societies to recover from. If we ever recover. I propose we take the time to understand exactly who is behind this. And why. We risk too much by rushing our response."

Vennor wrapped her hands around her cup, savoring the last of its warmth. "Trueno. I have to say that I agree with Enayat. The evidence is there, even if it's thin. We should act before the Settlers cause irreparable harm to the Arks. They will be held accountable for their actions." She paused. "And I expect cooperation from everyone."

Trueno offered her a strained smile.

Vennor's wrist glowed blue. It was the incoming she had been waiting for. Rising, she addressed both men. "Gather the others. I'm going to take this call."

CAS HAS A SURPRISE__

Rayne

RAYNE'S PALM rested on the door handle. Slinging her bag higher onto her shoulders, she put her ear to the cold steel and listened. Inside, a tangle of voices rose in overlapping conversation—urgent, moving fast.

Something thumped against the door. Startled, Rayne jumped back. When the noise faded, she pushed the handle down. The door swung open.

It was hard to see at first. The cool air smelled faintly of damp earth. She inhaled, holding her breath, and listened. There was no one.

She stepped inside and closed the door behind her. Down the tunnel to her right, faint light from the atrium spilled across the tiled floor and pooled into a rivulet at the top of a staircase. She made her way toward the stairs to check in.

As she approached, voices floated up.

"... Unusual for this time of year," she heard Tamas say.

"You're checked in. You're going to the south block today. On you go."

Rayne paused at the top of the stairs, taking in the atrium below. The vaulted ceiling arched high above a web of stone staircases that spiraled down the walls and converged at the center, where Tamas stood beside a tabletop, sleeves rolled, posture proud. A loose cluster of people surrounded him, murmuring as they waited for their block assignments.

She descended quickly, skipping the last few steps, her boots landing with a soft slap. No one glanced up as she slipped through the crowd—just another body moving through the storm shelter's rhythm.

At the table, Tamas held court like he always did, voice pitched for authority. "It was caught outside its own shelter," he was saying. "Poor thing. Back when they were plentiful, they used to dig burrows. That's how they survived the winter."

"Hey, Tamas," Rayne called as she drew near. "What did I hear running around in here?"

Tamas ushered two people through. "You'll just have to see for yourself." He gestured vaguely behind him, into the tunnels that stretched in all directions.

"I saw it," a voice said, just ahead of Rayne. It was Aden, standing next to his mother. "It was a brown puff ball and had big ears."

Rayne swallowed. "A puff ball?" She tried to imagine what kind of wild creature Cas had found this time.

"Yeah. It was puffy and fluffy all over. It squiggled around. A lot."

"Aden, let's go." His mother scooted him forward. "We're staying in the south block."

"I'm going to help feed it!" Aden called over his shoulder as his mother led him away. They entered the lighted mouth of a tunnel chiseled with the inscription SOUTH-3B.

Rayne drew level with the round table. "Tamas. What did Cas have? And how bad is it going to hurt me tonight?"

"It's not a porcupine, or whatever it was called. This one didn't seem prickly."

He waved his device over her palm. "Oh, look at that. You're heading to the west side. I guess the south blocks are full."

"Hey." Rayne drew her hand back. "Can you get me into the south? I have to work with Cas tonight."

Tamas raised one eyebrow and studied his device. The bank of overhead lights made sharp shadows on his face. "A special request for the Golden Pair."

Rayne's chest tightened. He was right to feel bitter. Rayne was uncomfortable with how abruptly she and Cas had been chosen. They had been named Game Designers over others who had worked just as hard. But that was the Seers' decision. It wasn't her fault. Tamas and his friends didn't know there was more to the story.

Tamas avoided her gaze and spoke into his Thread. "Can the south block take one more tonight?" He listened to the response, then gave a tight smile. "You're in."

Rayne walked past him, heading for the south tunnel. Tamas called after her, "But only for tonight. The stores will balance better if you eat from the west block tomorrow."

"Thank you, Tamas!" Rayne called back. She could have checked the Thread herself, to see if she could stay with Cas, but Tamas enjoyed playing the role of shelter facilitator. It made him feel important.

Tamas was a fan of Games that involved fending for yourself in the wilderness, where you had to eat bugs and make shelter from logs and leaves. He'd like her new Revolution Game. Hiding the cannons in the barn, evading the British Regulars—

Except her new Game needed hours of rebuilding before she could release it.

She made her way down the south corridor, heels thudding on the recycled porcelain floor. Along the alcoves, neighbors were unrolling bedding and slipping on gamescreens, vanishing into their digital sanctuaries one by one.

"There you are," Cas called as she rounded the corner.

He perched on a barrel, holding his overcoat shut like a shield. His things were piled haphazardly beside him, and something underneath the coat squirmed.

Rayne's hair whipped into her mouth as a gust of wind tore through the tunnel. She held herself against the sharp scent of rust and distant smoke.

"What did you smuggle in this time?"

"You always assume the worst, don't you?" Cas beamed at her, warmth radiating from his little alcove like a self-made sun.

She dropped her bag. "Only when I'm right. What's under the coat?"

He grinned. "Shelter setup first. Come on, you know the drill."

"I'm not lifting a single mat until you show me what you smuggled in." She crossed her arms. "If it bites, I swear—"

Cas pressed a hand to his chest in mock offense. "Bite? This sweet thing? I'd never."

"That's what you said last time. I still have scars."

"Okay, okay." He glanced around and motioned her closer. "But you have to promise not to freak out."

Rayne narrowed her eyes. "Does it have barbs?"

He hesitated just long enough to confirm her worst suspicion. "No barbs. Just... enthusiasm."

Cas cracked the coat open just enough for a small, speckled face to peek out—wide brown eyes, twitching whiskers, and impossibly long, furred ears flattened tight to its head.

"It *looks* like a ferret," he whispered. "But it's not. It's a cottontail."

Rayne took a full step back. "Cas. No. That's a wildling."

"I saw it outside," he said calmly, as if this were a completely rational decision. "It didn't have a shelter. It was just... out there. Alone. It's staying with us."

The cottontail stilled under the sudden exposure, its breath shallow and fast. Cas immediately pulled a rope sling from his satchel and wrapped the creature with practiced care, knotting it against his chest like a living talisman.

Rayne huffed. "You're wearing it like a baby."

"I *rescued* it like a baby."

"How much has the Thread told you?"

Cas raised an eyebrow. "Enough to know it's a relic. Used to be everywhere until the biomes collapsed. A keystone prey species—fed raptors, foxes, bobcats, even the occasional human. Total spring symbol. People used to keep them as pets, too."

He paused, gaze drifting. "But mostly they just got eaten."

There was that look again—the flicker of grief behind his easy charm. The fury he tried to hide whenever they talked about extinction or collapse.

"They made it through the small mammal die-offs," he added. "I figured... maybe that means something."

"Tell me what this little thing needs, and I'll start gathering." Rayne picked up her bag. "Then we have to talk. You will not believe what happened to my beta today."

Cas didn't seem to hear her. He gazed at the cottontail's head, which was unmoving. He placed a finger on the soft space between its ears. The cottontail sprang to life with a wild thump. Cas grunted. The thing must have kicked him square in the stomach. His eyes bulged in pain, but he did his best not to show it.

"That's my cue." Rayne turned, leaving him alone with the bucking animal.

On her way to the south block stores, she asked her Thread what cottontails ate. She saw images of pine needles, clover, and grasses. The Thread showed her enclosures inside people's houses, with bowls of water, dried fruits, and shredded greens.

This cottontail was going to have to settle for hay and twigs. Unless the Orchard had time to deliver a shipment of fresh produce before the storm kicked up.

The Orchard. Her mother had said something was off in the greenhouses—again. Probably like the time Kai was convinced the farmer drones were whispering behind her back. As if bots had secret plans to overthrow her composting schedule.

It was almost funny.

The NEWRRTH would never allow that. It wasn't some single-minded machine. It operated from thousands of nodes across the planet—an intelligent web trained on human behavior. Every decision it made was grounded in centuries of data: what worked, what failed, what might go wrong next.

It didn't think. It didn't want. It processed. It reacted. It offered probabilities—what was most likely, based on evidence.

When Rayne got to the food stores, she grabbed a sack of oats and tucked it into her bag. The NEWRRTH had kept the Arks thriving for nearly a century, guiding everything from crop rotations to emergency shelter protocols. The Threads in their bodies were synced to it, serving as personalized guides. Threads used the NEWRRTH's intelligence to track well-being and ease stress, keeping people healthy and aligned with the best possible outcomes.

People followed their Threads, or they didn't. But when they didn't, the NEWRRTH always showed them where they went wrong. Gently. Unfailingly.

The idea of rebellion against that? Ridiculous.

If everyone at the Orchard followed their Threads, there'd be no crisis. No uprising. No robot revolt.

She scooped a handful of wilted kale into her bag. No twigs. Oh well. She checked her Thread again, confirming she hadn't missed anything the cottontail might need.

She'd almost gotten back to Cas when she saw the glowing blue dot on her wrist. The incoming bleeped. She stopped and accepted the call.

"Rayne," a low voice said. "We need to talk." He came into virtual form beside her.

Rayne's stomach flipped. Enayat was a Seer. The NEWRRTH was a self-learning intelligence, but sometimes human intervention was required. That was the Seers' job. They made precise calibrations to keep the NEWRRTH aligned with the Principle of One, the law that prioritized life above all else—the lives of humans, animals, plants, and the Earth itself. It took years of training to sense the NEWRRTH, never mind learning how to directly manipulate it.

There was only one reason a Seer would contact her now, and it wasn't a good one.

"Hello, Enayat," Rayne said. "What can I do for you?"

"It has come to our attention that an anomaly occurred in one of your betas."

"Yes." She tried to keep her voice steady. "Yes, that's right. Something went wrong during my last playtest session. It's a Game based on the night before the start of the American Revolution—"

"When were you going to bring this to our attention?"

"There wasn't time. The storm got upgraded and I—"

"You are established in your shelter, I see." Enayat's avatar turned a shade darker. Blue-hued light glowed from behind his head.

Another blue dot appeared on Rayne's wrist. She accepted the second call and turned around. Her mother's aspect stood there, looking just as Rayne always imagined her: two fists on her hips, hair pulled back, a fierce expression on her face.

Rayne gave a small shake of her head. *Not now.* Her mother's face became stony when she saw Enayat.

Enayat continued. "We observed a significant error in your Game. I don't need to tell you the amount of data loss that caused."

Rayne cringed. Data loss was the worst thing that could happen in a Game. Data fed the NEWRRTH so it could continuously update its algorithms. The NEWRRTH's algorithms supported life on the planet.

She squared her shoulders. "Enayat, this wasn't something I planned. I swear. I can't explain exactly—"

"You will tell me what happened *exactly*," Enayat said, "or I will be forced to undo whatever you've gotten yourself into."

COTTONTAIL__

Rayne

Enayat finished speaking and vanished. Rayne caught her mother's gaze—of course Kai would call now. She always called at the most inconvenient times.

"Rayne, what did he want?" Her mother's aspect fell into step beside her.

"Not now. Please. I have to talk to Cas."

"Whatever this is, please tell me you're being smart about it."

"Ma, it's not what you're thinking. I'm not doing anything I shouldn't. Seriously."

Her mother always worried—but not without reason.

The last time her work veered too far from Ark expectations, it nearly cost her everything. One Game, one mistake. A prototype built with Cas that was too bloody, too graphic. They'd called it reckless. A violation of the Principle of One. A threat to social cohesion.

Kai had fought to keep her from reassignment.

Rayne still didn't know exactly what her mother said behind those closed doors. But she'd never forgotten the look in Kai's eyes afterward—strained, hollowed-out. As if defending her had cost more than Rayne understood at the time.

And now, Rayne was on the Seers' radar again.

Kai's gaze narrowed. "You're shutting me out again."

"I'm not," she said too quickly—then caught herself. This wasn't something she could explain, not yet. Not until she knew more.

"Ma..."

"You said you'd be careful."

"I am. I promise."

Doubt lodged behind her ribs—small, sharp, and undeniable.

She'd promised. But promises didn't always hold.

"Just be safe," said Kai.

<hr>

CAS LEANED over a little fire in a metal can. Curls of smoke drifted up toward the distant ceiling. He had flipped over a couple of wooden crates, collapsed them flat, and propped them at an angle. It served as a crude enclosure for the cottontail.

The furry little thing crouched against the wall. Its dark eyes watered. Maybe it was hungry. Or cold.

"I got some food for it." Rayne put her bag down by the fire. Reaching in, she grabbed a handful of hay and laid it inside the enclosure. She filled a metal bowl with water and placed it near the hay, then sprinkled a few oats over the ground. She kept her hands well out of the cottontail's reach, but she needn't have bothered. The thing hadn't moved.

"That should last it for the night." She settled next to Cas by the fire.

The flames snapped, casting golden light across the tunnel wall. "You always do this." Rayne stretched her hands toward it, grateful for the heat finally reaching her fingers. "Find the last wild thing and decide it belongs to you."

Cas didn't smile. "I don't want it to belong to me. I just want it to live."

She glanced at him sideways. There was something raw in his voice she wasn't used to hearing.

"You okay?"

He nodded, but didn't look at her. "Just tired."

"Listen. Something's up."

Cas glanced at her again. "Do you think the cottontail is ill?"

"I don't know about that. It's the Seers. They just contacted me. Enayat."

"Enayat?" Cas stiffened.

"About my new Game. The night before the Revolution."

Cas pushed a piece of hair out of his eye. It wasn't unheard of for Seers to review their work. They weighed in on accuracy, flagged concerns, nudged tone. But this felt different.

"I was about to cross the bridge. Everything was great, right? Dawn on the farm, the militia setting up, everything responding exactly how I programmed it. Then the soldiers—the Regulars—showed up too soon. And they weren't acting like my aspects. They caught me."

Rayne watched his reaction—subtle, but there. A shift in posture, a quick flick of his gaze. "Caught you how?"

"Like... tracked me. Surrounded me. And then they pulled me under the water."

"Pulled you under?" His eyes searched hers, brow furrowing.

"I tried to get away. I was going for the Old North Bridge, to trigger the militia sequence, but I didn't even make it halfway. One of them grabbed my ankle from under the water."

Rayne drew her arms around her middle. "They held me there. Dragged me under. Again and again. Like they were testing how long I could last."

Cas went still. "That's not behavior drift. That's something else."

"Exactly. They had their aggression limits. They shouldn't even be able to chase players through river, let alone—" she stopped. "Let alone hurt them."

"You think they were trying to hurt you?"

"No," she whispered. "I think they were trying to... study me."

In her mind, Rayne was back under the bridge. She felt the shocking cold of the river, the darkness closing around her.

The fire shone in Cas's eyes. "Was it just you? Did they pull anyone else in?"

"It was just me. The other aspects ran off. Just like they were supposed to. There were no other live players in the beta. I'm sure of it."

Cas nodded, pressing his lips together. "This sequence didn't appear in any of the probable paths?"

Rayne shook her head. "No."

"What about ghosting? Is Mo getting into your beta again, like that time in the Battle of Athens?"

"No. I would have seen his signature. And there's something else. I didn't realize it until now. I think the—the Regulars, or whoever they were—were panicking."

"Rayne, they don't feel anything unless you tell them to."

"Then why would they do that? Why would they attack me?"

"There are lots of reasons things go wrong in the Games."

Cas sighed. "It's probably nothing. The NEWRRTH is just being overprotective lately."

"You don't think I did it, do you? That I caused this somehow?"

Aden popped into the alcove. "There it is!" He headed for the cottontail's enclosure.

"It's so fuzzy," he breathed, kneeling in front of the barrier of wooden crates. "Can you hear me?" He reached inside and picked up a few oats. "Here. It's food for you. My Thread told me."

The cottontail kept still, its brown nose twitching. Cas broke Rayne's gaze and stood, ambling to the enclosure. "It's just scared, buddy. It needs time to adjust."

"I'm feeding it." Aden held his hand outstretched, offering a few damp oats.

Aden's mother rounded the corner. "Sorry to barge in. Come on, Aden. It's time to make our sleeping places. We can visit this..." She looked at Cas.

"Cottontail," Cas said.

"... this cottontail later." She guided Aden out by the shoulder. They disappeared down the corridor.

The cottontail hadn't moved. Cas reached in and pushed the water bowl closer to where it crouched. It turned its head toward the rippling liquid. How long had it been outside in the storm, looking for water?

"You didn't answer me." Rayne wiggled her hands by the crackling flames. She tried to catch Cas's eye.

Cas stood by the enclosure for another moment before responding. "No. I don't think you caused this." He sat back down by the fire.

"Say it like you mean it."

Cas looked at her fully this time. "You didn't make this happen, okay? Did you run through the data stories?"

Rayne pulled up the data the Thread had shown her. "Oh, yeah. There's a lot of stuff in there, but I haven't found anything yet."

She snapped the stories out of her Thread and created a projected image so Cas could see what she had already analyzed from her beta.

They started from the beginning.

LEGACY SETTLEMENTS__

Vennor

"THEY HAVE HIM IN CUSTODY," Vennor announced to Trueno and Enayat. "The Game Designer. The Peace Officers arrested him last night. They can't travel overland in the Level Six, so they'll hold him in his own shelter. Isolated and secured. For the time being." She returned to her seat at the head of the table.

"Very good." Enayat nodded. "I'll instruct the Officers to start a full data scan of his auric field." He pressed his right wrist until it glowed blue, initiating the call to the Officers in charge of the Designer. He spoke a few commands into the Thread, giving the Officers clearance to begin their information collecting.

A troubled expression passed over Trueno's face. "You know we can't hold him without informing him of his rights."

Enayat pressed his wrist again, ending the transmission. "This is a critical matter of Ark security. We have the right to hold him until we're sure he's not a threat. We're not playing legal games from another century."

"More tea." Vennor placed the order into her Thread. A full data scan would take a while, and might push the boundaries of lawfulness, but she believed it was warranted.

Her instincts told her this Game Designer was up to something. Whether it was connected to the anomaly or not, they would soon find out.

Trueno and Enayat continued to argue. She pushed her lower back into the chair, determined to ignore the squabbling. She had already made her decision.

"You're being unreasonable," Trueno repeated. "Our actions this morning will set the tone for an entire generation."

The door swung open, bringing the group to attention. Two more Seers filed into the room, one a distinguished-looking woman in a blue robe and the other in a wrinkled jumpsuit. "Nilo. Ana." Enayat gestured for the two youngest Seers to step inside. "Please join us. We're constrained for time."

Nilo strode toward the table, her blue robe trailing behind her. A silver-infused tattoo glinted at her neck. "We would have come sooner," she said, taking a seat beside Trueno. "But I was running experiments." She flashed an apologetic smile. Nilo was a couple decades younger than Vennor but was widely acknowledged to be the most prodigious talent in the Seer community. She was an expert at interpreting linguistic patterns to predict future events.

"We saw the anomaly in the Game betas." Nilo's speaking voice was a blend of natural resonance and tones projected through the filaments on her neck. Nilo had lost her hearing during Thread insertion, an unusual side effect of the process.

She used the micro-circuitry embedded under her jaw to receive vibrations to her inner ear. The circuitry glowed when she spoke, revealing a sparkling silver landscape beneath her skin.

"We tried to pin it, but it kept evading us. Have you been able to isolate it?" She flipped her sleeves out of the way.

Ana, the youngest Seer, took a seat at the far end of the table, her brow drawn. Her tousled red hair, liquid eyes, and sharp features always gave Vennor the impression of a huntress. Peering from under her bangs, Ana nodded to Vennor. "We saw the beta crashes. It's a puzzle." She tucked her hands under her thighs and gazed at the table.

When all five Seers had seated themselves, Vennor took control of the meeting. "Thank you for gathering. We'll get straight to it. Nilo, did you receive my request?"

"Yes." Nilo made a broad swipe in the air, projecting her Thread to the tabletop. Sweeping her hand through the holographic data, she resolved it into a moving column of numbers. "Here we are. A logic sequence. You asked me to resolve the question of whether the Settlers are, in fact, causing the anomaly in pre-released Game designs. Or if it could be something else."

Vennor squinted at the numbers, calculating. A memory of the antique child's toy—*what was it called? A kaleidoscope*—emerged in her mind as the bright display rolled past.

"Here we are." Nilo paused the stream. "Now, I've supported these conclusions by cross-referencing the modeling—"

A ping at the door interrupted her. A roving bot made its way inside the room. Vennor acknowledged the bot with a nod and accepted the fresh cup of tea from its tray.

When the bot left, Nilo's fingers hovered in the air, waiting.

Vennor noticed her hesitation. "You can speak freely about the Settlers." She put her cup down and held her palms open, an invitation. "I won't take offense. I came from the Legacy Settlements, but I don't belong there. Never did."

Nilo bowed her head in acknowledgment. "Your family. Yes."

"Not my family anymore. Proceed."

"Okay. The data shows two possible explanations for the anomaly. The first explanation is that it's random, some bit of code that's always been there but only recently came to our attention. The second is that it's human-made, created by someone for unknown reasons."

Trueno leaned forward to speak, but Vennor held up her hand and asked, "What does the Thread say is the probability of this being a random event?"

"Near zero. The anomaly isn't random."

"What does the Thread say about the probability that this is coming from inside the Atlantic Ark? That one of our own citizens is generating these attacks?"

"It's not likely," Nilo spoke with authority. "It's not a zero percent chance, but it's close. There's no reason for a citizen to interfere with the Designers' work. They love their Games. Without the Games, life in the Ark would be boring as hell and we'd all go mad."

Ana laughed, and her hand flew to cover her mouth.

Nilo chuckled to herself, neck tattoo glimmering. "What I mean to say is that without the Games, the NEWRRTH wouldn't be able to collect the data it needs to inform its algorithms and create personalized guidance for each of us. And citizens wouldn't have access to the kind of learning that takes place through the virtual sharing of experiences in historical settings."

She turned to face Vennor. "It's as you always say. 'Without the Games, we become what we fear the most: monsters stumbling in the dark.'"

Vennor nodded, her mouth turning up at the corners. "I have said that, yes. So the anomaly is not one of us, then. What about citizens from another Ark?"

Nilo shook her head. "Nope, it's not them, either. Same reasons. That leaves the only other option. Someone from outside the Arks is responsible."

"And what does the Thread say about that?"

"There's a high probability that it's true."

Enayat cut in. "And the Settlers would love to bring the NEWRRTH down. To prove they've been right all along."

Trueno leaned back. "Thank you, Nilo, for that elegant demonstration. The probabilities seem clear enough. But that's not the whole story, is it? We must be careful. If we act on this information without proof, we could cause a lot of harm."

"And if we do nothing, we risk a direct assault on the NEWRRTH," Enayat said.

Vennor closed her eyes and sighed. "I have to say, I'm relieved. As awful as this information is, it gives us a way forward. We understand what we're up against. And we can prepare."

Trueno frowned.

Vennor turned to each Seer in the room. "The Settlers are very different people from us. Many of them are extremists, motivated by hatred and fear. They live in squalor, in the shadow of what was once a great nation. They see us as a threat. We represent everything they've lost, everything they can never have. Some of them want to destroy us because to them, we're the enemy."

"What if it's a distraction?" Ana's head tilted, her eyes fixed on the stream of data from Nilo's Thread.

"I beg your pardon?" Vennor said.

"The anomaly." Ana glanced up. "What if the Settlers are

causing a disruption in our Games to take our attention away from something else?"

Vennor considered this for a moment.

"That would make sense, wouldn't it?" Ana continued. "That they're trying to distract us from a larger mission, like... breaking into our food banks or battery stores."

"Not in a Level Six blizzard," Enayat said. "They can't be mobilizing for an assault on the Ark in this weather. They'd be too exposed."

"I agree," Nilo said. "Nothing in our modeling predicts that. We're still watching their comm traffic, and we haven't picked up any unusual activity."

Ana shrugged. "Just something to consider."

Vennor drew a calming breath. "They wouldn't do that." The silence that followed made Vennor realize she had spoken the words aloud.

"They rejected the NEWRRTH." Ana kept her eyes on the table. "Why strike against it now? Why bring down the Arks after all these years of peace? It makes no sense."

"You know what the Settlements are like." Enayat jerked his head toward the outside. "The diseases, the fighting, the grueling labor. Maybe they've tired of their own scavenging lives and want a piece of our prosperity."

Vennor cut him a cool glare. "They have strong beliefs about what it is to be human. To be free. They blame technology for society's problems. They pride themselves on having their own intuition and imagination, without implants or artificial intelligence. They're the last people who live by the old ways."

"We used to live that way, too," Vennor continued. "Before the Great Divergence. Thankfully we've left that all behind." A memory came of her father, a large man, bent under a metal rod, barrels of fresh water hanging on either side of him. The liquid sloshed to the ground as he walked. The fire in her chest bloomed as she watched him. The conviction rose, even as a child, that she would never struggle under that weight. Never become what *they* were.

"But after all these years, why target the NEWRRTH?" Ana repeated. "The Thread hasn't shown us any data supporting the logic of an attack like this."

"That is an excellent question." Enayat put his hands on the table. "As it turns out, there is some data to work with. And someone who can speak to this issue." He paused for effect. "We arrested a Game Designer last night. He's in holding now. We're running a scan of his Thread activity to shed light on who is behind these attacks."

"And what exactly is he being charged with?" Trueno cocked his head.

Vennor sighed. "We haven't formally charged him. Yet. That doesn't mean we don't have a good reason to hold him."

Trueno shook his head. "Are you sure about this, Vennor? I thought you needed to take a step back. To rest. You said you weren't feeling as well as you'd like."

"My health is no longer an issue. I am back to all my duties."

"That's not what I meant." Trueno turned to her. "We know how sincerely you're committed to your work. But your history with the Settlers... it could affect your judgment in ways that could be dangerous. And that isn't good for anyone, least of all you."

Vennor met his eyes, unflinching. She had sworn to protect the NEWRRTH, and she would do just that. "I know you're worried about my involvement. But I'm feeling better than ever. And you will trust me on this."

Enayat abruptly stood up. The Seers turned their heads to him.

He clutched his wrist, eyes widening as he listened to the incoming call. "It's not safe to delay, I'm afraid." He tugged the square of cloth out of his pocket. "The scans of the Designer in holding have partially completed. There's already evidence."

Vennor turned away. She could guess what was coming.

Enayat's gaze swept over the expectant faces of his Seer colleagues. "There's evidence that he's been working with the anomaly. Programming alongside it. Directly and intentionally."

ARRESTED__

Rayne

There was shouting.

Rayne sat up, unsure of where the sounds were coming from. It was dark. The fire in Cas's sleeping alcove had gone out. She and Cas must have fallen asleep. Had she been dreaming?

She heard the commotion again. It echoed from far away in the corridors. "Cas?"

She patted the ground, searching for her bag. When she found it, she pulled out her flashlight and flicked it on. "Cas?" He wasn't near the fire.

"Shh. Turn it off." Cas sat inside the cottontail's enclosure with his back against the wall. His cheeks glinted in the flashlight's weak light.

The voices rose, getting closer. Rayne stood. "I'm going to check it out."

"No." A small shadow hovered next to Cas. She turned the

flashlight's beam onto the cottontail as it darted toward the water bowl, knocking it over. The liquid made a dark stain as it spread across the stone. The cottontail dropped to its side, legs quavering.

"Oh Cas. Is it—"

"Seizures. It was out in the cold too long, there wasn't food, I don't know what's wrong. It's just... these erratic movements, they could signal..." He took a few ragged breaths. "I don't think I can save it."

"You're doing what you can." She considered the creature, now struggling to its feet. "I'm going to go see what's going on out there. I'll be right back."

Rayne shoved her feet into her slides and grabbed her jacket as she left the alcove, clutching her small light. It must have been near the middle of the night, but people were coming out of their sleeping areas, awakened by the noise.

"What is it?" one neighbor whispered. "Is it a late check-in?" They heard the shouting again.

Doesn't sound like a late check-in. She began walking along the south tunnel. The soft orange lights came on above her head as she progressed. A few people followed behind her.

Vast slabs of polished stone in different shades of gray formed the floor and walls and ceiling. Her jacket was damp and cold.

Ahead, the shouting got louder.

"What's going on?" she heard a man ask. "My Thread said it could be a fire drill."

The corridor emptied into the grand foyer. A small cluster of people gathered in the center, the same spot where Tamas had processed their arrival earlier that day. One was fighting his way out of the group. He gestured wildly. He seemed so angry and helpless that she felt a pang of sympathy for him, and then his words hit her like a slap in the face.

"... WON'T TOUCH ME! IF YOU WOULD JUST LISTEN TO ME, I DIDN'T DO ANYTHING!"

Rayne dropped her flashlight. It was Vic. Vic, three years older and a skilled Game Designer, was a friend. He was... Rayne flushed. A childhood crush. She hadn't spoken to him in ages. Why was he yelling at the Peace Officers?

And what were Peace Officers doing in the shelter?

Two Officers grabbed Vic's arms. He bent double as his wrists wrenched behind his back. Stumbling, he tried to address them. They escorted him forward.

They were pushing him toward the eastern corridor. But where would they be going at this time of night—and in a Level Six? More neighbors, roused from sleep, trickled in from all directions. They gathered a safe distance from the spectacle.

A familiar, ringing voice called from the western block. "Stop! Stop! Please!" All around, neighbors tried to make sense of what they were hearing and seeing.

Vic craned his neck to see who was shouting behind him. "I DON'T KNOW WHAT THIS IS ABOUT, I SWEAR!" The Officers propelled him toward the east tunnel.

Rayne touched a hand to her temple, willing her Thread to speak up. She closed her eyes and tried to calm her mind. The image of the soldiers holding her under water kept cutting into her thoughts.

Had Vic seen something strange in one of his Games, too? Her skin prickled. What if the Officers came for her next? Or Cas?

"Vic! Vic! Let go of him!"

It was Jesla, Vic's partner, shoving her way through the small crowd. Jesla was a Teacher and always well put together, with swishy hair pulled into a messy bun. "Vic, tell them!" She caught up to the Officers and grabbed the nearest one. "Listen to him! He didn't do anything!"

"Jesla, I'm trying—" Vic's voice was muffled.

"What's going on? Where are you taking him? Wait!" They yanked Vic away. "Wait!"

Rayne, getting no information from her Thread, glanced around for anyone who might know something. Bewildered faces surrounded her. Some were speaking into their Threads with urgency.

"You can't just take him like this!" Jesla yelled. "You can't! Somebody help him! Please!"

Rayne slipped behind a young couple who were whispering to each other. The less attention she drew to herself, the better. Just in case.

Vic threw one last look over his shoulder, his face contorted.

The Officers grabbed him by his arms and shoulders, pushing him down the tunnel. He stumbled along, his feet dragging on the stone floor, as they walked deeper and deeper into darkness. The sound of their footsteps finally faded away.

Rayne bent to pick up her flashlight. Neighbors from all the blocks milled around, murmuring.

This was bad. The Officers wouldn't have made a trip through the Level Six just to ask a few questions. They had an order to take Vic and detain him. For what? She stared at the ground, dread beating through her ribs.

She couldn't do anything for Vic, and it was safer if she didn't.

In the center of the atrium, Jesla turned around. "Hey. Hey." She raised a shaking hand to cover her mouth, then let it fall. People were dispersing. "Can anyone tell me what's going on?" She turned to the other side of the atrium. "Anyone?"

One by one, people disappeared back to their sleeping alcoves.

"NO ONE WILL SPEAK UP?" Jesla turned again to the

scattering crowd. "What is *wrong* with you?" Her mouth twisted. "Are you all cowards? Is that what you are? Cowards?"

No one answered.

When the atrium was nearly empty, Rayne plowed ahead, brushing several people aside. "Enough, Jesla. Stop. Please." She reached for Jesla's elbow. "We have to get out of here." She glanced down the tunnel where Vic had gone. *Been taken.*

Jesla shook Rayne off. "Get away from me, Rayne. Everyone here is useless. How could they just stand by and let them take him?" Her eyes were wet. "How could you?" She started walking back to the western block.

Rayne walked beside her. "Jesla, this could be about something... we shouldn't talk about it here." She glanced around the atrium. The few remaining neighbors had their eyes on the ground, refusing to meet her gaze. "Please, we need to talk. I'm coming with you."

Rayne followed Jesla all the way back to her alcove. In the dim light of an abandoned flashlight, Jesla collapsed onto the floor, hugging her knees to her chest. Rayne lowered herself to the ground. The blankets on the floor had been thrown about. A pot of liquid had overturned near the entrance, chunks of something like potato scattered on the stone.

A surprise arrest.

Jesla drew her knees to her chest. "He didn't do anything."

"I know. He would never do anything to get himself in trouble."

"How would you know?"

"I... I don't know, I guess." Rayne paused. "I haven't talked with him for a long time." She hoped the meaning would come through clear enough. Vic never spoke to her anymore, didn't even like her, and probably never had. He thought of her as a little sister—if that—and nothing more.

"It's funny, you know?" Jesla rocked herself back and forth

on the hard floor. "I used to be jealous of you. The group of you working so closely together. Doing your Game Designer things."

Rayne remembered then that Jesla liked Games that involved singing in echoing cathedrals. Not the kind of adventures she and her friends designed.

"I hated that you were able to do things I couldn't," Jesla said. "Creating those amazing experiences for everyone else. Having Vic around you all the time." Her voice became thick. "We were just starting to think about our future together, Vic and me."

"I'm sorry, Jesla. Really, I am. You may not want to hear this right now, but..." Rayne twisted her palms together. "I think something is going on. With the Games."

"What are you talking about?"

"There's been a... change. I don't know what to call it. If Vic had an encounter like I did, it could be serious." She decided not to mention her conversation with Enayat. "I think the Seers have questions for him."

"The *Seers* are questioning Vic?"

"For a little while," Rayne said, hoping it was true. "But I'm pretty sure they'll let him go."

"What do you mean, you're pretty sure?"

Rayne shook her head. She didn't know. "Unless he caused the... thing that happened."

Jesla gave an incredulous laugh. "You're confused. Vic isn't mixed up in anything like that."

"I'm sure he's not. There's a lot I haven't figured out yet. But it's important that I find out what happened to Vic. Why he got arrested."

Jesla's eyes went cold. "Oh, I see. You want to know if they're coming for you next." She glanced away. "At least you're honest."

Rayne stiffened. "That's not it."

Jesla shrugged, not buying it.

Rayne hesitated. Then, quietly, "I do care what happens to Vic. I always have. He's a good person—better than me, most days. And yeah, I'm scared. But not just for me. Something's wrong with the system, Jesla. I've seen it up close. And if we don't figure out what's going on, Vic won't be the last person taken."

Jesla turned to face Rayne, her jaw working like she was grinding her teeth. Finally, she spoke, quieter than before. "You sound like him, you know."

Rayne blinked. "What?"

Jesla met her eyes. "Vic. He always thinks there's a bigger pattern. That nothing happens without a reason. It drives me crazy." A pause. "But he's usually right."

Rayne let out a breath. "Then maybe he was trying to tell us something. Before they took him."

Jesla's eyes narrowed. "What are you talking about?"

Rayne stood and began to pace the edge of the alcove. "I don't know yet. But Vic always had backup plans. Hidden messages. If he saw something—if the Seers think he's connected to the anomaly—maybe he left something behind. A clue. A warning."

Jesla sat up straighter. "You think he knew this was coming?"

"I think he suspected something. I know how careful he is —he wouldn't have gone down without a fight. Or a failsafe."

Jesla studied her. "And you want to find it."

Rayne nodded. "If there's a chance he left something... I need to find it before the Seers do."

Jesla didn't answer right away. Her fingers twisted around the edges of a blanket. "You're not the only one who wants answers."

Rayne hesitated, then knelt beside her. "Then help me. You know Vic better than anyone. You'd know where he might've hidden something. What he might've been working on. If we combine what we know..."

Jesla looked away. Her voice was quieter now. "We could figure it out."

Rayne offered her hand. "We don't have to trust each other. Not yet. But I could really use your help."

Jesla stared at the hand for a long moment, then took it.

"I'm not promising anything," she said. "But I want to know the truth."

Rayne gave a small, tired smile. "So do I."

THE LANTERN__

Vennor

Trueno's mouth fell open. "Are you saying... that one of our Game Designers has been *interacting* with the anomaly?"

Vennor pushed her teacup away, her focus sharpening.

Enayat's voice was steady. "Yes. That seems to be the case. He's been in contact with the Settlers—"

"With the anomaly, you mean," Trueno cut in.

"The *anomaly* has been collaborating with this Designer to create a new Game beta." Enayat lifted his hands and whisked them in front of his temple, drawing his Thread into view. It shimmered to life in the center of the table, then glowed green as it processed.

An image formed—first a canopy of trees, so thick and tangled it could have been anywhere equatorial. But then the view zoomed. A narrow trail snaked through the forest. Palm fronds rippled in the wind. And from above, unmistakably, flakes of snow fell.

Vennor peered at the images. She wasn't sure what it meant, this snowy rainforest.

Trueno blinked several times. "What are we looking at?"

Enayat's fingers danced through the holographic display. "We've extracted a data story from the Designer's beta. It's an entirely new Game, not based on any previous versions archived in the NEWRRTH. The Designer co-created this beta with the Sett—with the anomaly. The odd thing is the Designer did little to conceal it. It's right here for anyone to see. He didn't hide anything."

The Thread took them along a path in the jungle. Birds wheeled overhead. A brook gurgled over moss-covered rocks. The air moved thickly, clogged with haze.

Trueno stared at the images. "Do you think the anomaly created this beta to get into our data?"

"We don't know," Enayat admitted. "But it created this Game for a reason. And I intend to find out why."

"It could be an escalation." Nilo swiped through the images. "It wasn't getting what it wanted in the betas. The ones that crashed. So it started from scratch. Created its own beta."

"It *wants* something." Ana's voice was low. "It wants to get our attention. It wants to interact with us but doesn't know how."

"I suppose that's possible." Trueno gave a slow nod. "It could be trying to learn how to interact with us through our Games. The anomaly is trying to reach out. It made attempts through existing betas, but for unknown reasons, that wasn't successful. So it recruited this Designer. And is working with him to... open a new channel."

"We don't know that," Enayat said.

Vennor curled her hands together on the table. "It's a theory. The more we learn about the anomaly, the more I'm convinced we need to act. Soon. Let's discuss the possibilities for an intervention."

Enayat gestured to the images before them. "We have evidence that one of our own Designers collaborated with this anomaly. We know the anomaly is finding ways to progress. To test our boundaries. To find a weakness in our intelligence, in our coding. And when they do—*if* they do—it would cause irrevocable corruption of the NEWRRTH. This is an unprecedented *attack*." He spat the last word. "To that end, I propose creating a new set of Games using the Lantern."

A shocked silence fell over the room.

"You must be out of your mind." Trueno's color rose. "The Lantern? Do you remember what happened last time?"

The Thread sprang alive with visuals. Vennor's chest tightened as she recognized the Lantern upgrade from several decades ago. The images flashed by in quick succession. They saw an earlier generation of Seers releasing the Lantern, a long-promised upgrade, hope written across their faces. The horror when they realized what they had unleashed. The panic that followed. Citizens rushing into the streets. Shelters filling with angry parents and crying children.

Vennor caught a brief display of The Center for Future Guidance, a previous version of the Seers' own headquarters, engulfed in flames. Vennor could feel the heat on her skin as if she had been there herself.

"Are you in support of this?" Trueno fanned his arms at the images, turning to Vennor. "We can't go through this again. It's too dangerous."

The original Lantern was a catastrophe. Developed as a patch for malfunctioning code inside the NEWRRTH, it should have been a smooth fix. But things went horribly wrong. The patch destabilized the neuro-grid, causing the Games to implode. People's aspects got caught in the virtual destruction, trapping them inside chaotic data loops. Dozens of citizens Disconnected from reality. Several died.

In the months it took to reboot the system, people revolted. Their faith in the NEWRRTH had been shaken to the core. They fought, ransacked the Orchard's food stores. Schools shut down and lessons halted.

It had nearly collapsed the entire Atlantic Ark.

Enayat's face remained impassive. "We have no other option. Releasing a Lantern is our only hope of saving the Games. Protecting the NEWRRTH."

"I will not support a Lantern upgrade," said Trueno. "There's no way to guarantee it will work as intended."

"Trueno." An idea occurred to Vennor but hadn't fully formed yet. "Listen. It could be an elegant solution. It'll create a barrier between the anomaly and the NEWRRTH and encourage the NEWRRTH's self-repairing code to overwrite any corruptions."

"The original Lantern malfunctioned because of a human error made during installation." Enayat dismissed the images on the Thread with a slash of his wrist. "Think what could be done with it now. We'll be able to release an entirely upgraded version of the NEWRRTH. One that is impenetrable to outsiders."

"But the chaos—" Trueno tore his gaze away from Vennor's. "People, families in misery. Entire neighborhoods turned hateful and suspicious of one another. The shortages, the rioting, the—" His hands trembled, and he dropped them to his side. "The outcomes we worked our entire careers to avoid."

"We can improve the Lantern." Ana's eyes were on her lap, her hands pulling at her sleeves.

Vennor turned to her with interest. "And what would you propose?"

"We can develop a phased release. We don't have to let the

Lantern upgrade run all at once. We incorporate the code gradually." Her hands moved to the table as she spoke. "We design an array of new Games, releasing the Lantern into them over a period of time. We do that by…" She faltered. "It's a little complicated. There are a lot of what-ifs. But it could give us time so that any problems with the Lantern—I mean, *if* there are problems—could be handled as they came up. Before it affected people."

Vennor considered this. "I see. And the anomaly? Wouldn't it try to stop this phased upgrade?"

"That's one of the big what-ifs. But another reason to go slowly. To give us time to outmaneuver the anomaly. So if it evolves—"

"We evolve faster." Nilo grinned. "That could work."

Ana blushed. "It'll take longer, but we'll achieve the outcome we want—peace and unity. We'll leave the anomaly behind. And maybe we can skip the suffering this time."

Vennor was intrigued. It was her life's work to eliminate suffering. Perhaps this young Seer would be more of an asset than they'd hoped.

"The Designer," Enayat said. "The one who has been in co-creation with the anomaly. It's already working with him. That's what it wants. It wants *him*. And he's cooperating with it. Encouraging it! What if this Designer continues to collaborate with the anomaly and interferes with the Lantern's upgrade?"

The Seers began talking over one another. Vennor raised her hands for quiet. "This idea has merit, Ana. Well done." Her voice hardened as she turned to Trueno and Enayat. "We will speak with this Designer. See what he can tell us about the anomaly. Whether we can accomplish a new Lantern upgrade, I'm not yet sure. But we will not allow the anomaly to compromise us."

"You've got my support." Nilo sat tall.

Trueno shook his head. "I strongly advise against it. We're talking about the future of the entire Atlantic Ark. Of all the Arks. We would put our lives—"

"We are moving forward with this new directive," Vennor said. "Prepare your recommendations for a phased Lantern installation. We'll leave no room for error." She gave a curt nod of dismissal. "Report to me first thing in the morning."

Trueno's eyes flashed as he left the room.

"Ana, I'd like to speak with you. Come to my chamber."

<hr>

ANA CRACKED THE DOOR. "You wanted to see me?"

Vennor waved her inside. Seated on a green velvet sofa, she motioned for Ana to sit across from her. Vennor's chamber in the Center's underground shelter was furnished with the barest of necessities—a desk and a few chairs, a small couch. An ancient wooden bed hulked in the corner, draped in quilts.

"Thank you for coming. I trust that you've been taking proper care of yourself." She indicated Ana's pale skin and hollow cheeks.

Ana nodded and then remembered to speak. "Yes, I've been eating. Sleeping. The usual."

"I want to commend you for bringing this idea to us. A phased release. Very smart."

"Thank you."

"You're young, but you've already surpassed our expectations."

Ana fidgeted with the outer edges of her jumpsuit's pockets and glanced around the room.

"You and I are cut from the same cloth." Vennor handed Ana a glass of water. "We're both deeply aware of the suffering in the world. And you have an incredible intuition. I see that. There are others in the Guild of Seers who are interested in your progress. You're getting noticed." She settled back against the soft cushions. "You might even have my position one day."

Ana's eyes widened. She cupped her glass in both hands. "I don't know about that."

Vennor laughed. "Don't worry. I have plenty of years ahead of me." She shifted in her seat. "But we mustn't get ahead of ourselves. I called you here to discuss something sensitive. About the Lantern."

"I can start working on an alpha model right away."

"I look forward to seeing that. You know how deeply I care for the people of the Atlantic Ark. How fiercely I believe in the NEWRRTH."

Ana nodded.

Vennor's voice took on a serious tone and she leaned forward, clasping her hands in front of her. "I have every hope that we can release a version of the Lantern that successfully safeguards our NEWRRTH and shuts out the anomaly. Without harm to anyone. But if we can't..." She smoothed her hands over her lap. "It will be a colossal disaster. Maybe even worse than before. If the Lantern upgrade fails this time, it could mean the end of everything we've built here. The end of hope for our Arks."

Ana took a long drink of water and set the glass down with a shaking hand.

"But there's something we can do," Vennor continued, her voice softer now. "I've thought of a way to prevent disaster from occurring. It's not without risk. Are you willing to help me?"

"Of course."

"It'll involve developing a special piece of code," she said to Ana. "A fail-safe. In case the Lantern upgrade doesn't proceed as planned."

Ana nodded again. "Okay."

"I knew I could count on you." Vennor stood up and walked to her desk. She opened a drawer and took out a small box. "This is for you."

Ana took the box, turning it over.

"Open it." Vennor smiled.

Ana's mouth parted when she saw the crystal. It was a piece of clear quartz, with several smooth sides and a rough base. Its cloudy spires met in a rounded point.

"What is this?"

Vennor smiled. "This," she said, taking the crystal from Ana and holding it up to the light, "is a symbol."

"A symbol of what?"

"It's a symbol of our resolve." Vennor replaced the crystal in Ana's palm. "A reminder that we can never give up fighting for humanity, no matter how bleak things might seem."

Ana turned the crystal over in her hands, silent. Her brows pinched together as she brushed its translucent ridges. Vennor noted the tightness in her shoulders, the way her fingers hovered before curling protectively around the stone.

Good. She understood the seriousness. But not enough to be afraid. Not yet.

"The code we'll write," Vennor said, keeping her tone even, "won't interfere with the Lantern itself. It's a protective measure—meant to neutralize any attempts to halt or sabotage its activation, should resistance arise."

Ana studied the crystal as if reverse-engineering the implications in her mind.

"It won't activate unless we direct it to," Vennor continued. "It will sit dormant, invisible to the Thread. A precaution, nothing more."

That's all it was. A safeguard. A quiet line of defense to ensure the Lantern couldn't be derailed. To keep the anomaly contained. To protect the Ark from unraveling—no matter what interference emerged.

"We'd embed a sequence in the Lantern architecture. Something that could intervene if the anomaly breaches containment. A last resort. It wouldn't activate unless all else failed."

Ana nodded slowly, processing. "You want it to be able to control parts of the system."

"Only under the most extreme conditions." Vennor's voice was calm, but her eyes didn't leave Ana's. "Think of it as a fire-break. It would isolate, contain—delete, if needed."

Ana exhaled. "That's... a dangerous function."

"That's why we'll embed the protocol manually. Off-grid. No logs. I want you to keep this between us for now. Just until we understand the full scope."

Ana didn't answer at first. She glanced down at the crystal in her hand, then held it out slightly, as if offering it back.

Vennor closed Ana's fingers gently around it. "Keep it."

With a swift motion, Ana tucked the crystal into her jump-suit pocket. "I can write that code. It's complicated, but... I can do it."

"I knew I could count on you," Vennor said with a quiet nod.

Ana hesitated. "I just hope we don't have to use it."

Vennor smiled, though something in her chest constricted. "So do I, Ana," she said. "So do I."

GOODBYE__

Rayne

Rayne guided Jesla through the quiet corridors, retracing the path from Jesla's alcove toward her own.

The lights in the western alcoves, briefly bright during the commotion, had dimmed again for sleep. Neighbors had returned to their mats and blankets, pretending the Peace Officers hadn't just dragged someone out screaming.

It was the middle of the night. Only the soft pad of their footsteps echoed through the tunnel. Their breath rose in faint clouds, fading into the dark.

Rayne's ears still rang faintly from the surge of adrenaline. But with each step, her pulse slowed. The cold stone walls felt less suffocating. Her nerves began to settle—just enough to think clearly again.

"Did Vic say anything about what he was working on?"

Jesla shook her head.

"Had his routine changed in any way?"

"No."

"Do you know if he was coding a new beta?"

Jesla shook her head again. "No."

"No—I don't know? Or no—he wasn't working on one?"

"I don't know! He coded new betas all the time."

Rayne's mind spun. She tried to think like Vic. "You didn't hear him say anything about a weird thing in his betas? Like a crash he wasn't expecting? Maybe something in a new Game he was playtesting?"

Jesla screwed up her face. "I told you, no. I have no idea what you're talking about."

It was all Rayne could do to keep her voice steady. "Would anyone else have been coding with him?"

"His mother." Jesla stopped abruptly.

Rayne halted beside her. "His mother was coding with him?"

"No. His mother needs to know." Jesla pressed her temples. "I have to tell her."

"Shit." Vic had taught Rayne to curse when they were children. She wished he was here to tell her what to do next. "Of course. Healor Lynn doesn't know yet. Maybe she'll have some idea about what to do."

Jesla turned. "I need to call the Haven."

"Go, then. Just—try not to jump to any conclusions. Okay?"

Jesla was already moving.

"Come find me when you're done."

"I will." She disappeared into the tunnel's shadows.

Rayne checked her wrist for blue dots—no messages, no contacts. She let out a shaky breath and leaned back against the cold stone wall.

When she remembered the cottontail, her heart dropped. She'd left Cas alone with the sick creature. He didn't yet know what happened with Vic. He would be too consumed with worry for the animal. *If it's still alive.* As she hurried along the corridor toward the southern passages, she wished for the grounding presence of her Oak.

Cas wasn't in the sleeping alcove.

The cottontail was gone too, its makeshift enclosure flattened, as if someone had stepped through it in a hurry. Rayne reached for the overturned water bowl and set it upright. A thin film of moisture clung to her fingers. She wiped them on her jumpsuit, heart thudding harder than it should.

She shouldn't have left Cas alone with the cottontail. She'd told herself he could handle it—nurturing the animal, calming it, the way he always did. Maybe she should've stayed to help.

Then again, what choice had she really had?

The Peace Officers had dragged Vic away in the middle of the night. Jesla was shaken. Something bigger was happening, and if they didn't track it now, they might lose their chance.

She gripped her flashlight and turned, scanning the corridor. No sign of him. No flicker of light. No sound.

How long had she been gone?

It was still too early for anyone else to be awake. As she continued down the tunnel, the hush pressed in around her, thick with leftover tension. As if the shelter itself hadn't caught its breath since Vic was taken.

At the entrance to the underground kitchens, she heard gentle scraping sounds.

She entered through the southern food store and walked into the airy space, with its spotless white floors and walls. A globe of lights hung in the center of the ceiling, casting a warm glow over the honeycombed shelves filled with canisters of cornmeal and cranberry biscuits and sealed jars of pickles and peaches. Each canister showed the letter "S," indicating its correlation to the people staying the south tunnel.

In the three connecting kitchens, there would be "N," "E," and "W" stores. The Thread managed its inventory according to how people spread themselves out in the tunnels, and recommend changes in food stocks depending on the number of people and length of each stay in the shelter.

She found Cas by the freezers. "Cas, what are you doing?"

He squatted with his back to her. She spotted the empty rope sack spread across the ground. Cas had placed the limp body of the cottontail on top. He reached over, and with great care, took a handful of dried leaves from his pouch. He folded the leaves into long strands and stuffed them into the sack around the cottontail.

The animal was small and vulnerable on the ground, its body slack and still, with one leg sticking out at an odd angle. It never struck her before this moment how quickly life left the body. One moment you were alive, kicking and thinking. The next moment, you were gone.

"Cas?" She knelt at his side. She put a hand on his shoulder to pull him around. He didn't react.

"Are you... burying it?" Custom dictated a loving burial in the Earth for all living things, but there was no going outside now. The ground would be frozen for weeks, maybe months, to come.

The cold of the room worked its way up her legs. She let her hand fall and stood up.

"I'm doing what I can. It's not much." Cas used the back of his hand to wipe his nose.

"Can I help?"

He shook his head and finished preparing the bundle. He'd worked a lining of leaves around the furry body, almost like a nest. Or a burrow.

"Do you want to say the rites? I'll do it with you."

Cas turned to her. His eyes were raw. "I don't think I can."

Rayne took a breath. "We are One," she began. "We are all."

Cas's lip trembled. He stood with the leaf-wrapped package in his hands. They said together, "We are the living. We lay this body with loving intention to rest in the Earth. Sky, water, fire, wind. We are One."

Rayne opened one of the heavy freezer doors.

Cas hesitated, then stepped forward with the bundle in his arms. "I'm so sorry," he whispered to the cottontail. "It's where you'll have to stay until we can dig a proper hole in the ground." He placed the sack gently on an abandoned upper shelf. Rayne eased the door shut, the seal clicking into place with a soft hiss.

With another swipe at his nose, Cas bent to gather the green leaves that had fallen to the floor, brushing them into his palms with deliberate care. His movements were slow, reverent.

She watched him, torn. This wasn't the right moment—but there might not be a right moment.

"I think you need to know what just happened."

He glanced up, his eyes rimmed red.

"It's Vic. They arrested him."

Cas straightened, the leaves crumpling in his grip. "What?"

"They took him right from the western corridor. Peace Officers. He was yelling, Jesla was yelling. No one knew what to do." She stepped closer. "No one helped him."

Cas froze, his arms still full of leaves. His fingers dug into the stems, not moving.

"I'm sorry. I know this isn't the time. You're still—" Her throat tightened. "I just thought... you should know. And I'm worried, Cas. What if we're next? What if it has something to do with the beta?"

Still, he said nothing. The silence dragged out between them, heavy with unspoken thoughts.

She lowered her voice. "I think we need to start digging. The Thread might hold clues—about Vic, about the anomaly. About what's really going on."

When he finally spoke, his voice was quiet and brittle. "I'm not in the mood to talk about it now."

"I get it. I do. You're grieving, and I'm terrified, and it's a lot all at once." She swallowed. "But Vic is our friend. If there's any chance we can help him... we have to try."

Cas exhaled, slow and steady. Then he nodded, almost imperceptibly.

"Yes," he said. "We should help."

"Then let's go."

ROCK STARS__

Rayne

"Here's what I think." Rayne steered Cas back into their sleeping alcove. "We need to playtest a beta. One of yours. The stadium. Sit down."

Cas shrugged off Rayne's directive and went to the empty enclosure. He picked up the fallen wooden pieces and stacked them against the wall, then sank to a blanket in the middle of the floor. "You want to playtest my concert? How's that going to help?"

Rayne arranged herself on her blankets. "It's the quickest way to look at both things at once." She swept her temple to display her Thread. "Show us my American Revolution Game code again." Her Thread blazed to life, rolling through the data stories they had been poring over the night before.

"But we couldn't—"

"That's right, we couldn't figure out why my beta crashed.

The second problem is Vic. Where the hell is he and what do they want with him? Call Vic."

The Thread went dark.

"See?" Rayne said. "I thought so. The Seers disabled his Thread. We've got to work with what he's left behind."

Cas sighed. "Slow down. You want to trace Vic's Game aspect? But he wasn't in my concert beta. I was working on that myself."

"No, he wasn't in your concert. But the same—disturbance—could be affecting all our betas. Including Vic's. We have to search for common themes. We already know my Games might be compromised. That's why we have to play one of yours."

Rayne dug around in her bag for her gamescreen. "Put yours on," she said.

Cas glanced at the wooden slats against the wall. His eyes shone. "I don't feel like playing right now. I haven't even finished designing this beta yet."

"Cas." Rayne held her screen between her hands. "You know I'm right. Plus, some distraction will be good for you right now. Help take your mind off things."

Cas sat silently. Then he rooted around for his own game-screen and pulled it on. "You're so damn stubborn."

"Only when you deserve it." Rayne cracked a smile. "Now keep an eye out for anything weird."

***

THEY DROPPED INTO THE CONCERT. The roar of the crowd hit like a wave—louder, messier, more electric than Rayne expected. Smoke clung to the rafters. The whole stadium reeked of sweat and beer and something sharp, like ozone after a storm.

Backstage, shadows flickered across crates of lighting gear and half-empty water bottles. Rayne gripped a bass guitar, the strap rough against her shoulder. Cas stood beside her in a glittering floor-length gown, a lace train trailing behind him and elbow-length fingerless gloves flashing under the colored strobes.

Rayne caught a glimpse of herself in the mirror bolted to the side wall—there was a feather braided into her hair, shimmering violet. Of course there was.

They emerged into view of the audience, and the sound hit with a physical force, vibrating in Rayne's chest. A dozen spotlights pinballed over the stage. Fans screeched and hooted as Cas flung out his train with a flourish and slid behind a gleaming grand piano.

Rayne squinted into the crowd, trying to steady herself. A giant stuffed elephant sat in a box along the stage's edge, waiting for its dramatic reveal.

Cas wrapped one hand around his mic and waved. The cheering surged, practically blowing the stadium roof off. His whole face lit up, and for the first time all night, Rayne saw something spark in him.

The stage became a pulsing mass of satellite imagery. Holographic mountains, deserts, and oceans passed over the band. Thousands of handhelds twinkled from all over the stadium. Rayne's mind came alive with music. Her fingers played. Her mouth opened, and the growling song came out in perfect harmony with Cas.

Drums the size of refrigerators hung on either side of the stage, rotating to the beat. The throbbing pulse made Rayne's heart race, pressing against her ribs until she felt it would burst.

Cas tossed his hair and sang. He pounded the keys and pointed at the crowd. They roared.

"This is violent ocean weather!" Cas sang. As the song gained momentum, he bounced on the piano bench, whipping

the crowd through the next verse. *"This is the best kind of violent weather!"* The lights swirled around him.

For a beta that isn't finished, this is pretty damn good.

Rayne's senses were overwhelmed. It was difficult to focus on the aspects around her.

It was time for Rayne's solo. Her fingers flew over the strings. She shimmied up to Cas, and they danced and sang with each other in front of his microphone.

They caught their breath after the second chorus. Rayne scanned the crowd again, this time making out a few individual faces at the front. She caught the eye of a pair of people dressed head to toe in neon blue who were flailing in time with the beat. Nodding to them, Rayne pounded out the last notes. As the song ended, she held her bass high overhead. She breathed in the waves of joy from the fans. *Her* fans.

Cas launched into the next number. Already Rayne's fingers were finding the notes.

There was a click. Rayne's fingers fumbled. The holograms disappeared. The drums stilled. The spotlights went dark. Cas's skin took on a strange hue as the glow of ten thousand personal electronic devices bathed the stage in a blue-white glow.

The joyful roar of the crowd faltered, then became something else. Screams.

She let go of her instrument, grabbed Cas's hand, and yanked him to standing. The piano bench tipped over. They pushed past the guitar player's aspect, fell over a tangle of cables, and scrambled backstage.

Out in the stadium, the sound became a thunderous snarl. Something large groaned and crashed. The floor shook. Had the fans started a stampede?

"I'm guessing this isn't part of your beta," Rayne shouted.

They bumped into several people as they made their way off stage. It was even darker in the wings.

"No! Definitely not!"

People pushed and shouted around them. Rayne tried to make out faces, but it was too dark. Her hand slick with sweat, she held onto Cas and pulled him toward where she guessed the control panels were. If they could get the lights back on, they might see what was causing the disruption.

Glass shattered nearby. Panic filled her throat.

There was a man in their way. She slammed into his chest with a thud. Unlike everyone else, he wasn't moving.

"Hey!" Cas shouted. "Who—"

The man grabbed Rayne's wrist. His face in shadow as he pulled her close.

"What's going on?" Cas bumped into her from behind.

"Don't move!" the man hissed into her ear. "And don't speak until I tell you to." He smelled sour, like dried sweat. Something cool touched her throat.

She gasped. "Cas, he's got a—"

"I said, *don't speak.*" He jerked her forward.

Rayne reflexively twisted her arm, but the man tightened his grasp.

She hard exited the Game, taking Cas with her.

"WHAT WAS THAT?" Cas removed his gamescreen. "I didn't design any of that. The lights—"

"I know, I know." Rayne took off her screen and put it aside. "Let's get the code."

"You hard exited my Game! What the hell!"

"Take a breath. Shit. This is exactly what happened to me." The Thread delivered a stabilizing signal—slowing Rayne's heart rate, nudging her system to release calming neurotransmitters.

Cas clenched his fingers. "Okay, give me a minute." He stood and paced the short length of their alcove, then stopped in front of the cottontail's empty enclosure. His chest lifted in a long breath, muscles loosening as his Thread administered its own calming protocol.

"Show us what happened," Rayne said, her voice low. She exhaled slowly, the way she had when she'd first surfaced from the river in her own beta.

The Thread responded, casting its display across the alcove. Data stories from the final moments of Cas's concert began to unfurl—timelines, movement scripts, audience feedback loops. Dozens of threads spun outward in delicate spirals.

Rayne barely looked at them.

"No," she said. "Not those. Thread, run a sublayer scan. Look beneath the behavior scripts. Filter for unregistered overrides."

Cas raised his eyebrows. "You think it's the same as in yours?"

"I think it might be worse." She flicked through several panels with swift motions, her focus needle-sharp. "In my beta, I found something—buried in the soldier protocols. A line of behavior override code I never wrote. It was elegant, hidden between command strings like it belonged there. I thought it might've been a glitch. Until I saw the signature."

Cas leaned in. "Not Ark-coded?"

She shook her head. "Not from any Ark. It didn't just hijack behavior—it rewrote the core logic without breaking the architecture. I need to know if the same blueprint is hiding here."

She tapped in a new command. "Thread, isolate anomalous

command strings embedded within behavior protocols. Search for encrypted syntax patterns."

The data stories collapsed, replaced by a thin column of raw source code. Lines scrolled upward, flickering with subroutine markers and null values. Cas watched in silence.

"There," Rayne murmured.

She froze the scroll on a string tucked deep within the applause response matrix. Her pulse picked up. "Look at this segment. It's nested like the one I found in mine. Same encryption markers. Almost identical structure."

Cas squinted at the code. "But... why embed it here? This doesn't even trigger player interaction."

Rayne's eyes didn't leave the display. "Because it's not meant to. It's watching. Testing variables. Like it's... learning."

"Adaptation servers are subject to data explosions at this time stamp."

"What?" Cas tilted his head at the Thread's statement. "What does that mean?"

"Adaptation servers are subject to data explosions at this time stamp," the Thread repeated. "The Thread has identified the source of the disruption. The voice is coming. It's lost in the data storm."

Rayne and Cas exchanged glances.

"I think it's trying to identify something specific. Translate," Rayne said.

The Thread went completely white.

"I got dried fruit this time to feed it!" Aden galloped into the alcove.

Cas jumped about a mile. "Aden! You—you surprised me."

Aden froze when he saw the wood slats stacked against the wall. "Where's the cottontail? I have a treat." He straightened his arm and opened his fingers to reveal a crushed brown currant.

"A treat. How nice." Rayne shut down the weird blank Thread.

"Listen, buddy." Cas brushed off his pants. "I have some news."

"Did the cottontail find its home?" Aden asked.

"No, not that. The cottontail has... rejoined the Earth." His voice hitched. He put his palms on Aden's shoulders. "I wasn't able to save it."

"That's okay." Aden shrugged. "Some things can't be saved. My Thread told me." He popped the currant into his mouth. "I'm having breakfast with Ma now." He wormed out from under Cas's hands and loped down the corridor.

"What *was* that?" Rayne asked.

"Aden isn't old enough—"

"Not Aden. The Thread."

Cas shook his head. "I have no idea. And I don't think we're going to figure it out, either."

Rayne scoffed. "Of course we're going to figure it out. We haven't even tried—"

"What's the Thread even talking about? Adaptation servers? Data explosions? 'The voice is coming?'"

"It's confusing, sure. But we can work with it."

"I've never seen that. Have you? And my beta is all crapped up now because you hard exited."

"I'm sorry, I—"

"We're just Designers, Rayne. We have to report this."

"You're joking, right?" She took a step back. "The Seers *arrested* Vic. We have to figure out why before they come for us."

"Maybe it's not for us to meddle around with. I'm tired." He put his hands over his face.

"Let's take a minute." Rayne raked her fingers through her hair. "Why don't we get something to eat?"

"I'm not hungry." Cas sat down again on the blanket and pushed his thumbs over his eye sockets.

"Yes, you are hungry. You need to eat. I'm going to get us something. I'll bring it back here, okay?"

Cas turned away.

"Cas. We can do this." Rayne tried to meet her friend's eyes.

Getting no response, she turned and left for the food stores.

A REPORT__

Vennor

A SMALL FIRE crackled in the grate of the Seers' underground library. Faded fabrics hung on the walls, depicting landscapes from an earlier time on Earth. Vennor's Thread, open before her, displayed Ana's model of the phased Lantern. It repeated over and over, showing the upgrade unfurling. Slowly at first, then spreading to thousands of Games. The upgraded Games exploded to life.

The fire hissed, shedding sparks in the darkness of the room. Vennor leaned back in her chair, allowing herself a moment of relief from the stress of the day's meeting.

An eternally stable, peaceful future finally within reach. Vennor couldn't help but feel a sense of awe. And trepidation. If they released the Lantern into the NEWRRTH, there would be no turning back. They had to be sure.

She brushed the simulation away and closed her eyes. "Tell me about the anomaly," she said to her Thread.

"The anomaly appeared 314 hours ago in a beta Game—"

"Not that. Tell me what it wants."

"No source code is available for the anomaly. Unable to determine its origins."

She had been through this line of questioning with the Thread. It was time to try something new. "Did the NEWRRTH send the anomaly?"

The Thread was silent.

"Is the anomaly here to teach us something?" Again, nothing.

An incoming flashed inside her right wrist. "Incoming," her Thread announced.

"Decline." She had asked to be left alone.

Her gaze lingered on the fabric hangings that decorated the room. The harmonious designs reminded her of the tranquil intervals in human history. When no war raged. When people harvested flax and cotton, spun fine colored thread, and dreamed up patterns to weave into cloth. But those times were always temporary. In every period of human history, there was more violence, more senseless loss of life, waiting just ahead.

The door opened. Nilo announced herself in her melodic voice. "I know you requested not to be disturbed. But you'll want to see this."

Vennor lifted her head, surprised. Nilo clutched the ends of her robe as she walked in. An aspect trailed beside her. "I think he can help us."

Vennor appraised the aspect of a tall, slender, brown-haired person with a kind face.

"Let me explain," Nilo said. "He called us a few minutes ago. I think it was intended for you. I accepted the incoming—"

"And...?" Vennor asked. She did not like the hint of rebuke in Nilo's tone.

"And this could be the missing piece that completes our plan. For implementing the new project."

<hr>

THE LEVEL SIX showed no signs of abating. They would be in the shelter for another few days at least. After the morning meal, Vennor swept into the shelter's conference room. "We have found the perfect champion. We need to transport him here. Immediately."

Ana's head snapped up. "After the Level Six clears, you mean?"

Vennor scowled. "Of course. Once it's safe, we'll send overland transport for him. Bring Trueno and the others. The discussion will continue."

Ana spoke into her Thread, summoning the Seers. Vennor paced. She felt restless, eager. The longer they waited, the more danger the anomaly posed. But now they had a chance. A way to manipulate the situation. To outsmart the anomaly and leave the Settlers behind. They now had the extra assurance of not one, but two Game Designers.

One Designer who could create beautiful things, and one Designer who could end them.

The door to the conference room opened. Nilo entered, followed by Trueno and Enayat.

Ana dismissed a call on her Thread. "He's six hours away, and will leave immediately after we're cleared for overland travel."

Vennor nodded. "Good. We'll be ready for him." She turned to the others as they took their seats. "In the meantime, Ana launched our work on the Lantern. You'll agree that it's a brilliant start."

The time for caution was over.

RAYNE BALANCED two bowls of rice porridge in her hands and made her way through the tunnels. The shelter hummed with early morning conversations. "Excuse me." Rayne passed a family just emerging from their alcove. Their voices swirled around her as she went by.

It became even more crowded as she left the western block and entered the atrium. She spotted Cynthia and her grandsons across the echoing space. Catching Cynthia's eye, she raised her eyebrows in a question: *How's the new Game?* Clem spotted her, and they both waved. Cynthia smiled, gave a thumbs-up. *Good.*

Rayne pushed through the crowd, listening to the voices around her. "... you should have seen the water we swam through, it was so blue..." said a man. "No, I haven't played it yet, but I heard you could fly in a metal transport..." came another voice. The rhythms of barrel music began echoing somewhere deep inside the shelter.

Rayne's heart lifted at the familiar sounds. It was going to be a good day.

"Everything all right today, love?" a neighbor asked.

"Just bringing breakfast to Cas." She held the bowls high to avoid getting bumped.

"He should eat in the commons."

Rayne pushed past her. She hated being short with people, but there was no time to explain. "We'll have to disagree about that," she called over her shoulder.

Slipping into Cas's alcove, Rayne put the bowls down on the blanket. "I couldn't manage the tea."

Cas lifted his head. He was hollow-eyed.

"I had to go all the way to the western block. That's where the Thread wanted me to get my food." Rayne lowered herself across from Cas on the ground. "Can't disappoint Tamas. Wouldn't dare take away the bliss of having all the food stores balance out. You should eat this while it's hot."

Cas pushed the blankets aside and sat up. "Do you know how many people used to freeze to death?"

"What?" Rayne reached for a spoon, then stopped.

"In the winters. People and animals used to die all the time from exposure to the weather. Before the NEWRRTH."

"Fantastic. Real great morning talk, Cas."

"I don't mean to get all dark. I'm just trying to remind us how hard life was before the Thread. And the Games."

Rayne smiled. "Breakfast first, words later. I'm cold and tired. You are too. Right now, you need to eat. Then your Thread can help you process the cottontail's passing. It wasn't your fault."

"You keep telling me what to do, Rayne."

Rayne made a face. "I don't."

"You do. You're always on my case. I can think for myself."

"Okay, Cas. Think for yourself." She pulled a spoon from one bowl of sticky rice. "But take my advice. This idea about reporting the anomalies. It's not smart." She took a bite of the hot porridge. "Mmm. This is good. The kitchens must have found more salt."

"I mean it, Rayne. I've never felt a disruption like that in a Game. Like a wall coming down. That blank Thread? It was scary." He pushed his bowl away. "And I'm not hungry."

Rayne couldn't help but laugh. "What is this? The great awakening? Come on. Everything's going to be all right. Just eat."

"You don't get it. We need to be careful. This anomaly could bring down the Games."

"The Thread will lead us where we need to go. It always does."

"Haven't you noticed? The Thread's been useless."

"You don't mean that," she said, swallowing. She didn't like the way he looked at her. His nostrils flared and the tips of his ears reddened. She spoke carefully. "The anomaly is not a random glitch, Cas. It's *sentient*. Maybe the Thread isn't helping us because it's already been corrupted."

"Do you hear yourself?"

"We just need to be careful. We need to stick together, and we'll figure it out. We always do." She reached out and squeezed his hand.

"We're getting help." Cas pulled his hand away. A note of firmness crept into his voice. "I hope you accept it when it comes."

INTERROGATED__

Vennor

VENNOR KEPT her hands under the table so the rest of the
Seers wouldn't notice her clenched fists. "Thank you for assem-
bling again. We're ready to take the next step."

Trueno's eyes, rimmed with red and swollen from only a
few hours' rest, widened in alarm. "The next step? But we
haven't discussed the *first* step. The precautions we need to put
in place. We can't launch this upgrade without investigating all
the possible outcomes."

"Yes, yes." Vennor hoped her impatience didn't show.
"That's why we're here now. To interview our Game Designer
in holding."

Trueno shook his head. "I hope you've thought this
through, Vennor."

"I have." Vennor forced her hands to relax, nodding to
Enayat. "Let's begin. Connect to the Designer in holding."

Enayat established a secure connection and activated the

Thread in the middle of the table. "Bring us to the Designer's shelter." As they waited for the call to go through, Enayat continued, "His scan is continuing. But we have enough evidence to question the parameters of the beta he's created. How far he's—they've—progressed in coding."

"Perhaps we should start with why the anomaly wanted to work with him," Nilo suggested. "What it wants. And what it's capable of."

"I doubt we'll get far with that line of questioning," Enayat said.

Trueno crossed his arms. "And I doubt we'll get far with this... what did you call it? This *meeting* with a Designer being held against his will and without a formal charge."

Vennor faced him. "I have a hard time believing that Vic will voluntarily share information about how to take down the anomaly *that he's been cooperating with*." She took a breath. "Don't question my decision again."

Trueno stared at her for several moments before glancing away.

The Thread showed a small room with no windows. Two Peace Officers stood in front of a young man who sat cross-legged on the floor. They had cuffed his wrists behind his back. One Officer spoke. "Connection established." The Officers moved to the side so the Seers had a clear view of their subject. He stared at their aspects as they assembled around him.

Enayat pushed up his sleeves. "Vic, we securely connected you to the Seers at the Center for Future Guidance. We have brought you to this room because you are under investigation for crimes against the NEWRRTH."

Vic's head lowered. Vennor couldn't tell if he was smirking or afraid. "What do you want with me?" He raised his head, eyes hard. A handsome boy.

"You have been tampering with the Games." Vennor kept her tone neutral.

Vic huffed. Defiant.

"Designers are allowed—encouraged, even—to create at will. You can dream up any Game with the help of your Threads. But the freedom to create and play doesn't grant you the right to collaborate with entities hostile to the NEWRRTH."

"I didn't do anything."

"We have proof." Vennor motioned to Ana. "Show him."

Ana told the Thread to show them the new beta Vic designed. The ashen cloud swirled. A narrow path wound through the trees, following a river with muddy banks. A tuft of land appeared in the middle of the water. An island.

Vic's jaw tightened.

Ana streamed the scenes in fast forward motion. A powerful gust of wind bent the trees. Then, a blizzard of gray snowflakes. A towering rock with a crack through its side. The path stopped at the rock. Ana stopped the stream.

Vic gave a short, barking laugh. A ripple of apprehension crossed Ana's face.

"You didn't create any of these scenes, did you?" Vennor asked.

Vic didn't answer. It was impossible to tell what he was thinking behind his forced smile.

"You know we only want to protect you." The Officers shifted.

"Who programmed this Game with you?" Vennor regarded their subject more closely. Vic's nose was a little too long, his chin too pointed. Even with his mop of dark curls, Vic's face was not that pretty after all. But the Designer had a certain flair, a delicacy of movement.

Vennor asked Ana to let the beta run again. Vic faced them

all with a cool glare. One that said he would weather any storm that came his way. It irked Vennor.

"Tell us." Trueno cleared his throat. "Do you believe what you did—conspiring against the NEWRRTH or not—was aligned with a life affirming outcome?" It was a prudent question. Any actions that deviated from the Thread's guidance were not associated with progress.

"I acted under the One Principle." Vic's eyes narrowed. "Are you trying to scare me? I don't fear you or any of the Seers. Or the Peace Officers."

Vennor remembered a vintage film she'd seen in a Game of a man cornered by a hungry lion. Vic had the same inscrutable manner as the wild cat—fearless, ready to strike.

The Seers exchanged glances. "This is going nowhere," Enayat murmured.

"If you believe your actions were life-affirming, in accordance with the Principle of One," continued Trueno, "then why won't you tell us about your collaborators?"

Vic scoffed. "Because you wouldn't understand. None of you." He swept his gaze across the room, eyes hard. "You sit there pretending you're guiding the future, but you can't even see what's right in front of you." He leaned forward slightly. "I see it. I'm building it. And you're too afraid to ask the real questions."

Vennor waved a hand. "Let him know the charges he faces." Charging Vic was a gamble, but it was one worth taking. If they couldn't get any information about the beta or the Settlers, he'd be dealt with. In a way.

Nilo set a list of charges on the Thread. She added a countdown.

"You leave us no choice," Vennor said. "In ten hours, we will begin the cleaning of your data from the Game network.

After which you will no longer be a Designer. We will delete all your data from the central Archive."

Vic closed his eyes.

Vennor continued. "In five hours, we will release a report to the public. You will be labeled as a threat to the Game, guilty of crimes against the NEWRRTH. You will be marked as a non-player. The public will be instructed to ignore you. And if anyone tries to contact you, they will be sent to us for questioning."

The Seers watched Vic. After a moment, Vennor said, "That will be all."

"Wait," Vic mumbled. "Stop the countdown."

Vennor raised an eyebrow. "You'll cooperate?"

"Yes." He gazed into the distance. "I need my Thread activated. Please."

"Before we do that, we require a certain amount of information from you. Do you agree to share what you know without hesitation to benefit the Games and the Thread? All in alignment with the Principle of One?"

Vic seemed to consider this request.

"Release the cuffs," Trueno said.

Vennor's eyes narrowed. *Don't rush this.*

One Officer knelt behind Vic and unlocked his cuffs. Vic rolled his broad shoulders around.

"Do you agree to the terms?" Vennor repeated.

"I agree." The ghost of a smile on Vic's lips.

Nilo whispered, "Go on, Vennor. Give him his Thread."

"Turn off the countdown," Vennor said. "Let's begin."

KAI'S DISCOVERY__

Rayne

"Incoming. Incoming." Rayne snapped to attention. She'd been dozing in an alcove in the western block. For two days, she and Jesla had been asking the Thread to give them clues about why Vic had been arrested. But it had led them nowhere.

She left Cas alone in the southern block. He did this thing sometimes, getting angry at everyone and working on his own for a while. When his stormy mood blew over, he'd come around.

Jesla stirred sleepily beside her. "What's going on?"

"Accept," Rayne said to her Thread. "What is it?"

"Level Six has abated to an acceptable level. Return to overland housing is appropriate."

She exhaled. *Not the message I was expecting.* Enayat's angry face flashed in her mind.

"Okay to return home?"

"Confirmed." The Thread showed her a stream of weather data. The storm had played itself out.

"It's done." Rayne turned to Jesla's questioning expression. "We can leave."

Jesla fell back against her blankets. Her eyes were blood-shot from all the data scanning they had been doing. She pressed the back of her wrists to her eye sockets. "Great. Now we can focus on getting to Vic. Wherever they're holding him."

"We should pack up here."

A whiff of dried sweat wafted through the air. After three days in the shelter, they were beginning to stink. They stuffed their bags with blankets from the floor. Rayne thought about reaching out to Cas. Was he ready to hear from her? Probably not.

"Hey." Jesla had finished packing. "Can I ask a favor?"

"Mmm-hmm."

"It's going to be lonely at our apartment. You know. With Vic gone. Would you..."

"Oh! Yeah. You should come home with me. Stay as long as you like." Rayne nudged Jesla's arm. "You're always welcome."

They joined their neighbors trekking through the western corridors. People jostled and laughed around them, happy to be returning home. When they reached the atrium, cheerful banter multiplied from all directions.

At the top of the long staircase, Rayne saw an unmistakable figure in a long, dark coat. A stream of people parted around Cas. Was he waiting for her? He stared right where she was walking with Jesla. Maybe he wanted to apologize and get to work again. They were so close to discovering what this anomaly was. Once they isolated it, they might even have a handle on what had happened to Vic.

When she looked up again, Cas was gone.

Rayne swung open the door to her house. Jesla hesitated on the threshold.

"Are you okay? Coming in?"

"Sorry." Jesla shifted to her other foot. "It's not that. It's just —I haven't seen Vic in almost three days. I don't know if he's still—" She closed her eyes. "I can't believe I let them take him away."

"Vic can take care of himself."

Jesla chewed her lower lip. "This was a mistake. I should go back to our apartment in case someone comes by."

"No. Let's get you settled in here. Then we can sort out Vic."

Jesla didn't move. "If you're sure." Her eyes darted around the darkened room. She stepped in. "Nice place."

"Thanks." Rayne motioned to the hallway. "Come on in. Washroom's down there. I'll be right back."

Jesla put down her bag and kicked off her footslides. "You're sure we'll be safe here?"

"Why wouldn't we?" Rayne took off her own footslides and wandered into her bedroom. "Things have been quiet for a while."

"How do we know?" Jesla said from the kitchen. "Things change when we're not paying attention."

"Yeah. It doesn't do any good to worry, though." Rayne dropped her bag in the corner of her bedroom and returned to Jesla in the kitchen. "Start retraction," she said to her Thread.

The shutters over the windows rolled back with a clang. Blinding light poured into the cottage. They shielded their eyes from the whiteness.

"That's bright," said Rayne. "Good to see the sunshine, though. You ready for a shower?"

"I'm tired. Think I'll rest for a bit."

"Suit yourself." Rayne took her arms away from her eyes. Snow sparkled through the windows. Jesla's face was buried in her hands. Was she crying?

"Dirties," said a voice from the living room. Luci trundled over from its docking station. "You missed Luci."

Jesla lifted her face. She wiped her nose with the hem of her T-shirt.

Luci stopped in its tracks. "You. No sitting on the couch."

"You have a Luci?" Jesla cracked a smile. "Why didn't you tell me?"

"It was... a gift. Luci, I know we're dirty and we need to wash up. Give us a minute, okay?"

She took Jesla to the living room. Luci nudged between them. Standing at the center of the oval rug, it guarded the couch. Luci was not much to look at. Its body was roughly the size of a toddler's, proportions all wrong, its single arm equipped with a cotton pad. It had a cartoon face etched onto a featureless black box.

"Luci," said Rayne. "Can you go back to rest for now?"

"Not a chance."

Jesla put her hand on Luci's casing. The bot beeped warily at her. "I'll be careful. I won't get anything dirty. I promise."

"Incoming." They both checked their wrists. It was for Rayne. She left Jesla to fend for herself with Luci and walked toward her Oak. She accepted the call from her mother.

"Hi, honey," Kai said. "Are you back home?"

"Ma, you can see I'm here. Look, I'm sorry I never called you back while we sheltered. We were... it was busy." She leaned her full weight against her Oak's bark and felt the comforting release of energy.

Her mother dismissed Rayne's comments with a wave. "I know. Oh, the Oak is doing well."

"Release and retract windsails," Rayne told her Thread. To her mother, she said, "Sounds good, Ma."

"You're not listening, honey. Sit down for a minute. I have an update."

The large sails around the Oak retreated with a zippering sound and flapped back into their compartments in the wall. Her Thread displayed the amount of energy captured by the windsails during the storm. It was a good reading.

"I'm listening. What's your news?"

"Remember when I told you about the problem with irrigation here at the Orchard? The farmers thought they had watered the lettuces, but they hadn't, and we had to follow all sorts of protocols to check their Thread connections."

Rayne surveyed the courtyard outside. The snow glittered over every twig and needle. It was breathtaking. The wind animated tiny plumes of snow on top of the drifts. There didn't seem to be any damage, only a few large branches down. Except—

"Luci! Come over here." Luci was spreading a cloth over the couch. "The bird feeders! They all fell down. Why didn't you fix them?"

Luci rode over. "Because of the pneumonia."

Her mother's aspect put her hands on her hips. "I'll wait."

"Sorry, Ma, just a minute. Luci, help me with the feeders. Grab the birdseed and put on your trackers." They took off down the hallway. "Hang on, Ma. I'm going outside." She pushed her feet into her tall rubber boots. Luci stuck its appendages into rubberized footings. Thick grooves on the bottoms prevented Luci from slipping in the snow. Rayne opened the front door, but Luci stayed put. "Fine," Rayne mumbled, and grabbed a scarf to throw around Luci's neck. "Satisfied?" The bot made a spiteful beep, and they stepped outside. The cold air bit at her cheeks. Her legs sank into the fluffy snow with each step.

By the time Rayne had finished with the feeders, Luci had already cleared a path to the door and was cutting the fallen branches into manageable pieces.

"Thank you, Luci," Rayne said. "I'll let Ma know we're okay." She hurried back inside and gave her mother a thumbs up. "Sorry." She sat on the floor and pulled off her wet boots. Luci trundled in behind her and slammed the door shut.

"It's fine. I'm glad there isn't much damage," Kai said. "But you need to hear this."

"Sorry. What were you saying about the farmers?"

"Right," Kai said. "It took forever to get the farmers to realize they'd forgotten to water the lettuces."

"Oh. The lettuce thing. Yes."

"What happened was—the Thread of the first farmer—it was like it disappeared. Our engineers were surprised. They had never seen anything like it. But the two of them, they had this old device, a tracer of sorts, and they pulled it out of storage —or wherever old software lives—and sent it after the Thread."

Rayne was paying full attention now. Her mother continued. "It found the broken Thread and followed it. It led them to a new location. A new home. I'm not using the right words. A place we had never seen before. A new Thread. It was... well, new."

"You used old software to find a new Thread? What does that mean?" Rayne said. "Are you sure it wasn't a mistake? The NEWRRTH makes adjustments sometimes—"

"We checked the energy signature. It was the farmer's Thread. But it snapped. Broke off. And when we found it again, it was connected to... something else. Rayne, we suspect sabotage." Kai narrowed her eyes. "I believe it's connected to Vic."

Rayne frowned. "You know about Vic?"

"Everyone knows about Vic." Kai lowered her voice and glanced around. "They warned us."

"Who warned you?"

"I can't say here." Her mother hurried through the greenhouse. She was probably headed to her office. "The Land Keeper Council told us there were... things happening in the NEWRRTH. That we should be careful."

Rayne placed her hands on the porcelain kitchen counters. The Game anomalies. Vic's arrest. Now the farmers have new Threads? She shook her head. There was a connection somewhere. But she was missing it.

Something clattered behind her. Whipping her head around, Rayne saw Luci dumping Jesla's bag with a flourish. "Luci! What are you doing?"

With its single arm, Luci started picking through Jesla's belongings. "I knew I smelled something disgusting."

"Put that back right now. You only touch *our* things. Never someone else's. Go rest!" Luci released Jesla's clothes and they tumbled back to the floor. The bot went right past its docking station and rolled into Rayne's bedroom. With a sigh, Rayne put Jesla's things back into her bag.

"Rayne, honey, I don't know what to do." Kai sat down in her office chair and put her face in her hands.

"I don't know either, Ma. But the Council is right. Don't do anything yet. We need to know more about what... or who... wants to sabotage the farmers. It's lucky you discovered what you did. We can use it. But let's not draw the wrong attention right now. We need to keep following the Thread. Right?" She pushed Jesla's gamescreen on top of her clothes, then zipped the bag tight. "Right, Ma?"

Her mother was silent.

TRACING VIC'S ASPECT__

Rayne

"THERE'S SOMETHING ELSE." Kai closed her office door.

Air escaped from Rayne's lips. She didn't realize she had been holding her breath. "There's more? Ma, how could there be—"

"Sh. Listen. Something happened to me, too."

Rayne glanced at Jesla in the living room. Jesla was talking to someone's aspect and wasn't paying attention to Rayne's conversation. Still, Rayne left the kitchen and walked to her bedroom. Kai's aspect followed. She closed the door.

"What happened, Ma?"

"I did my own work with the farmer drones. When they lost their connection to the Thread." Kai glanced around and spoke quietly. "I saw something. Or... that's not it, exactly. I made something happen."

"Okay."

"Promise not to tell anyone."

It took all of Rayne's energy to nod.

"When the engineers sent the tracer down the farmer's Thread, I took a different approach. I connected to the lettuces."

Rayne's face must have shown her confusion.

"I used my Thread to connect to the lettuces. Directly."

"But how..."

"I used the Thread. And pushed into the living tissue of the plants. To see if, you know, they could speak to me."

"Did they?"

Kai's eyes widened. "Yes."

Rayne sat on the edge of her bed, pushing her fingers into the blankets. It was possible that her mother was Disconnecting. It happened sometimes when people had difficulty distinguishing the virtual world from real life.

"Did you hear what I said?"

"Yes, Ma. I just—are you feeling okay?"

"I'm feeling fine. You're not listening."

Rayne breathed in and out, in and out. "I heard what you said. You're saying—you're saying you can connect directly with the lettuces?" It came out as a question.

"Rayne, this is what I've been studying. I have known for years that it is theoretically possible to connect to the network of living plants. I never knew how, until this happened."

"I thought you were studying... fungus?"

"Yes. The mycorrhizas that connect every living green thing in a hyphal web. But I wasn't sure it would work in a hydroponic environment. The greenhouses here, they're... well. There's no soil. That's where the fungal networks operate."

Rayne didn't understand any of that, but it seemed believable. *Real.* That was the important thing. "You're sure it wasn't a Game you were in?"

"Of course not. I was present in reality!" Kai turned toward her office door. "Oh. There's someone here."

"Who?"

"We need to be careful. Rayne, I'm sorry. But you can't tell anyone about this."

Rayne scanned her mother's face. "If you need help..." Rayne wanted to offer her mother something. An action to take. Anything. But her mind came up blank.

"I'm fine. Thank you." Kai was still looking at the door. "And I'm not cracked." She ended the call.

Rayne swayed, lightheaded. Her mother believed she had connected with the network of living green things. Trying to process what Kai said was like trying to peer into a bright light.

Luci bent down in the corner, hovering over Rayne's bag. Taking hold of it, Luci shook it upside down. Rayne's things toppled to the floor.

"Luci, why are you being difficult?"

"You haven't seen difficult. Mind your own business."

Rayne closed her eyes and tried to gather her thoughts. She wished she could pause time and think through these events. She opened her mouth to speak to her Thread, then snapped it shut again.

She hadn't asked her mother the obvious thing.

When Kai connected to the lettuces, what had they said?

Opening the bedroom door, Rayne crossed the kitchen and approached Jesla in the living room. Jesla noticed her approach and said, "Hold on, Rayne's here."

"Sorry to interrupt. There's something—"

"You've come at a good time," said Healor Lynn. Her aspect sat next to Jesla on the couch. She wore the standard charcoal jacket of a Haven healor, but there was something different about her. An air of authority. Her eyes were piercing.

"We were just discussing the possibility of negotiating with the Center for Future Guidance."

"Negotiating with the Center? About what?"

"About releasing Vic."

Chimes tinkled behind H. Lynn's aspect. The Haven was a peaceful place, but Vic's mother looked anything but serene. She crossed and re-crossed her legs. "I know it's risky. But it's the only sensible option. The overland routes have cleared enough that we can go—"

"The Center will never negotiate with you."

H. Lynn's face fell.

"But I have another idea."

"Rayne. We're not making any progress using the Thread. We need to do something in person."

"I'm telling you, they won't help. It might make things worse. We don't know what they intend to do with him."

Jesla leaned forward. "But you said yourself the Games are deteriorating. The Center is the only place we can see him. Make sure he's okay."

"The Thread might not be deteriorating. It's more complicated than that. I think there's an alternative approach we can take."

Healor Lynn and Jesla waited.

Rayne straightened her shoulders. "There's a program we can use. It's an old application, actually. It could send a tracer after Vic's energy signature. We can see where he was, what he was working on before he got arrested."

"You just thought of this?" Jesla tapped her temples. "After all that time we spent—"

"If we try it and don't get what we need, we'll travel to the Center. Deal?"

Healor Lynn glanced at Jesla, then at Rayne. "It couldn't hurt."

Jesla grunted. "Fine. But let's hurry, okay?"

Rayne activated her Thread. "It won't take long." To her Thread, she said, "Show me the tracer. The one my mother used in the Orchard in the past few days. The program that deployed protocols to the drone farmers."

The Thread glowed blue. After a moment a series of numbers and phrases scrolled by.

36-02-02-20-03-27 — *Public Openshell — Plantation — Collection* — 14,900

"What's Openshell?" Jesla peered over Rayne's shoulder.

"It's an old software program." Rayne watched the Thread. Her heart sped up. "My mother found this when her engineers were figuring out a... um. Describe Openshell."

"Openshell was public domain software." Her Thread's soothing voice started its explanation. "People used its code to upload fixes or contribute improvements to the NEWRRTH. It was discontinued because of modifications that overwrote its own source code."

"Did it behave like a cryptoworm?"

"No," the Thread continued. "A cryptoworm causes a malfunction in a closed system. Openshell is a roadmap for data collection."

"Can we use Openshell to trace an aspect?"

"Possible."

"Show me." Jesla and Healor Lynn leaned forward.

"Describe the target," the Thread said. "Openshell is booted and standing by."

"Rayne. Hold on." Healor Lynn's forehead creased. "Where did you say you found this application?"

"Do you trust me?"

"I trust you. I'm just not—"

"Then let's keep going. We're looking for Vic," Rayne said to her Thread. She located the signature of his aspect and presented it to her Thread.

"Openshell engaged." Vic's signature became a thin green line. It started vibrating. Then it shot away into the distance. Jesla grabbed the couch cushions as if to steady herself. "Where's it going?"

"It's following Vic's aspect. We're going to see where Vic was the last time he was in a Game." The green line branched apart. A few strands moved in different directions, swimming through the dark. The green filaments continued to multiply.

"Where are you going?" Rayne muttered.

"Is it malfunctioning?" Jesla leaned forward.

Rayne spoke to her Thread. "What is this?" She pointed to the branching green stands. "What are these?"

"Redirecting to other aspects."

"No. Stay with Vic."

H. Lynn's expression became confused as she tried to follow the branching. "Which one is he?"

"No idea," Jesla said. "Rayne, what's happening? Why is it doing that?"

The green lines stopped. All at once they turned around and headed back.

"What the..." She told the Thread to throw up several safety screens. The lines kept approaching. Some of them paused, others raced onwards. Curving, moving. Tracing something.

Vic's signature was in the middle of all of them. They were converging on him.

Creating an image.

"What's going on?" Rayne demanded, her heart in her throat. The green lines were getting closer and closer to Vic's signature, as if they were being pulled in by some invisible force. "Thread, what's happening?"

"The tracer is malfunctioning," the Thread said. "It is recommended that you discontinue use at once."

She was not about to give up now, not when she was this close to finding Vic. "Fix it."

"Malfunctioning cannot be fixed. Discontinue use." The strands, dozens of them now, pulsed in a twisting display, forming and reforming as they advanced.

"Why are they coming at us like that?" Jesla stood and backed away.

"I said fix it!" Rayne shouted, her patience at an end. Without thinking, she reached into the code and yanked hard. The green lines froze.

Rayne's heart pounded as she stared at the lines, now unmoving. What had she done? She had never tried to directly manipulate code like that before.

Rayne lowered her hands. The green lines began advancing again. Slowly, they came together in a glowing green sphere. The sphere rotated in front of them.

"Stop. Stop this now," Healor Lynn said.

"Don't worry," Jesla said. "Rayne knows what she's doing."

Rayne snapped her wrists and made the Thread's hologram disappear. "Vic's aspect is being interfered with." She sat down on the couch, knees wobbly. "Something surrounded him in the last Game he played. Protecting him, maybe. Or interacting with him. I can't see what it is. But whatever was with his aspect in there saw us coming."

"What does that mean?" H. Lynn asked.

"It means we have to find him. Fast. I have a lot of questions. Like what the hell he thinks he's doing."

She hoped Cas was ready to talk.

ANOMALY ESCAPES__

Vennor

"You've made it too slow." Vennor glared at Enayat. "The Settlers will attack us before the upgrade is complete. It needs to spread more quickly. If the Lantern takes too much time, we'll be defenseless."

Enayat frowned. "I'm sorry, but I can't make it go any faster. The upgrade process is delicate. We're building in time to make fixes as it releases."

Vennor sighed. She knew Enayat was right, but she couldn't help feeling anxious. The whole situation was spiraling out of control, and they were no closer to finding a solution.

Enayat placed a hand on her arm. "We need to be patient. This will work."

Vennor nodded, but she still couldn't shake the belief that something was going to go wrong. "Double its speed. This is not the time to hold back."

"But Ana said we should—"

"Double the speed of the Lantern."

Enayat put his hands deep into the pockets of his jumpsuit. "Ana said the Settlers aren't capable of keeping pace with the Lantern at its current speed."

"Don't tell me what Ana said." Vennor walked down the center of the ancient wool rug in front of her desk. Despite its thick texture, it didn't make her office feel any warmer. The soaring stone ceilings kept the Center's air perpetually chilled.

The Lantern has to work. It has to. "Is there anything else I should know?"

"Nothing," Enayat said.

"You're certain Vic has no contacts or friends among the Settlers, who might be encouraging him to collaborate on a plan to take us down?"

"I questioned him several times."

"And?"

"He doesn't seem to understand the danger he is in. That we're all in. The urgency of the situation." Enayat's gaze fell to the ground. "He's on his way to the Center now. As you requested."

"Good. We can use his talents here."

"I know." Enayat hesitated. "Vennor. There's something that concerns me." Another pause. "I'll tell the Seers when we meet, but I wanted to share this with you."

"What?"

"When I questioned Vic about his collaborators, he talked about a life outside of the Games. Outside of the NEWRRTH. He believes the anomaly represents a... a way out."

"That sounds like Settler propaganda."

"I don't know," said Enayat. "It sounded like he was speaking metaphorically."

Vennor retrieved a fresh glass of water from a silver tray

next to her desk. "I see." She took a sip. "I don't want to make any moves until we have more information. Vic's a valuable asset and we need to do whatever we can to keep him on our side." She replaced the glass on the tray. "In the meantime, alert me when he arrives. You'll be questioning him further. We'll find out everything we can about his contacts among the Settlers. We need to be sure he isn't working against us."

"What do you want me to do about the Lantern?"

Vennor paused. Ana's words echoed in her head. *Don't rush the process.* But what could she do? If the Settlers got into live Games, no one knew what kind of havoc they would cause. It could be worse than the original Lantern. Chaos. Her mind swam.

"We need to get this right. Keep going with this version of the Lantern. See that it is strong and works as swiftly as possible."

"I will not fail you." Enayat lifted his eyes to hers. "I promise."

She smiled, although she didn't feel like smiling. "I trust you."

"Thank you, Vennor."

"You are an excellent Seer." Enayat bowed his head.

There was a faint rumble. Her desk shook. "Flay's here. Go back to work. I'll bring the others to meet our guest."

Enayat gave a half bow and left.

Vennor summoned Nilo and Ana to her office. When the young Seers arrived, Vennor greeted them at the door. "Walk with me. We're going to the garages to greet Flay."

"Who?" Nilo asked.

"Flay, the skidder driver!" Ana hissed.

Nilo brought her shoulders together in a shrug. "Why are we meeting him?"

"Flay is our transport manager." Vennor moved down the

carpeted hallway toward the elevators, Nilo and Ana keeping pace behind her. "He has traveled overland with a special guest. I expect you two will offer a warm welcome." She stepped into the waiting elevator.

"Special guest?" Ana asked. The three of them faced the closing doors.

"The Designer you recruited to join our cause." Vennor pressed the button for the basement. "I've rarely seen a young person so committed to the integrity of the Games."

The skidder driver waited for them in the underground garages. A bleak expanse of stained cement, the garages gave off a musty smell, a stagnant mixture of chemicals and rain. The top of the skidder was up, and Flay was taking readings that involved several wires connected to the vehicle. On either side of him, the enormous wheels of the skidder towered. Their treads were packed with snow. The driver was a skilled transporter, that much was clear. Tall, with his hair cut short, he wore a wool coat over his jumpsuit, and had a pleasant manner about him.

"It's good to see you," Vennor said.

"It is an honor," Nilo said. Her tone was formal.

"Yup," the driver said. His back was to them as he took his readings. "I'm Flay."

"My name is Nilo, and this is—"

"I'm Ana."

"How was the journey?" Vennor asked. "Did you have any difficulties?"

"Nothing we couldn't handle." Flay said. "There was a snowslide, but we made it through. The skidder's a little banged up. That's to be expected." He continued to peer at his readings, which gave an impression of a man who was more interested in his work than the people around him. He pressed a few buttons on a small metal box.

"Excellent." Vennor smiled. "Is our guest a good traveler?"

"He's been quiet. Hasn't been any trouble."

"Good."

Putting his instruments down, Flay turned to face them.

Nilo gasped and took a step back. "Sorry, I—"

"It's okay," Flay said. "Most people react that way." He came toward them, wiping his hands on a rag hanging out of his pocket. Nilo and Ana gaped at the right side of his face, the side where everyone's Thread implant was. It was a mess of lumpy scar tissue. His cheek was red and puckered all the way to his ear.

"What hap—"

"Bit of a problem with the insertion, but my reception's just fine." He winked.

"Nilo doesn't mean to be rude," Vennor said.

Nilo's expression of horror turned into a broad grimace. "Sorry. It's just impressive."

"Thank you. But I'm a driver, not a performer." He jerked his chin at Vennor. "Are we done here?"

"Yes. Where is he?"

A figure jumped from the cab and hit the concrete floor with a soft thud. "There you go," Flay said.

As Vennor approached the guest, a blue dot appeared on her wrist. She quietly answered the incoming. "Trueno. What is it?"

"Bad news." Trueno was out of breath. "It's the anomaly. We found evidence. Just now. It's gone into a live Game. It crashed the first live Game."

Her limbs went cold. "We're on our way." She turned to Flay. "Turn the skidder around and get the hell out of here."

Flay's face fell. "But—"

"Turn the skidder around. You'll be receiving a series of

coordinates from us. It's time to send the messengers. To the other Arks. You need to reach the Pine Barrens first."

Flay remained rooted to the spot.

"Get out," she said. "Now!"

"This way." Ana grabbed their visitor's arm and steered him away from the skidder. "What are we dealing with?" She hurried with Vennor as they ran toward the elevators.

"It's the anomaly." Vennor's vision blurred as she moved. "The Settlers. They've gotten into a live Game. They did it. They actually found a way in..." She wiped her eyes before she lost her footing.

Nilo hadn't moved. She bent and put her hand to her temple, murmuring into her Thread. Their visitor kept pace beside Ana and Vennor as they reached the elevator. His dark coat flapped.

"Nilo!" Ana shouted. "Come on!" Ana pressed the elevator button. Nilo sprinted toward them.

The doors opened and they all piled in. Ana pounded the button for their level. "How is that possible?" she asked. The elevator began its ascent.

"It shouldn't be possible," Nilo whispered as the elevator glided up. Was she speaking to herself or to all of them? "It shouldn't be possible."

Below them, the skidder's engine roared to life.

TASK FORCE__

Rayne

THE WARM WATER felt good on her skin. Rayne made slow circles on her scalp with the juniper root bar. Replacing it in its dish, she picked up her lavender soap and inhaled its sweet scent. Dirty suds gathered in the drain before washing away.

She stepped out of the shower and grabbed a towel. After drying off, she tapped a few fingerfuls of aloe on her face. She sent a pulse of gratitude to the herbalists who grew the ingredients and mixed the concoctions that cleansed their bodies.

"Continue. Tell me more about those green lines in Vic's aspect retrieval. I want to know why the tracer branched off."

"Pausing inquiry. There is a broadcast alert. Broadcast. Broadcast. Broad—"

"All right! Send me the broadcast then. Just a minute."

Rayne paused in the bathroom and gazed at herself in the mirror. Her face was pinched and pale, despite the soothing heat from the shower. She pulled on her jumpsuit and wrapped her hair in the towel. After kicking the door shut behind her, she stood still for a moment, savoring the heat in her clothes.

Jesla sat on the couch, her knees crossed, hands wrapped around an oversized mug of peppermint tea. She had already showered and wore a warm suit of Rayne's.

"There's a broadcast," Rayne said. Luci wiped the living room table, brushing invisible crumbs from a plate of untouched cranberry biscuits. Jesla nodded, pointing to her temple. Rayne sat next to her and brought up her Thread between them so they could watch together.

They caught the end of the Celebration song. The song was popular among Teachers for helping students learn the Principle of One. But it was a joke for Designers. They made up verses that sounded like the actual words but were much funnier.

Jesla watched fixedly as a panel of people sang along, putting their hands on their hearts as the song finished.

> You will be me,
> I will be you.
> We are life.
> I am your daughter,
> I am your son.
> We are One.
> We are One.

"Good day," said a woman sitting at a long table. Her face, with high cheekbones and deep brown eyes, was strikingly beautiful. She wore a pale yellow jumpsuit and a yellow fringed shawl around her shoulders. "My name is Vennor. I am speaking to you from the Center for Future Guidance."

A checkerboard pattern of the same yellow hue filled the background behind her. Above her head was an inscription: *Progress Through Unity*. People in colorful jumpsuits sat alongside her at the table. Rayne recognized Enayat's dark eyes and scowling mouth.

"I am speaking to you from the Center for Future Guidance because we—the Seers of our collective future and keepers of the NEWRRTH—have found a critical threat in the Games."

Rayne stood.

"We are committed, as always, to maintaining the Games for all to enjoy. But this error may disrupt the Games in unpredictable ways. This... threat..." Vennor's eyes went to a person out of the frame. She cleared her throat. "This threat is a serious risk to the future of the Games. To our peace and unity. And to our ability to uphold the Principle of One."

"What is this?" Jesla sat forward on the couch cushion.

Vennor continued. "We will not tolerate this attack on our freedom. The future of the Games—and the peace of our people—depends on our actions today. We must overcome and subdue this threat. And we will. Whatever endangers the Principle of One must be eliminated." Vennor's eyes were hard as she stared into the feed. "I assure you, we will protect the Games."

"It can't be." Rayne's mouth went dry.

"We are working with Game Designers to identify this entity. They have been assisting us in our efforts to eradicate it from the Game."

Game Designers? Plural?

Jesla bit her lip. Turning to Rayne, she started to ask a question. The broadcast interrupted her.

"Our Game Designer collaborators have risen to this challenge. As we knew they would. But we cannot accomplish this task alone. We are therefore announcing a new effort, the formation of a group of concerned people, just like you, who will join against this threat. The Game Preservation Task Force will carry out the identification and termination of all entities hostile to the Principle of One. We are calling on all Game Designers, Creators, Farmers, Builders, Teachers, Healors..."

Rayne's head spun. She sat back down on the couch.

Vennor appeared to be reading from a list.

"They want regular people to volunteer for this task force?" Jesla asked. "To find errors in the Games?"

"I think so. This is insane."

Vennor continued. "We need your help—yes, your help—to identify and eliminate all entities hostile to the Principle of One."

Luci moved closer to the broadcast. "They're cleaning the Games. Good."

Rayne shook her head. "She's sending regular people into the Games to find the anomaly. This is dangerous. Remember the last time something messed with the Games? There was nearly a war."

"It's a Game," Luci said. "You follow the rules."

Rayne stared at Luci, who had finished polishing the table. "When have you ever followed the rules?"

"I follow rules every day. It's how I learn limits."

"You have yet to discover any limits, Luci."

"Rayne!" Jesla pointed to the broadcast. Vennor was still talking.

"I know this is unexpected, and I know there are many of you who are skeptical. But I assure you, we would not be making this call if the situation was not dire. We need your help to protect the Games and ensure that our people can continue to enjoy them for generations to come."

"This is what you've been seeing in your betas, isn't it?" Jesla asked.

"Yes." Rayne's heart sank. Vennor just announced to the entire Atlantic Ark that the anomaly posed a threat to the Games. Did this mean the anomaly had escaped the betas? Was it affecting live Games being played now by hundreds of citizens?

"And to lead this effort, the Seers have appointed a leader," said Vennor. "Someone who can gather the intelligence necessary to restore the integrity of our Games. I am very proud to present our Game Preservation Task Force director."

If the anomaly had infiltrated live Games, what did that mean for Designers like her? Was there going to be a prohibition on designing Games now?

Jesla gasped and put her hands over her mouth. "Isn't that—"

Rayne lifted her gaze. Cas stood next to Vennor. The image zoomed in on his face as he spoke. He wore a wobbly smile. "If you discover the location of any entity hostile to the Principle of One, please contact the Game Preservation Task Force. If you have information about any entity hostile to the Principle of One, please contact the Preservation Task Force. Please contact the Preservation Task Force if you have seen beings that are hostile to the Principle of One. We appreciate your vigilance and dedication to the NEWRRTH."

"I volunteer." Luci stepped forward, facing the broadcast.

Cas finished speaking. He took a step back, looking relieved.

"Here are the locations of every place you can make a report." Vennor flicked her fingers and a confetti of red dots appeared on a map. "To make a report, find your nearest location indicated by these markers. If you suspect any activity—

any activity *at all*—that is not aligned with the Principle of One, make a report."

The broadcast ended.

Rayne felt as if she were falling. "It's Cas."

"I know."

"He's leading this... what is it? Some sort of anomaly hunt? Why would he do this?" Rayne's wrist lit up. It was Mo. Then Rook, Briz, Cha. Her Designer friends. They wanted to talk. Of course they did. They probably had the same questions she did. Rook with his bearlike enthusiasm for coding mysteries. Mo and his curiosity about all things technical. Briz and their fascination with vintage programming practices, and Cha, master of brilliant Game design.

There was no way she could speak with any of them right now. She placed a hand over her wrist, declining all of their calls. "What is he doing? What do they want from him? He's just... Cas."

Another blue dot flashed. It was Cynthia.

Rayne accepted the call. Cynthia's hair was a tangle of white around her pale face. "Rayne, did you see the broadcast? What's going on?"

"Cynthia, listen to me. Are the boys playing Games right now?"

"Yes—" Cynthia dashed into her living room, where her grandsons sat with gamescreens over their eyes. "Should I—"

"End their Games, Cynthia. Do it. I don't have any more information, except what you heard on the broadcast. Just keep them out of the Games for now. Please."

"Thank you, Rayne." The boys started wailing as Cynthia reached for their screens. Rayne ended the call.

Jesla put a hand on her shoulder. "It's going to be okay."

"I don't know how you can say that." Rayne's voice shook.

"This is bad. This is really bad. I can't believe... he did this without me."

"You know what Cas is like. He does things a certain way because he thinks it's the right way to do them."

It was true. Cas's mind frayed around the edges when he was worried. Without Rayne to protect him, to speak up for him, he wasn't always careful with his words or his moods. But he was an extraordinary Designer. People didn't give him credit for his genius. Had Cas discovered something in the Games without her? She wanted to believe he would have told her about something this important.

Except that Cas wasn't speaking to her. She hadn't seen him for days. Why did she have to leave him all alone with that cottontail? He was her best friend, and they were in this together. She should have been there for him. But partnering with the Seers and leading this new Task Force... that was extreme.

And Rayne was sure Vennor wasn't telling Cas the whole truth.

Jesla had her hand on Rayne's back, patting. "It'll be okay. Remember when we were kids? All the times Cas tried to keep us safe? Like when we hid in that old factory. We wanted to finish playing our Games but Cas ran around yelling for us because his Thread warned him about the poison in the ground."

Rayne almost smiled. "Oh, yeah. The mercury in the soil. His Thread told him it was toxic to humans. He wanted to save us. He wanted to save the insects, too. Bring them to an unpolluted patch of ground."

"We had to convince him the insects had already moved on. Remember when he made us hang the bird feeders? Because of the pesticides in the wild berries? It was a little too late for us." She gave a little laugh. "But he's like a walking

Principle of One. He knows what's going on, Rayne. He cares about you. About life. He won't do anything stupid."

Rayne glanced out the window, where her bird feeders still hung from their metal pole. "Yes, I know. I know."

But she couldn't shake the feeling that she had already lost him.

RAG IN THE SNOW__

Rayne

It wasn't yet dawn. Rayne pulled her robe over her sleeping suit and headed for her Oak. She woke in a dark mood. She wrapped her arms around the tree's solid trunk. Its embrace dislodged a bit of her heaviness.

Stepping away from its cool bark, she began heating water for tea. Jesla stirred in the shadows of the living room. Rayne tried to be quiet so she wouldn't wake her.

Settling on a stool at the kitchen counter with her mug, Rayne peered out at the night. The woods were black, the sky a deep navy. As she sipped her tea, she thought about the tasks ahead.

For days, she and Jesla tried to pin down Vic's last known location in the Games. Openshell had proven to be a bust. So they had recruited a group of friends, fellow Designers and Teachers, to help them find Vic's aspect. They searched all places that Vic had touched for a clue. Rayne tried everything—

even using her hands to manipulate the Thread's code again—to prevent herself from succumbing to the fear that she would be arrested like Vic. Or worse.

They'd found nothing.

The floor creaked and Jesla entered the kitchen, her hair in disarray. "You're up early," she said, yawning.

Rayne nodded. "Couldn't sleep."

Jesla groaned and rubbed her eyes. "I know the feeling." She shuffled to the cupboard for a mug.

After pouring herself a cup of tea, Jesla joined Rayne at the counter. They sat in comfortable silence for a few moments, sipping their drinks. Jesla broke it with a sigh.

"What are you going to do? About Cas, I mean."

Rayne shrugged. It had been days since she'd seen him on the Seers' broadcast. Almost a week since their fight in the shelter. And now he was directing the Seers' new Task Force.

"I don't know," she said. "I miss him."

She considered reaching out to him, but worried he would report her to the Seers. They had arrested Vic for interfering with the One Principle—the most serious charge in the Atlantic Ark—and it seemed his only error was being targeted by the anomaly in a beta. They would suspect her of foul play, too.

But Cas was the only one who knew what she was going through. He was the only one who understood what it was like to have your life turned upside down by a Game beta.

Rayne finished her tea and asked her Thread to run through the weather for the week. All was clear for the next few days. But an air vortex had descended, holding them captive in a frigid polar weather band.

"Temperatures reaching life-threatening levels in the following days," her Thread told her. "Limiting outdoor exposure recommended."

"How long is this pattern holding?"

"The vortex will remain in place for at least seventy-two hours. Recommend limiting time outside and having access to warming shelters if exceeding thirty minutes of exposure."

"All right. We'll stay inside. Thanks for the update."

Luci disengaged from the docking station, rolled into the kitchen and started mopping the floor.

Jesla put down her empty mug. "I had a dream."

"What about?"

"There was something about the trees."

"What about them?"

"Something was wrong with them. I think something was wrong with the woods."

"What did you see?"

"Flashes of lightning... oh, I don't know." Jesla shook her head. "It's gone now."

Rayne frowned and sipped her tea.

Jesla headed for the shower. Rayne followed her Thread's instructions for moving her body. She did a few sun salutations, leg lifts, and squats. After a few minutes, she felt warm and limber. She tossed her robe over a chair.

Luci made a beeline for it. "Maybe one day I won't be here to clean up after you."

"I'll try to remember that."

Rayne was about to pour another cup of tea when she heard a branch snap outside. She tensed and turned toward the window. A pale orange glow had just touched the tops of the evergreens. There was no wind, no movement. But she could have sworn she'd heard something.

She crept to the window and peered out. Her eyes scanned the darkness. And then she saw it. A flash of white in the distance. It was gone as quickly as it had appeared. She thought about calling for Jesla, but decided against it. If it was just an animal, there was no need to alarm her.

She asked her Thread to bring up images of the woods. "Please select a latitude and longitude."

Rayne pointed to a spot near her cottage on the Thread's map. "Here."

She waited as images of her neighborhood came into focus. "Conduct a visual scan of the trees around this location." She heard whirring as one by one the outdoor cameras powered up and connected to her Thread.

Soon she had a live aerial view of her neighborhood. She wasn't sure what she was looking for. An owl? She had never seen one. A deer? That was possible. But she didn't think so.

Then it hit her. She stilled as the thought dropped into her mind. *What if the anomaly can take physical form?* As soon as the question came, she dismissed it. There was no place for a person to live without being detected. And it was too cold for anyone to stay outside in these temperatures.

Still, she felt a shiver of excitement.

She asked her Thread to continue its sweep of the woods and watched the snowy fields, the roofs of cottages, icy trees, and the steady pulse of the windmills. An occasional gust of wind made the stark branches sway. She waited until the scan made a complete rotation in a radius of about five miles. "Stop," she told her Thread.

"Continue in adjacent locations?"

Why not? If the anomaly wasn't here, maybe it had taken form somewhere else. "Yes. Move here." She pointed to a spot about twenty miles away. Her mother's Orchard.

"What are you doing?" Jesla said. She pressed a towel against her wet hair, and she had dressed in a clean suit.

"Oh, I'm just—well, I had an idea. It's nothing." She angled her Thread's projection so Jesla could see it. "Just thought I saw something outside. An animal or something. It's gone. But I was thinking... if we can see the anomaly in the Games, do you think it has a physical form somewhere? I mean, is it projecting an aspect into the Games like we do?"

Jesla looked impressed. "That is an idea." She thought for a moment. "Couldn't we just ask the Thread?"

"It'll just toss out a million data stories. I'm doing a visual scan of the woods." She watched as images of the Orchard's sprawling greenhouses came up. She told her Thread to widen the radius again.

Next to her, Jesla spoke to her Thread. "How does the anomaly project itself into the Games?"

Rayne kept her scan going, but leaned over to listen to the answer. Jesla's Thread said, "We may view the anomalies in the Game in multiple ways. The primary visual representation takes the form of a three-dimensional object projected into the Game environment."

"What is its original form?" Jesla asked.

"There are many possible forms. The anomaly may project itself from a physical object. It may be a hologram. A shadow..."

"What about a person?"

"Please be specific," the Thread said.

"What if it's a human being?" Jesla asked.

"There is no sign that a human is connected to the anomaly."

Rayne smirked. "I'm thinking the Thread doesn't have a clue about what the anomaly even is—"

"Rayne! Look!"

Rayne glanced back at her own Thread. Images of the snowy forest surrounding the Orchard scrolled by. "Tell it to stop," Jesla said. "Go back. I saw something."

"Pause scan. Review the last fifteen seconds of tracking." The Thread froze, then jumped back to where it had been scanning. It was empty forest.

"There!" Jesla pointed to a dark stripe on the snow. "What is that?"

"Stop." Rayne peered at the shape. It was unrecognizable. "Do we have enough resolution to zoom in?"

"Zooming in," her Thread replied. The shape was like a rag someone had thrown out. It was still.

"Put up an IR map." The image became grainy with infrared colors. The trees were orange and green. The object on the ground glowed red.

"It's alive. It's alive!" Rayne said. "What is it?"

"Identify the object in view." Rayne's heart pounded.

Whatever this was, it would not be alive for long in this cold. "Identifying a human with body temperature of eighty-nine-point-oh-nine degrees Fahrenheit, blood pressure—"

"Oh shit. It's a person."

"—establishing DNA signature as Kai of the Orchard in sector seven..."

"Wait. Repeat that!" Rayne said.

"This is Kai of the Orchard in sector—"

"It's my mother! We need to help her!" Rayne felt panic closing in.

"What do we do?" Jesla said.

"Call the Haven. Get a transport to the Orchard. Give them the coordinates. Go!"

Rayne's hands shook as she placed the call to the Orchard. *Please, please accept the incoming.* She thought of all the Keepers who lived there. Did they know her mother had gone outside? Protocols prohibited solo outdoor work when it was this cold.

Finally, the connection clicked through to one of the Orchard's offices. "Hello? Hello? Is someone there?"

"Communication not authorized."

"What? Who is this?"

"Communication not authorized."

"Hello?" Rayne said. She tried to access her mother's Thread. There was no answer.

She tried the Orchard again. And again.

"We have a problem," Jesla said. She held her hand up to a woman at the Haven, who paused mid-sentence and crossed her arms.

"What?" Rayne said. "What's going on?"

"The Haven won't send a transport," Jesla said. "There's some sort of outbreak. All their vehicles are already out."

"But my mom is out there. Alone. In the freezing cold." *And the Orchard's communication is down.* "We're going. Get your bag."

Jesla's jaw opened and closed. "We can't. It's too cold to stay out for that long."

"Call transport directly. Have them go straight to the Orchard. Pick us up on their way to the Haven. You know how to do that?"

"Yes, I—"

"Do it. Get your bag. Meet me at the front door."

Rayne sprinted into her bedroom. She ripped off her sleeping suit and put on her heavy warm jumpsuit. She pulled on her wool socks and grabbed an extra pair. She tore the blankets off her bed. Her bag was right where Luci left it after cleaning it out. She stuffed her socks and blankets inside and raced back to the kitchen to fill a few water bottles.

Jesla was speaking to her Thread when they met at the front door. "Hax? This is Jesla. You're our closest option. Yes, it's a rescue mission. Yes, I spoke to the coordinator. I don't know if he cleared it! I'm telling you this is an emergency. You can intersect our route from the Orchard. I'm sending you our coordinates now. Please hurry."

"Put those on," Rayne told her, pointing to a pair of snow-shoes. "I'll wear my skis."

They bundled against the cold as best they could. A blast of freezing air swept through the open door, stealing their breath away as they stepped out.

GAME OF GAMES__

Vennor

"Slow down." Trueno jogged to keep up with Vennor. "Think about this for a second. Please."

"I have been thinking." They passed under the glass arches that framed the Center's courtyard. "That's why I need to get to the simulator." Down below, snow sparkled like mirrors over the tree branches. The brightness made Vennor's eyes ache.

"You don't know what you're doing." Trueno's voice rose a notch.

"I care about what happens to the NEWRRTH. Right now, the NEWRRTH is being threatened. All else is irrelevant."

They reached the double doors leading to the other side of the Center's offices. "Pine Barrens Ark. And the others. Where do they stand on this?"

Vennor paused. "They will support whatever we decide to do."

"Are you serious? You haven't brought this to the Guild of Seers?"

She started walking again. "We've sent messages."

Trueno slipped past and swung back to face her. "We have to give them a chance to take part in this decision. They have a right to vote."

"We have to act. Now."

Trueno put his hand on her shoulder. "And we will. In treaty with the Guild."

Vennor watched the top of Trueno's head, the way his hair fell over his collar. It was something to do other than look into his eyes. "I have a much clearer picture of what we're facing than you do." She put a hand on the doors, and they glided open.

"You think you do." Trueno followed her into the gallery, with its view of the globe that was Earth. He glanced up at the planet with its blue seas and white clouds pasted in a motionless swirl. "You want the Settlers to go away. But you're so angry that you're lashing out at them and everything they stand for. Are you willing to take this all down with you?"

She walked straight past the globe without a glance. *Sentimentality from another age.* In modern times, their loyalty lay with the intelligence that kept them alive.

Trueno blocked her way. "I care about the NEWRRTH, too. You've always been its fiercest protector." Trueno took her hand and held it. His eyes were earnest, entreating. "Rushing the process is wrong." He kissed her palm and held it against his cheek.

Vennor ignored the heat that spiked from her palm to her belly. "Are you stopping me or not?" She withdrew her hand.

"I'm asking you to stop. Please."

She regarded him in silence, seeing his soft gray eyes, the lines of his face. Wanting him.

No.

She pushed him aside and strode into the hallways. Trueno didn't follow.

The lights above her flashed green as she unlocked door after door. They reflected off her skin, making her face glow as she progressed deep into the Center's corridors. She would make Trueno understand that the Lantern could lead the Games—and the NEWRRTH—into a new era. One that protected their world from the Settlers. From anyone who dared challenge their peace. Their *freedom.*

It was time to show Trueno and the rest of the Seers what the Lantern would achieve.

She flew into the control room at the end of the corridor. A wall of windows showed a bank of orange clouds in the sky.

"Cas. Show me what you have." Cas looked up in surprise. Nilo stood in front of him. A Thread lay open between them. Perhaps they had been arguing. No matter. They would deliver what they could, and the rest would be up to her. "What do you have for me?"

She didn't notice the group of Scrubbers until they were right behind her. One approached holding a palm tablet. "Just a routine health scan. Hold still."

"I will not. Step back. We're in the middle of important work."

The Scrubber didn't move. "I realize that, and I'm sorry, but the Haven ordered everyone at the Center for Future Guidance—well, everyone in the Ark—to have a scan. There's a Phase Three outbreak. People are piling into the Haven's emergency centers, and they want to contain—"

"I said, *step back.* You can scan me after we've finished. Leave."

The Scrubber glanced at his colleagues and shrugged. They all left.

"We're almost there," Cas said, when the Scrubbers had cleared the room.

Nilo nodded and lifted her chin to expose her tattoo. "There's an issue." Deftly, she reoriented the Thread, so it faced Vennor. "Look."

"What is this?"

"It's the Game you asked me to design," Cas said. "But it's—"

"This?" The Game appeared haphazard, nothing like the demonstration she had imagined. It was a mess. "I don't understand."

"It's unstable." Nilo pointed at the Thread. "But we think we know why."

"It's like a puzzle in multiple dimensions," Cas explained. "You're supposed to put the pieces together, so they form a picture. But we can't do it until we enter the Game. It's how I figured out—"

"How *we* figured out," Nilo corrected.

Cas continued. "How we figured out how to keep the anomaly out of this beta. It hasn't been able to penetrate this modeling."

Vennor frowned. She had expected something much more polished.

"This is the Game I asked you to Design? That will keep the anomaly at bay while we release the Lantern?"

"It's like a Game before the Game. To shield it." Cas swallowed. "But it's not that simple. The more complex the beta, the harder it is to finish from the outside. This one is... well, it's the most complex beta I've ever designed."

"Have you playtested it yet?"

Cas closed his hand protectively over the Game's code. "It's not ready for that, we're still—"

"Then let's go. Have my gamescreen brought to the conference room," Vennor said to her Thread. "We're going to test the Lantern in this beta. If we see any hint of the anomaly—if anything you didn't code appears in this Game—you start over. Understood?"

Cas stood, dumbstruck.

"Ana, send me the Lantern code."

Ana's virtual form appeared next to them. She sat in her office several doors down. "You want the Lantern? But I haven't finished it yet. I'm still going through the audits in alpha. It hasn't passed the thresholds."

"Send it directly to my Thread. Now." Vennor ended the call and pressed her temple, ready for the transmission. She remembered the look Enayat gave her yesterday when he told her that the anomaly—the Settlers—had destroyed several live Games at once. She pushed the image of his flustered face out of her mind.

The code arrived. "It's time to test our model. Are you ready?"

Nilo hesitated. "Shouldn't we invite another Seer to monitor us while we play? In case…"

"They have other priorities."

Cas glanced around, finally finding his voice. "You understand, this isn't stable yet."

"How long do we playtest the Game until we know the Lantern is effective?"

"In theory," Cas said, "We know the Lantern will work. We just don't know how long it will keep working. And we don't know how long we can stop the anomaly from interfering."

"I want to know how long it will work in this Game. Begin."

Cas pushed a lock of hair out of his face but didn't make a move to start the Game. "What'll happen to us?"

She raised an eyebrow.

"The Game will seal the anomaly out," Nilo said. "The

Lantern will be operating in the background, so nothing out of the ordinary should happen. But I can't say for sure."

Vennor leaned forward. "Better to live on the wild side than never experience anything at all."

Cas wrinkled his brow. "There's a chance..." He picked his words. "It's impossible to say how we will subjectively experience the Lantern. But there's a risk..." He shifted. "We might need to hard exit. That means—"

"I know what that means," Vennor said. "You told me that the anomaly can't penetrate the modeling you've set up."

"Yes, but—"

Her voice rose. "Are you saying you cannot complete this task? Are you unable?"

Cas's lips thinned. "No. We can do it."

Vennor's gamescreen arrived on a roving bot. Sitting in one of the chairs in the room, she turned to Cas. "Begin."

Nilo and Cas claimed seats on either side of her and put their screens on. "Are you ready?"

"Ready." Vennor lowered her gamescreen over her eyes. Her heart pounded. The next few moments would change everything.

Cas took a deep breath. "We're going in."

COMA__

Rayne

T H E   S K I D D E R   S H U D D E R E D to a halt in front of the Haven. Inside the cab, Rayne cradled her mother's head in her lap. "We're here," she said softly. "We made it. You're going to be all right."

Her mother had stopped shivering several minutes ago. According to Rayne's Thread, that was a sign she had progressed from moderate to severe hypothermia. She had minutes to get to a warming chamber.

Hax jumped down from the cab. A hatch unlocked and swung open in the wall next to them. Padded robotic arms reached out for their patient. "You'll have to help me," Rayne said to Jesla. "I can't lift her!"

Hax reached up and opened their side of the cab. "Hand her down to me." They struggled for a moment to position Kai so she wouldn't fall. Hax grabbed Kai's blanket and made a stretcher. The three of them carried Kai to the circular hatch.

The robotic arms closed around Kai's blanket-wrapped form and slid her back into the bright warmth of the Haven.

Rayne's fingertips were numb with cold, but she touched her mother's wrist as she slid past. Kai's skin was like ice.

"The Healors have her now," Jesla said. "They'll do whatever they can."

Rayne nodded and wiped her cheeks. Jesla turned back to the skidder. "Thank you, Hax," she said. "Let's unload our stuff. We need to let you go."

Hax blinked at Rayne for a moment. She could tell he wanted to say something encouraging, but she stopped him with a shake of her head. "Thank you for getting us here so fast."

He gave them a half salute. "When duty calls..." He reached into the cab and handed them their bags, then laid their snowshoes and skis against the bay wall.

"Thank you," Jesla said.

"Who are you?" Turning, they saw a Healor approaching. "And where did you find that transport?"

"It's for my mother. We found her out in the woods by her Orchard. She wasn't supposed to be alone—"

"This is not an authorized transport," the Healor said. She listened to her Thread. As she approached, Rayne saw her name clipped to her coat. Rhode.

"I'm leaving now," Hax said, backing away. "Just dropping off a patient."

"You are not leaving," H. Rhode said. "Stand by. You will receive additional coordinates."

"I'm sorry," Hax said, jumping into his cab. "This isn't cleared with my coordinator. I have to go."

All Rayne wanted was to run inside and find her mother, but she kept her feet planted. "We're the ones who asked for this skidder," she explained. "Like I said, it was an emergency."

"In case you haven't noticed, we're in a Phase Three. It's all hands on deck." Rayne blinked as she took in all the surrounding activity. Every bay was occupied. Healors darted around, herding people and vehicles into the portals. Directing them out again. The air was a chorus of engines and shouting.

"H. Rhode," Rayne said. "Not to be rude, but my mother is in critical condition and I need to know she's okay."

"And I'm trying to find out how many patients we can save with this additional skidder," H. Rhode said.

Hax leaned out the window of the cab. "I don't know about any crisis, but I'll talk to my coordinator." He turned to consult his Thread.

"Please," Rayne said to H. Rhode. "My mother. I need to find her."

H. Rhode's expression softened. "Go inside there," she said to Rayne. "She'll be in one of the triaging areas."

Rayne glanced back at Hax, who was busy with his Thread. "Let's go." She and Jesla picked up their bags, snow-shoes, and skis, and made their way inside the Haven.

The doors swooshed open and then closed behind them. Inside, a translucent glass dome let in a flood of light. A flowery scent lingered in the air, and along with the warm temperature, the lobby was soothing. Along the walls, rows of herbs and fungi hung in pots.

"This place gives me the creeps," said Jesla. "It's so quiet." The Healors scurried around in their charcoal uniform jackets, but some wore vests and sweaters. Assistant Healors wore matching black scrubs. Robotic arms brought patients through portals and whisked them into diagnostic tents. The tents emitted soft beeps as they rushed past, floating on silver robotic transports to be triaged and admitted.

"Do you see her?" Rayne asked. "I'll look along this side." There was a distinct feeling here. It was like when Rayne had a question, and before she could ask her Thread, she felt the answer reach out and touch her heart. It was a feeling of peace and calm.

She glanced at face after face coming through the portals. "Over here!" Jesla called. "She's in a pod."

Rayne dropped her things and ran to the corner where Jesla was standing. Inside the pod, Kai lay curled up in a fetal position, wrapped in clear, plastic tubing. It looked like a cocoon. "Ma?" Rayne asked. "Can you hear me?"

"That's your mother?" said H. Rhode. She followed them inside the bay. "She was just scanned."

"Ma." Rayne reached out to touch the side of the pod. "I'm here. You're safe now."

"She's being warmed," the Healor said. "The pod is programmed to monitor her vital signs. The more her body temperature rises, the more it will open."

"How long until she's awake?" Rayne asked. As she spoke, the pod started rolling away from them. "Wait. Where is she going?"

"They just admitted her to our intensive care unit," H. Rhode said. "That's where the pod is heading. You're not cleared for access. I'm sorry, you'll have to wait here. Try to stay out of the way."

Kai's pod whispered as it sped away.

Rayne felt tears pricking behind her eyes. "Ma," she said. A Healor bumped into her, apologized. Rayne didn't move. There was nothing she could do.

Jesla was speaking into her Thread. "Yes, we just arrived. Kai was admitted. Intensive care. Hypothermia. She's heading there now. Okay. Thank you."

"Who was that?" Rayne asked.

"Healor Lynn. I told her we're here. She's coming down."

Rayne slumped against the wall. Vic's mother would know

what to do. Healor Lynn was a smart, capable person. Rayne put her head in her hands while they waited.

"What a surprise to see you both," Healor Lynn said as she rounded the corner. "Although I'm sorry about the circumstances." She gave each of them a hug. Rayne could feel the Healor's ribs through her jacket.

When she pulled away, Rayne saw purple circles underneath H. Lynn's eyes. "I'm sorry," she mumbled. "We shouldn't be bothering you. With all that Vic is going through."

"It's always a pleasure to see you," H. Lynn said. "You know that. Now let's go up to my office. There's not much we can do while Kai is in intensive treatment." She put an arm around each of their shoulders as they picked up their bags and started walking. "Leave those skis and shoes. I'll send for them later. We have a lot to discuss."

A pod crossed in front of them. Inside, a person lay prostrate and unblinking, covered in a foil blanket. Rayne couldn't help but stare. "What's wrong with—"

"Confidential." H. Lynn picked up her pace. "You ever hear the old term 'shitstorm'?" H. Lynn gestured toward the commotion. "I'm pretty sure this is a classic example." She guided them to the stairwell. "The elevators are being used for patients. We're going this way."

They climbed the stairs. As they reached the second floor, Rayne's shoe caught the edge of a step, nearly tripping her. Her stomach lurched, and she gripped the handrail.

"Careful." H. Lynn put a hand out to steady her.

"We haven't eaten for a while."

"Then it's time to get your blood sugar up." H. Lynn helped Rayne regain her balance. "And boy, do I have a story to tell you both."

H. LYNN'S DISCOVERY__

Rayne

THEY FILED INTO H. Lynn's office. The Healor closed the door. She removed her jacket and hung it on the rack in the corner. "Sit down, please."

"When can I see my mother?" Rayne took a step closer to the door. "I... I want to be with her now."

"Oh, Rayne." Healor Lynn sat down on a curving pink chair. Jesla sat beside her. "Please, sit."

"She's going to be okay, right?" Rayne pulled a chair over from a small table and sat down facing the two of them.

"You've had a shock." Healor Lynn handed her a small jar. "Rub this on your temples. It'll help you relax."

Rayne was about to protest when she saw Jesla rubbing the balm into her temples. She used her fingers to dab a little on. It melted on her fingertips like beeswax. It smelled of mint and dry grass. She closed her eyes and took a deep breath.

"Send two hot meals to my office," H. Lynn said to her

Thread. Turning to them, she said, "I have a few things to tell you. After we traced Vic's aspect, and we saw all those green lines branching out and coming toward us, I did some digging of my own. Then this morning, I got a call."

Rayne opened her eyes. "From the Center for Future Guidance? Was it Vic?"

The Healor lowered her head. "No." Her voice was quiet. "It was your mother."

Rayne's heart stopped. "What did she say?"

"She said she had something to show us. Something that would prove her findings."

"What?" Rayne asked, queasy. "What was she talking about?"

"She didn't say," H. Lynn replied. "She couldn't. She was in the middle of the forest, freezing to death."

"She went out into the woods at night to call you?" Tears pricked beneath Rayne's eyelids.

"It was early this morning. Before sunrise. I told her to go inside, begged her, told her she was acting irresponsibly. But she was adamant about showing me something first."

"What—what did she show you?"

The door opened, and a bot wheeled in a cart. It offered Rayne and Jesla each a large bowl of vegetable soup and two doughy biscuits. They picked up their trays and watched it leave.

Rayne hadn't realized how hungry she was until she smelled the food. She swallowed a biscuit in two bites, barely registering its salty flakiness. Then she picked up the bowl of savory stew and took a sip, hot spice burning her tongue.

"Kai didn't show me anything," H. Lynn said, watching them eat. "Our connection was interrupted."

"I wasn't able to reach the Orchard at all this morning," Rayne said. She put down the bowl and tore into the second biscuit. "Something about communication not being authorized. Who would have done that?"

"I don't know," H. Lynn said. "But I have an idea." She shifted so she could open her Thread in front of them both. "I came across something interesting when I did a little more digging."

Freya's Path.

The phrase appeared on her Thread. The words dissolved. The Thread spun through images of women draped in feathers. Colorful drawings, painted pictures, stone carvings flew by. One curious image showed two cats in a harness leading a tall woman in a crown.

H. Lynn dismissed the graphics. Her Thread went dark. "I don't know where to begin."

"Who's Freya?" Jesla took a bite of her biscuit.

H. Lynn sighed. "Freya is—was—a goddess. From an ancient Norse civilization. And from a revived version of pagan worship starting in the twentieth century. The Norse people claimed she embodied love and witchcraft and war. They also believed she could... well, that she descended from a line of gods that could predict the future."

A cascade of goosebumps swirled down Rayne's body. She had never heard of Freya, but she felt a familiar pang for the people of the past. The people without Threads who longed for control over their unpredictable world. Wasn't that the deepest desire in all of recorded history? To know the future in order to prepare for what was to come?

Until the NEWRRTH, of course.

H. Lynn animated her Thread again. A building came into view. "The details about the goddess Freya aren't important. But she is connected to something that Vic told me about the Great Divergence." The Thread zoomed into a window of the building, one of many in a great city, to a family huddled over a cooking fire. The walls were black with soot, the windows streaked with grime. Outside, broken glass glittered on the sidewalk, empty storefronts gaping.

"I don't like looking at these," Rayne said.

"It's part of our history." Jesla patted the corners of her mouth with a napkin. "The Great Divergence is just one of the difficult periods in our past we must confront if we want a true handle on our future."

H. Lynn interjected before Jesla could go further. "Back then, our world was falling apart. We survived because of the NEWRRTH. Look. There's one thing I didn't realize." Her Thread morphed to show a roomful of people gathered in rows of seats. A speaker held their attention at one end of the room, gesturing to an old-fashioned screen behind his head. "Vic showed me a while ago. Not everyone was in strict agreement about how to move forward."

"We teach this all the time," Jesla said. "Some people wanted to use the NEWRRTH differently than others. But every nation on Earth agreed it was our only chance for survival."

"That's true. But I didn't piece it together until now. What Vic found is... different from those debates. People tested versions of the NEWRRTH and discussed various possibilities for deploying it, sure. But there was one group who broke away from the others. This group thought the NEWRRTH was supposed to be something else. Something more. The next step in our evolution. They believed people should join the NEWRRTH. *Evolve* with it instead of using it as a tool or guide."

The Thread went dark again. A single image appeared. It was a woman with tawny skin and curly hair clipped short. "This group called themselves Freya's Path. This was their leader," H. Lynn said. "Her name was Entra."

"Wait." Rayne put her empty soup bowl on the table. Despite the healing balm on her temples, she felt an invisible band tighten across her brow. "There were people who wanted to merge with the NEWRRTH?" She shook her head. "But how does that matter now? They're all long gone. The NEWRRTH is impenetrable."

"That's what I'm trying to tell you," H. Lynn said. "Freya's Path kept their work secret. They never committed their findings to the Archives." She frowned. "They believed the NEWRRTH could become a hive mind. A collection of countless minds. Like a cloud. And... this is the hard part. There's some evidence that they succeeded in joining it."

Rayne thought about Kai, and how hard she had been shivering on their drive to the Haven before she suddenly stopped, her body at its breaking point. She had been so lifeless and cold. It didn't seem wrong to want to leave the physical behind to join a virtual world. As a Designer, she did that all the time and helped others do that in the Games. But leaving your entire life? Merging consciousness with others? Rayne didn't see the point of that.

"This group—Freya's Path—they joined the NEWRRTH?" Jesla said. "Like the way we send our aspects into a Game?"

"I don't know how they did it. Only that they could be still active inside it. They may have been interacting with Vic. All those green squiggles going around him and branching off from his aspect. And Kai—your mother, Rayne, she knew about them, too."

The silence stretched on. Rayne was so stunned, she didn't know what to say.

"Look at it this way," H. Lynn said. She tucked her hair behind her ears and pressed her hands together. "The sheer amount of data the NEWRRTH has about our world makes it impossible for us to comprehend it all. Maybe there's a way to access information that hasn't been discovered. Maybe there's even a way to use that information to see the future."

Jesla finished chewing her biscuit, then glanced upward, as if trying to read the cracks on the ceiling.

"All I know for sure was that Entra was attempting some kind of merge with the NEWRRTH directly. The few records she left behind after the Great Divergence don't tell the whole story. Entra was a psychologist. And a geneticist." She paused. "She was a Teacher."

"A Teacher?" Jesla said.

"Rayne," H. Lynn said. "I think your mother went out to the woods this morning to tell me about what's happening to the NEWRRTH. I think she was going to say the NEWRRTH is turning into something else."

A blue dot appeared on H. Lynn's wrist. She accepted it, walking a few paces away. "I see. Did she have signs of... No? Is there a reading on her brain activity now? Okay. Thank you."

"How is she?" Rayne moved toward H. Lynn. "Is she awake?"

"No," the Healor said. "But she's been stabilized. We won't know for sure until she wakes up, but they see no signs of brain damage." Rayne winced. "It's too early to tell, though. She's warm now. She's comfortable."

"So..." Rayne assembled her thoughts into a single question. "What are we going to do about Freya's Path?"

PLANTING A SEED__

Vennor

"WHAT DO YOU MEAN, we have a problem?" Vennor snapped at Trueno. "We just showed you a solution. A solution that will stop the anomaly safely, with no suffering, and bring the NEWRRTH a quantum leap forward. Just think what this upgrade could do for us. For all the Arks." She sat down heavily.

The Scrubbers stared at the ground. The results of Vennor's scan hung in the air, a group of numbers glowing red. The Scrubber who held the palm tablet spoke. "Please, don't you think we should do this in private?"

The Seers sat in varying degrees of exhaustion around the conference room table. The air in the room was stale and damp, with a smell of mold. Vennor's lower back ached. She took a deep breath and asked her Thread for a soothing cocktail of endorphins.

"I don't need privacy to discuss an issue that affects us all. We'll do this now."

"If we release this version of the Lantern," Trueno said carefully, "it could destabilize the health of our population." He pointed at Vennor's results. "Do you see? Your scan showed sequence changes in your circulating DNA. Those patterns weren't there on your last scan. The Lantern changed your genetic code, Vennor. We don't know what it could do to others who are exposed to it."

The Scrubbers eyed one another. "We have to carry on with our scans."

"Of course." Vennor waved her hand. "Go."

The Scrubbers filed out silently. Vennor watched them leave. *That miserable lot just ruined everything, and for what?* When the door shut behind them, Trueno leaned forward, his elbows on the table. "What's wrong with you, Vennor? Does vengeance burn so brightly that you can't see what's right in front of you?"

Vennor closed her eyes and tapped the center of her chest, just under her collarbone. It helped soothe the tension in her upper body. The tapping usually worked, especially in combination with the endorphin release.

Enayat stood and cleared his throat. "We could plant a seed."

"A what?" Vennor's eyes opened.

"A player who carries the Lantern coding. Someone we could monitor, scan, to make sure there aren't any adverse effects. And if there's nothing to be concerned about, this player will seed the Lantern in other players. Spread the upgrade organically. Just like we planned."

"And what if the anomaly reaches us first? And destroys the live Games?" Nilo asked.

"We use the model Cas developed to keep the Games safe

until the Lantern can be released in each one. We make the model available to all Designers, make it mandatory—"

"I will be the Seed." They all turned to Vennor.

"You can't be," Ana said. "You've already had a reaction to the Lantern. Plus, if anything goes wrong, we need you at the helm."

"The Seed would function like a viral host," continued Enayat. "Borrowing from the old infection model. Once activated, it would spread the Lantern like a virus to every person who interacts with the Games. In a timeframe we can control. Which is tight, given how far the anomaly seems to have already penetrated."

"So a single player would be the first host." Nilo's eyes flicked as she made some calculations on her Thread. "And we monitor this person while they release the Lantern inside a Game. To make sure there are no adverse effects."

"Precisely."

The room erupted in conversation.

Vennor lifted her palm and everyone went quiet. She turned to Ana. "How long will it take to have a viable version of the Seed?"

Ana rose and went to a small table in the corner. "Not long. I have some ideas for a prototype." Enayat joined her and they started working with a Thread open between them.

Trueno pressed his temple, consulting with his Thread. "Vennor, I don't like this."

"Not here." Vennor gestured to follow her into the hall. Vennor closed the door behind them. "The Games are already breaking down. This is our only chance."

"It isn't." Trueno put his hand on her elbow, stopping her. She lifted her eyes to his. He inched closer, his breath quickening. The moment stretched between them.

"The anomaly," he said. "It shows all the signs... of their return."

She took a step back, releasing her arm from Trueno's grip. "I won't have this discussion with you again."

"Please, Vennor."

"There's no evidence they exist. We can't make life-or-death decisions for the NEWRRTH based on a fantasy. You want to show me their signatures? Do you have one letter of code or shred of a record from anyone, anywhere?"

Trueno's mouth twisted. "It's not about proof."

"That's right. It's about faith. Your faith in this delusion. Entra and her Path. But I don't believe in dreams and whispers. I can't. And I won't stake the future of the NEWRRTH on it."

"What if they're real?"

"I don't believe they are. Even if they were, even if Freya's Path is active right this minute, there's nothing we can do about it. We have to focus on the here and now, on what we can control." She faced the view outside, where darkness advanced over the icy trees.

"You believe this Seed will work?"

"If we get the coding right, it will expand the NEWR-RTH's feed far beyond the anomaly's reach, without overwhelming the platform."

Trueno lifted his hand to touch her again, then thought better of it. "There's still a risk. We're making an educated guess that the living Lanterns will survive their infection."

Vennor nodded. Calculated something in her head. Then she said to her Thread, "Show me where Vic is being held." The Thread lit a pathway on a map through the offices of the Center, leading to the other side of the complex.

"We already interrogated him," Trueno said. "He told us what he knew."

"We no longer need his knowledge of the anomaly." Vennor gave a half smile. "He'll serve a higher purpose now."

"WHATEVER IT IS, I won't do it." Vic crossed his arms and faced Vennor. Trueno had gone back, alone, to the control room.

"I understand this is difficult, Vic." With a wave, Vennor dismissed the two Officers who stood guard outside his room. This would go better if it was just the two of them.

She paced in front of his chair. The brown carpet was worn and flattened. Iron bars covered the single, rain-stained window. A tiny strip of dark sky was visible at the top. She had selected this office because of its location in a separate wing at the Center, well removed from the Seers' meeting room.

"It's an enormous responsibility. But I think your unique talents make you an ideal candidate."

"Candidate for what?" Vic's eyebrows scrunched together.

"A special task."

"What's that supposed to mean?"

"You'll be... let's call it the *key* to the NEWRRTH's evolution. Honestly, it's a tremendous honor for you. And simple. You will enter a Game of our design. You will interact with a handful of players. Then you will exit the Game. That is all we ask of you."

"No."

"You don't have a choice." Vennor sank into a chair that felt cold through her back.

"I do have a choice. And I'm choosing not to do your dirty work."

"You will help us. Because you want the charges dropped, and your access to the Games restored."

Vic bristled. Vennor opened her Thread in front of him and scrolled through Vic's charges. A countdown clock appeared, like the one they had shown him before, ready to tick the minutes away until the Seers wiped him from the central Archive.

"Don't forget what we can do—legally and within the Principle of One—should we decide you are no longer cooperating with the Center for Future Guidance."

Vic shifted in his seat. "What other Designers are working with you on this special project?"

Vennor did not answer.

"You don't have any, do you? No Designer would help you with this. Because Designers know not to fuck with the NEWRRTH. We work with it, you see? We—"

"A Designer is, in fact, collaborating with us. I believe you know him. His name is Cas."

Surprise—or was it a glimmer of fear?—passed over Vic's face. "I see. Cas is talented."

Vennor stood and stretched her back. "So you'll prepare to enter our Game. Soon. I brought what you need." Vennor placed Vic's gamescreen on the small table between them.

A muscle in Vic's jaw twitched. "If I'm going to help you, I have one condition." He placed his hands on the table, eyes locked onto his gamescreen.

Vennor cocked an eyebrow. "You are not in a position to bargain with us."

"I know. I just—" He licked his lips. "I'll help you. But I'm asking for one thing. I think you'll agree it's not too much." His gaze shifted to Vennor. "I'd like to work with Cas. The two of us. We can make it happen. Whatever you're working on. We can make it better. Together."

Vennor consulted her Thread. The probabilities were favorable in a scenario where Vic and Cas designed the first

Game of the Lantern together. In fact, there was a stronger chance the Lantern would work if Vic collaborated on its release. His Design skills, in combination with the protection Cas developed, made it almost certain the Lantern would succeed.

"We'll grant you that." Vennor closed her calculations. "We'll restore your full access effective immediately." Standing, she straightened her jacket. "The Officers will bring you to Cas shortly. You'll await instructions." They were so close now. They had a perfect plan.

Turning, she left Vic in the little office and made her way back to the control room. Every minute counted.

There was one thing left to put into place.

SAFE ROOM__

Rayne

Rayne sat by her mother's pod all night long. The convalescent tent opened to a bed where Kai lay wrapped in insulated blankets. Tubes stretched from softly beeping machines, disappearing beneath the covers. Kai's face was serene, her heartbeat strong and regular.

"It's almost morning, Ma." Rayne picked up her mother's hand. It was warm. "I'm still here with you."

"I'm so sorry." Rayne's eyes stung. "I don't know what to believe right now. Is Freya's Path causing the anomaly? It's so hard—it's hard to wrap my head around this. I can't access the Orchard anymore. I should have tried harder to understand what you were telling me." She squeezed Kai's hand. "I'm listening now. I'm... I'm going to prove it to you." She took a deep breath. "I'm going to figure it all out."

She settled into her bedside chair when an incoming came

through. It had no signature. Warily, she accepted it. "Who is this?"

"Rayne. It's me." A shadowy aspect appeared in front of her. Her heart leapt. Was it—

As the face turned toward the light, she gasped. "Vic!"

"I don't have much time. Listen. I'm here with Cas. We've been working all night."

"Are you okay? We've been trying to find you for days. Cas is with you?" Rayne tapped her wrist, summoning Jesla.

"Cas? No, he's stepped out—"

"Where have you been? They must have revoked your Thread, we couldn't see you anywhere. Please tell Cas I'm sorry. I didn't have a chance when we were in the shelter together, he was upset with me—"

"Rayne. They're tracking me. I'm in a safe room for now, but they have protection protocols on my ass. You need to hear this."

"Got it." Rayne beat back her questions. "Go."

"The Seers are planning to release an upgrade. It's big," Vic said. "It's a mind-virus. Or something that behaves like a virus. Players are going to burn it straight into the Games. That's what Cas is helping them do. He's building a special Game just for this purpose." He glanced behind him, as if to reassure himself he was alone. "And they're using me to detonate this thing."

Vic tapped his palms on his chest. Rayne noticed each callus and crease on his broad fingers, the lean muscle in his forearms. The irises of his eyes were a watery green, reminding her of the ocean. "What do you mean? Detonate... what?"

"They're planting mind-virus code inside my living tissue. Once I enter this Game—I'm helping Cas design it, so I have some control over the parameters—whoever touches me will become infected with the virus. They're calling it an upgrade. But it's not. It's an infection that completely alters our bodies, our DNA. And they want to upgrade—infect—everyone in the Ark so that the anomaly won't be able to reach us—"

"An *infection?* What are they trying to do?" An image came to her then—something tall and shimmering, like a ghostly goddess made of smoke. "Is it true you've been in contact with..." She couldn't bring herself to finish the question.

"What? Listen. We cannot let this mind-virus out, you understand? We need to prevent this upgrade from releasing. It'll totally corrupt the NEWRRTH, bring it out of alignment with—well, it's not what they—just don't trust Cas right now. I know you two are close, but Cas is not on our side. Not now, anyway. Get the other Designers together. You'll need help. The Seers want us to join—"

He was gone.

"Vic. Vic!" There was no response.

She howled in frustration, then remembered where she was. "Sorry, Ma." Her mother hadn't stirred.

"You called?" Jesla poked her head through the door. "Is everything all right?" Her gaze slid to Kai.

"My mother's fine. It was Vic. He found a way to contact me."

Jesla gasped. "Vic? Was he—is he okay? How did he—"

"We need someplace to talk. And I need to work with the Thread. Let's ask H. Lynn if there's an unused room somewhere."

H. Lynn sent them to a storage space on the first floor. She promised to check on them later. With a last glance at her mother, Rayne took Jesla down the stairs.

The storage room wasn't hard to find. Tucked into the rear of the Haven, its double doors were dark. As they pushed inside, silvery light trickled through a bank of grimy windows and spattered soft shadows on the tiled floor. It smelled of old plastic. Piles of discarded equipment lay scattered around.

Perfect.

"Over here." Rayne guided Jesla to a wide ledge under the windows. They wove around a bank of outdated pods and scrapped monitors. "We can sit here." They hopped onto the cold metal, getting as comfortable as they could.

Jesla didn't take her eyes off Rayne. "Where is Vic? Is he okay?"

"There's not much I can tell you." Rayne blew the air out of her lungs, resetting her adrenaline. She looked around at the unused appliances, shadows everywhere. "He showed up on my incoming. Said Cas was helping the Seers build something. An upgrade."

"We already knew that, right?"

"Yes, but not the specifics. The Seers are planning some kind of mind-virus upgrade to the NEWRRTH. And they're using Vic to release it."

"What do you mean?"

"It's okay. We've got this. I asked him where he was. He said he was in a safe room."

"A what?"

"A safe room. It's a place Designers go to get in touch with other Designers. It's a holospace the NEWRRTH creates in basic operating mode that only exists in the moment you create it. It got cut off quickly after that. I'm sure they're tracing him."

Jesla shook her head. "I don't get it, Rayne. What are the Seers planning? And why does Vic have to be the one they use for it? It makes no sense."

Rayne put her head in her hands. "Could it have something to do with the Orchard? Maybe the Seers figured out how to tap into the Orchard so they can build... whatever they're building." She sparked her Thread and threw out a few search commands. It came up with nothing. No connection between the Seers and her mother's experiments.

What was she missing?

Jesla blinked. "But why so secretive? Wouldn't we all welcome an upgrade?"

"I don't think..." Rayne's voice strained. A massive upgrade. Disruptive anomaly. Vic under arrest for designing... something. "Maybe I'm wrong, but there's something going on with the NEWRRTH. Freya's Path could be disrupting something in there. If they still exist. I'm pretty sure it's connected to the anomaly. Whatever it is, it's threatening enough to the Seers that they want to release a new version of the NEWRRTH. And they want Cas and Vic to create a Game where they can make this upgrade and leave the anomaly behind."

Rayne's Thread churned, reflecting her tumultuous thoughts. "It's possible Vic was communicating with Freya's Path. You know those green lines we saw when we used Openshell? H. Lynn was right. It could have been Freya's Path interacting with him. The Seers must have found out, so they arrested him to make it legal to shut his Thread down, cut off his access to them."

Jesla turned to the windows. Streaks of grit obscured the view of the woods. At ground level, the frozen forest was ominous. "He won't get out of there, will he?"

"Honestly, Jesla... I don't know. I don't know what's going to happen to him. I should have trusted my instincts. I'm so sorry."

"It's not your fault."

"I have to reach out to the other Designers. We have to stop this—whatever they're calling this upgrade. This group... Freya's Path. I have a feeling there's something we need to know about. Something we should be listening for."

"What can I do?"

Rayne saw the worry in Jesla's eyes. "We need snacks. And water. Can you make a trip to the kitchens and bring back some supplies? I don't want anyone besides H. Lynn knowing where we are. And bring our bags, too."

Jesla nodded and scooted off the sill. "What are you going to do? This Freya's Path group sounds dangerous. Please don't get yourself arrested, too." She crossed the room and disappeared into the hallway.

Rayne sent a rapid-fire alert to all the Designers she knew and trusted.

Stop playtesting betas NOW.

NO going into unknown Games.

Be ready. More info coming at u

She retrieved the data stories she had asked her Thread to compile. The first one unspooled.

"It began with the introduction of expressive code," her Thread recited. "The ability to manipulate living code inside the NEWRRTH—"

"I don't need the history of the damn universe. Tell me what you found on the viral model. How could this mind-virus affect the Games? And the humans who play it?"

The Thread swirled for a moment. "Mind-virus activation has never been initiated in the NEWRRTH. There is no historical precedent. Data modeling predicts—" A complicated graph appeared. "—a nine-point-nine percent probability that humans will develop a mind-virus powerful enough to alter the state of the neural-machine connections..."

The Thread continued. Rayne shifted her gaze to her incoming alerts. Four of her closest Designer friends pinged her back.

Cha: Whats going on

Rook: You find the anomaly??

Mo: Where u been R2?

Briz: Lots of weird shit up here you all seeing this

Rayne paused the data stories. She set up a safe room and invited the Designers to join her. There was a lot of information to share. And they had to come up with some sort of plan.

If it wasn't already too late.

DELETED__

Rayne

RAYNE PACED the virtual safe room as she told the Designers everything she knew. It wasn't much. After she finished, they all began talking at once. Rook threw his arms wide and spun around, telling them to calm down. He was sure, he told them, they could design a Game that would lure the anomaly. Then they would trap it.

"What would we do with it then?" Briz said, hands on their hips. "And how do we escape arrest?"

Cha waved both of them off. "We don't need to interact with the anomaly. And we don't need to design a whole new Game. The Seers already have a beta."

"The Game Cas is working on." Mo's brow furrowed. "All we have to do is get in. Put a damper on the upgrade. Get out."

Rayne sighed. "It's not that simple. The Seers are using Vic to release the upgrade. Vic called it a mind-virus. Has anyone heard about that kind of program?"

They reflexively pressed their temples, but Rayne stopped them. "I already asked the Thread. It doesn't know anything useful."

Briz stood. "I do." The Designers turned. "A mind-virus is a piece of code that hooks into a person's genetic material inside a Game. I came across it when I was looking into old computer viruses." They all nodded, acknowledging Briz's obsession with historical coding practices. "It's the kind of thing that can mess with a person's biology inside a Game. It affects chromosomes in particular. The Seers are inserting a piece of code into Vic that can connect to someone else, infect another aspect in the Game. Except it's not just spread among aspects. It's changes people's DNA in real life, too."

Rayne's stomach churned. *Mind-virus activation. That's what the Seers wanted to hide.* Cas wouldn't know about that. If he did, he wouldn't be helping them. He was too sensitive to the well-being of others. If the Seers were planning to use it, they must have had a good reason. But what could that reason be?

"What's the point of changing people's DNA?" Mo asked. The chattering started again. Rook threw his hands up in frustration. "Come on, we need to focus!"

One by one, they came up with ideas and then shot them down. They went round and round about their options. Finally, Rayne suggested they take time to work with their own Threads. Grumbling, tired, they agreed to come back together after thirty minutes.

Exiting out of the safe room, Rayne felt the chill from the windowsill seep into her bottom and down her legs. *The heating really sucks in here.* As she pulled her hands close to her body, her wrist lit up. A call. *Already?* She sighed, gathering her thoughts. "Yeah." She pushed down her irritation and accepted the incoming. Two Designers stepped forward.

Rayne shot to her feet. "What is this?" She scrambled back, bumping against a bed on wheels, just catching herself from falling. The bed rolled away and crashed into something metal.

"Rayne." Vic's aspect reached out, as if to steady her. "We've come about something urgent."

"We're ready to begin the NEWRRTH's transformation." Cas had shadows under his eyes. "It's going to be beautiful. We're calling on all Designers to be part of the upgrade. We wanted you to be the first."

"Cas, listen, there's something you should—" Rayne sputtered. *Wait a second. They're both inviting me to join the upgrade?* Vic had warned her about this. Rayne struggled to take a breath. "I thought—I thought—"

"It's not important what you thought." Vic's gaze bore into her. "This is about your mother."

Her mother? "I don't know what you're talking about. And I won't be part of any upgrade. Or whatever else you're planning. No thanks." Rayne moved to end the call.

Vic raised his hand. "I know how to bring your mother's aspect to you."

Cas glared at Vic. "Don't lie to her. You can't promise that."

"It's true." Vic's eyes locked on Rayne's. "You join this Game, and you'll be able to talk to her. Ask her anything you'd like."

Rayne wanted to believe him.

"And," he continued, "you'll get the chance to join us, if you'd like."

She willed herself to look away from Vic's pleading expression. He didn't seem to be lying. Cas grunted in irritation.

"Why?" Rayne barely got the word out. "Why are you doing this?"

Vic had his answer ready. "Because we need your help. We need the help of every Designer."

"Because it's the right thing to do, Rayne." Cas pressed his palms together. "For once in your life, do the right thing. Protect the NEWRRTH with us. And if that isn't enough for you, do it for me." His eyes filled.

Rayne choked up. "I—Cas, you know I—"

"Sending you the Game summons now." Vic tapped a few commands into his Thread. "Please. Come."

Rayne decided. She would accept their Game summons. See for herself what this mind-virus upgrade was, and how she might work with it. After all, Vic and Cas would be there. They'd be just as vulnerable to the infection, wouldn't they?

The door to the storeroom banged open. "Vic!" It was Jesla. She ran with their bags slung over one shoulder along with a large tray of food. "Vic! Is that you? Are you okay?" She dropped the tray on a metal exam table, where it landed with a clang, and wove through the junk.

Vic's aspect smiled at her. "Jesla, it's good to see you. I've missed you. Yes, I'm fine. We're working on—"

"We're about to play a very important Game, Jesla." Cas's voice was clipped. "Do you mind giving Rayne some time?"

"Your mother, Vic, she's so worried about you."

Vic closed his eyes. "Tell Healor Lynn she'll be seeing me soon, okay?"

Jesla nodded. Her jaw worked, as if she couldn't choose her next words.

Rayne lifted her bag from Jesla's arm and felt around for her gamescreen. It wasn't there. She dumped the contents of the bag onto the floor. "Did you see my gamescreen?"

Jesla shook her head, still gazing at Vic's aspect. "I just grabbed the bags. Didn't go through anything."

Cas crossed his arms. "We're standing by."

Rayne panicked. "I don't have my gamescreen. It's not here."

Luci. That sodding bot had dumped their bags when they returned from the shelter. Rayne's gamescreen must have fallen somewhere inside her cottage. In her haste to leave yesterday, she didn't check to see she had packed it.

"You can use my gamescreen," Jesla said with a shrug.

"We don't share screens." Rayne lowered her head. A failure even before starting.

"It won't matter." Vic turned to Rayne. "Use her screen. You'll show up as Jesla's aspect in the Game, but you'll still be directing gameplay. You'll still be... you."

Designers never shared their gamescreens. It was poor form to show up in a Game as someone else's aspect. Was Vic trying to tell her something? Maybe he did have something to show her. "Okay. Jesla, are you sure you don't mind?"

"Not at all." Jesla pulled her gamescreen out of her bag and handed it over.

Before Rayne snapped it on, she tapped her wrist a few times and spoke a rapid message. She did her best to leave a trail so the other Designers would know how to follow her. Then she flipped through the notifications on Jesla's screen. She didn't see any new invites.

"Where's your summons?"

Vic pulled his screen on. "Sending it through to Jesla's screen now."

"There it is." Rayne felt her heart racing. She couldn't believe she was doing this. Was she ready? Maybe. She checked that her message had gone through to her friends. It had. For now, she'd play along with whatever Vic and Cas had in mind.

She swiped Jesla's screen.

"Rayne?" Cas's voice cracked. "Thank you."

A suffusion of warmth spread through her chest.

"Are you ready?" Vic asked.

SMOKE HUNG in a blue haze near the ceiling. The bar was dark, the windows curtained. A sign above the door said *Mighty Fine* in red neon. The smell of stale beer stung her nose, and she tasted it in the back of her throat.

"Get you another?" The grip of the bartender's hand was strong. Rayne wanted to pull away, but she couldn't. "We've got lots on tap." The bartender's eyes searched her face. Why did she seem familiar?

Rayne's aspect-body felt like lead, and she wasn't sure she could remain standing. She saw an empty pint glass in her hand, a lace dress that left her—Jesla's—knees bare, and dirty white hexagonal tiles beneath her feet.

"No, I think I'm meeting someone," she slurred. She slid the glass along the top of the bar.

A pink-haired woman in a white dress fell back in her chair and laughed, the drink in her hand tipping precariously. Red vinyl booths lined the walls. Pinball machines rattled and music blared. The song jarred her nerves, something about not needing education. On the tables, candles flickered inside thick red glass jars.

Bells jangled above the door. As it opened, Rayne glimpsed a vertical sheen of skyscrapers. A puff of putrid air told her it was a humid afternoon in a big city. If this was Cas's Game, it was Manhattan. Late 1980s.

"Rayne?" Cas appeared at her side. She steadied herself against the brass bumper.

Vic came up on the other side of her, placing a hand on her lower back. A jolt of electricity zipped down her legs. Vic's gaze raked Rayne up and down. "Weird that it's *you*." Rayne wasn't sure if he meant her or Jesla.

"Where are we?"

"Doesn't matter." Cas tapped his fingertips together. "We're here. Let's get started. You will not believe what we're about to experience. It's going to blow your mind."

"Hold up. Wait." Rayne struggled to get the words out. "Did you... the Seers... mess with me already? Why am I feeling... like this?"

Vic reached for her hands. "You're not used to being Jesla's aspect. It can be disorienting. We got you." He slid his arm around her waist. "Let's sit down." He guided her to a booth along the wall.

"Where's my mother? You said I could talk to her."

"We don't have time, Rayne. We are making history here!" Cas smacked his fist with his open palm. A few patrons glanced at him, then went back to their own conversations.

"Is this the new Game you designed? Where the upgrade gets released? Are we really doing this?" Rayne asked.

"This isn't the new Game," Cas said. "It's an antechamber. A waiting room." He smiled. "You're going to *love* this."

"Slow down, Cas. I think Rayne needs a minute." Vic deposited her on the vinyl bench. Cas scooched around to her other side. She slumped against Cas's shoulder. It felt comfortable to be near him. Like they were friends again.

Vic remained standing, but dipped his head so his eyes were even with Rayne's. "I told Rayne she could speak to Kai. I wasn't joking around. Wait here." He pushed his way through the tables to the back of the bar. They lost sight of him.

"Damn it! He's supposed to stay HERE!" Rayne winced and tried to lean away from Cas.

A man approached their booth. "This one giving you trouble?" He jerked his thumb at Cas.

"No, we're just talking. We're fine," Rayne said.

"Get out of here." Cas dismissed him with a wave.

"Hey, I know you," the man said, staring at Rayne. She

closed her eyes. She couldn't handle this. Not even in a Game. "You look like you could use some help."

"Go away," Rayne breathed.

He leaned in close to Rayne's ear. "You're not okay, are you?"

Rayne felt a hand on her neck. Her body went rigid. She opened her eyes and saw herself reaching forward, pushing the stranger's arm. "I'm fine. I'm just a little under the weather."

The man's other hand grabbed her chin and tilted her face upward. He put his face right next to hers. Those dark eyes. They reminded her of Enayat's.

"Get away," she breathed.

His fingers were on her neck, her cheek. His grip tightened. She turned her head and tried to bite him. Cas picked up the candle and tossed it. It bounced off the man's forehead, splashing hot wax down his neck. The man cried out in surprise. "You—you burned me, you little f—"

"You! Get ahold of yourself." The bartender appeared behind the man, and he grunted in surprise. Grabbing his wrist, the bartender hustled him toward the door and pushed him out into the languid sunshine, where he stumbled. The door slammed shut with a resounding jingle of the bells.

In a low voice, Cas said, "That wasn't supposed to happen." He slouched back onto the vinyl bench.

Rayne slumped beside him. "What the hell." She wiped her mouth with the back of her hand. The pinball machines chimed and whooped.

"I don't know what Vic is doing. He needs to get back here."

"He won't be able to reach my mother. She's in a coma. Did you know?" Rayne put her hands on the table. "Your seedy bar is a bit too authentic. I'm getting out of here."

"No! Wait. Listen—you can't."

"I've had enough. Cas, what were you thinking? This is not you. And this is definitely not for me."

"You haven't even seen... Please, I haven't even shown you—"

"Cas is right," the bartender said, sauntering back to their booth. "You can't leave."

Over the bartender's shoulder, Rayne spotted Vic making his way toward them from the back of the room. Next to him, Kai's face was luminous in the smoke-filled interior. She glanced around nervously, her gaze settling on Rayne.

"How is that possible?" Rayne whispered.

The bartender snorted, then broke into hysterical laughter. "Oh, it's possible. It's exactly how we arranged it." She reached for Rayne's arm.

Cas bolted out of the booth. "Not her!"

Rayne struggled to her feet. The bartender's palm closed over her wrist. That poufy mane of black hair, it was almost like—

Vennor.

A searing pain exploded in her forehead as Vennor-the-bartender squeezed her wrist. Tiny invisible claws descended the length of her spine, followed by a high-pitched whine that slammed through her head like a sledgehammer. Her skin drew tight over her bones. She felt shadows descend. There was an almost audible click as Jesla's aspect disengaged and crumpled to the tiled floor of the bar.

Rayne didn't have time to think. She hard exited the Game.

SOMETHING FOR YOU__

Rayne

RAYNE DROPPED TO HER KNEES. Her hands flew to her head, but the pain was gone. There was a dull ringing, like an echo. She slid Jesla's gamescreen off. Eyes wide, she took in the room. *Reality, reality. I'm here in the stale-smelling storage room. At the Haven.* Hazy light shafted through the windows behind her. She leaned on a nearby table and pulled herself to standing.

A bubble of nausea ricocheted through her intestines. Her Thread sent a pulse of something—oxytocin?—into her system. The sickness cleared. Searching for a place to sit, she saw something on the floor. It was a shoe. No, it was a leg. She felt a pang of panic that someone had followed her here from the Game bar. *That can't be possible.* But a lot of impossible things were happening in the Games.

She pushed a pod out of the way so she could move closer to the person on the floor. How long had she been in the

Game? It couldn't have been more than a few minutes. She inhaled when she saw Jesla's face. Eyes open. Fresh blood on the side of one cheek.

"Jesla." Rayne knelt beside her. She reached out to touch her arm. "Are you—"

She found her breath and ran to the front of the room. "Help!" she screamed, throwing open the doors. Before they whooshed closed again, she yelled again. "Someone help me!" Lurching back to where Jesla lay sprawled on the tile, she saw two empty bowls and a handful of chopped vegetables scattered across the floor. Rayne bent down and picked up the bowls, gathering spilled carrots and peppers into them with shaking hands. She put her fingertips on Jesla's shoulder. "Thread! Scan her!" She thought about calling upstairs for help but stopped. She didn't know who she could trust.

The doors swung open. Healor Lynn stood there, surveying the dim room.

"Healor Lynn. Over here! It's Jesla. She's—"

H. Lynn rushed over but stopped short when she saw the body on the floor.

"I found her here. I was..." Rayne's voice trailed off as she realized she didn't know what had happened.

H. Lynn kneeled down and placed two fingers on Jesla's neck.

"Is she..." Rayne asked.

The Healor gave a brisk shake of her head. "I'm calling a trauma pod. There may be something we can do, but..." She made a summons on her Thread and kept scanning Jesla's body with her hands.

Rayne's stomach dropped. The room spun. "What... happened?"

"Weren't you here with her?"

"What?" Rayne's voice cracked. "No! I was in a Game, and when I exited, I found her—"

Her breath caught. The searing pain in her head. The bartender touching her arm. Jesla's aspect collapsing afterwards.

Not the bartender. Vennor.

"Healor Lynn, I think something happened in the Game we were playing."

H. Lynn gave her a sharp look. "Rayne, you're in shock. Let your Thread take care of your rebalancing. We'll understand in time what happened. For now, let's get her up to trauma so we can run a full scan." The door bumped open again and a pod entered. Gently, it extended its arms and scooped Jesla into its interior.

"Wait," Rayne said. She tucked Jesla's gamescreen under a sensor in the pod. "Here. Take this. It might be useful." The pod closed and glided out.

H. Lynn stepped closer, concern in her eyes. "I know this is hard, but you need to concentrate. I'm going to do everything I can to help you today. A light healing sequence is going to help you focus. You'll need to be alert. Justice may want to interview you. You're going to tell them what happened. It's best if this comes from you first."

"But I don't know what happened." Rayne pushed off the wall, trying to regain a sense of balance. "She was just—gone."

"We'll talk about that later. Let's go upstairs. I'll show you where her pod is." H. Lynn took her elbow and led her away. "I was looking for you. Hax is here. He has something to give you. He said you weren't answering your incoming."

"I was in a Game. With Vic." She didn't know what else she was supposed to say.

H. Lynn's eyes widened. "Vic?" Several emotions rippled over her face. "How is he?"

"He's fine," Rayne responded. *That awful bar.* Why had Cas designed a place like that? The man who had come to their table and whispered in her ear. The pain exploding in her head. At least they had spared Jesla that.

"Vic isn't in danger."

The lie burned in her throat. Vic said he was the one the Seers had chosen to spread the mind-virus. There was no guarantee he would be safe in any Game. Yet he had brought her mother to talk with her. Her mother, who lay unconscious in the Haven.

Nothing added up.

"Oh, thank the gods." H. Lynn sighed with relief. "Did he say anything?"

Rayne nodded. "Yes, he said to tell you not to worry. He'll be back soon." H. Lynn was waiting for more information. "I think he's working on... something." Rayne stopped. She didn't know Vic's plans.

The main entrance of the Haven buzzed with pods arriving through the portals. Rayne felt lightheaded as the healing H. Lynn activated worked its way through her body.

"Here he is." H. Lynn walked with Rayne to the front of the Center. Hax stood just outside the glass doors, a gray duffel against his back. His skidder was in view behind him. He wore a plain red overcoat and work gloves. He caught Rayne's eye as he came through the doors.

"Rayne." He smiled, reaching out and taking her hand in his.

"Hax." A blast of cold air swept around their ankles. The doors swished closed behind him.

"I have something for you." He swung the duffel to the floor. It landed with a clunk. A faint sound came from inside. He unzipped it. "I believe this is yours."

Peering inside, Rayne murmured in surprise. Luci was

bundled in several scarves, melting snow pooling around its little body. Lifting its head it said, "Well, that was unpleasant."

Hax wrangled Luci to a standing position. The scarves fell away, dropping slush onto the floor. Luci clutched something in its single arm.

Rayne stared. "Luci, what happened? What are you doing here?"

"It's clean now." Luci pushed its arm toward Rayne. In Luci's outstretched pad was Rayne's gamescreen.

Rayne took it, eyes widening. "Luci. Did you travel overland by yourself? How did you manage that?"

"It's an intrepid little bot." Hax zipped the empty duffel closed. "Found it stuck in the snow. Would have made it all the way here, except for a snowslide."

Rayne stared at Hax in disbelief. "You knew Luci was looking for me?"

"I had no idea." Hax laughed. "But it sure explained everything. Good thing you're still here. I tried calling you, but you didn't answer. How's your mother doing?"

H. Lynn stepped forward. "She's still being treated. Thank you for bringing Kai here. Your transport saved her life."

Hax reddened and waved his hand in dismissal.

"Yes, thank you," Rayne squeezed her eyelids shut and struggled to compose herself.

"Can't say it was my pleasure, but I sure am glad Luci got here. It was pretty worked up about needing to get to you." He pressed the empty duffel to his chest and turned to leave. "Tell Jesla hello for me."

Rayne opened her mouth to say something. The words clogged in her throat. *Jesla is gone. Dead?*

H. Lynn put her hand on Rayne's shoulder and gave it a firm squeeze, steadying her. "We hope to see you again under better circumstances."

Hax tipped his chin to them both, then disappeared into the wintry afternoon.

"Dirty man." Luci picked up the damp scarves crumpled at its feet. "Took me in his filthy cab."

"Luci, follow us." H. Lynn took off toward the trauma bays. Rayne wobbled after her, feeling H. Lynn's healing take full effect. "Can we check on Jesla?"

H. Lynn called over her shoulder. "I'm getting messages about her scans now."

"Scans? Is she...?"

"I'm sorry, Rayne. We're doing scans on her body to determine the cause of death. It's not clear yet why she... Why this happened. But we'll know soon what caused this."

Luci held the damp scarves high in its single hand. Its treads spattered droplets as it rolled alongside Rayne.

"I think it had something to do with the Game I was in," Rayne said. "With Vic."

H. Lynn stopped. Rayne almost crashed into her. "That's impossible. No one—*no one*—can experience a life-threatening event inside a Game. Our Threads prevent it. You don't know what you're saying. So stop saying it."

Rayne's mind spun. Of course their Threads prevented death in a Game. But this was different. Jesla's death had been *deliberate*. She was sure of it. But who would do that? And why?

H. Lynn continued toward the trauma bay. "Why don't you go sit with your mother? I'm going to be here for a while."

Rayne felt herself sinking into the pleasant feeling of the healing. "Okay. Sure." As she turned to leave, H. Lynn grabbed her arm.

"If what you're saying is true," H. Lynn said in a low voice, "You're accusing someone of violating the Principle of One. Who could that be? The Seers? They're up to something, that much is clear. So I'm asking you. Please, please don't speak about what you think happened. They'll blame Vic."

Rayne shook her head. "They're not blaming Vic. They're using him for something else."

H. Lynn didn't seem to hear. "All I'm asking is to wait for Jesla's scans to clear. I need to be sure we can trace nothing to Vic or the Game he was in. You need to calm down and concentrate."

"I am calm! There's no way I'm forgetting what I saw inside that Game. What I felt."

"You don't have to forget." The Healor sighed. "Just wait. That's all I ask."

No way I'm waiting for anything. Jesla deserves more than that. She had died on someone's orders. Someone who was operating without consequences. The enormity of that fact made Rayne's head spin. The risk of the mind-virus was real. How many more people would die before they could stop this thing from spreading out of Vic?

She rolled her thumb across the gamescreen nestled in her palm. "I'll be in my mother's room. You can find me there."

NEW PLAN__

Rayne

RAYNE LEANED OVER HER MOTHER, grasping the bed rails for support. Her vision blurred. With tears or from H. Lynn's healing, Rayne didn't know. Machines sighed and beeped. Behind them, Luci settled into a Haven docking station, powering up a self-diagnostic. It would take at least an hour for it to assess and fix the damage from the overland journey.

Taking a deep breath, she climbed onto the empty cot beside Kai. Her whole body sagged. The inside of her head felt like a room full of sharp edges. She closed her eyes and let her gamescreen slide out of her hand.

She'd felt this kind of grief before.

Breathe. Breathe.

She remembered standing in the middle of her father's workshop, surrounded by his tools and half-finished projects, feeling like someone had turned her to stone. Everything was silent except for the keening of her own breath and the sound of her mother's sobs coming through the open doorway.

The ground had opened up beneath her feet. It was an accident, they said. *A malfunction of the equipment that the Thread hadn't expected. It couldn't have been prevented.*

Just like that, her father was gone.

It was as though she was falling and falling, but never hit bottom.

It was only later, after she and her mother had received their first grief healing, that she could summon a memory of her father. He always smelled of cold and salt. Leaning close to her, he comforted her when she felt lonely. He would recite the poem that always made her smile.

> Don't fear the wind
> Little one
> For there is a mouse
> Who is kind and friendly
> By your side, through the night
> And who, tomorrow morning, when you
>   wake up
> Will bring you a gift of sweet grass.

One day, about a month after her father's death, Rayne found Kai in the Orchard, as she often did in those days. Kai was grafting apple trees in the Fruitlands. Her hands moved mechanically, weaving the branches together with expertise born of years of practice. Rayne stood apart, watching her for a moment before she spoke.

"You haven't been home much."

Kai paused, her hands resting on the pile of twigs. Her eyes were glassy with exhaustion. "I've been focused on my work. I'm sorry if I've been ignoring you."

"It's not just me. You've been ignoring everyone."

Kai sighed and put down her supplies. She sat down on the ground, leaning against the trunk of the apple tree behind her. "I guess I feel like I have to prove something."

Rayne's jaw tightened. "You have to prove what? That you can be better than Dad?"

Kai shook her head. "No. That I can be better than what happened to him."

"What does that even mean?"

"I've been thinking a lot about the day he died. How it shouldn't have happened. I keep wondering why the Thread didn't tell him, didn't warn him. But it didn't. Now I feel like I have to do better. Like I should be able to make sure no one else gets hurt."

Rayne swallowed. "There's nothing you could have done."

A breeze rustled the leaves, making the branches creak and whisper.

"It's like they're trying to tell me something," Kai said, squinting at the fruit trees. "But I can't quite translate it."

Rayne took a step back. Not this again. "Maybe the trees are talking to you, Ma. But you're shutting yourself off from everyone else. From me. You're not the only one who misses him, you know." She turned and took off toward their cottage.

Breathe.

The room in the Haven was bright, the windows drawing sunlight to the edges of the room. She sat up, dizziness poking at her skull.

She stared at Kai. Her mother's skin was pale, her cheeks sunken. *Communing with green things.*

Rayne had an idea. "Engage Openshell."

"Warning. The application you're requesting has under-performed—"

"I said *open it.*" She rested her head in her hands while she waited, the sound of her mother's even breathing beside her. She was sure the bitter taste in her mouth came from H. Lynn's healing. She spat it out, wiping the back of her hand against her lips.

"Describe the target," the Thread said. "Openshell is booted and standing by."

"The target is—" Rayne hesitated. Recollecting. "The target's name is Entra. She's a member of a group called Freya's Path."

A tiny dusting of code, like snow on a window, materialized in front of her.

Rayne narrowed her eyes. "Define. What are we looking at?"

The code shifted away from her, then froze and disappeared, like an underwater creature blending into the seafloor. "Unable to define its parameters," her Thread said. "Recommend discontinuing application due to low data utility."

The filaments of code appeared again, blinking in and out of existence. Ghostly. "Not accepting your recommendation. Stay with the target." She raised her hands, gingerly cupping the air around the shimmering thing to see it better. "What are you? What are you trying to tell me?"

The code broke apart like a dandelion puff dispersing in the air. She leaned away from it. As if it had been waiting for her to sit back, it began pulsing again. Then the code rushed around her with more intentionality than before. It took on a darker color, almost like smoke. Just as suddenly as it started, it stopped moving.

The change in movement came with a sound: a soft ping like metal touching metal. An alert notification that came through her Thread.

With trembling fingers, she reached for her gamescreen.

Slipped it on. The Game summons was waiting for her. With a startled jerk, she pulled the screen off. *What's going on here?*

Her wrist lit up with an incoming. It was the Designers. She closed her eyes and swore under her breath. They didn't yet know what had happened to Jesla.

With a sigh, she pushed the gamescreen away from her on the cot. She swiped to accept the call. Rayne could barely bring herself to look at her friends as their virtual forms appeared before her. As she talked about the new plan, she watched their faces change from disbelief to horror to resigned determination.

Then fear.

THE SEERS GO IN__

Vennor

From the window of the dark-paneled boardroom, Vennor watched a turkey vulture circle above the forest. *A good omen.* Its great black body and ungraceful face were associated with death and other sinister ideas, but the vulture represented cleansing, rebirth, and renewal. And its role in the ecosystem was essential—without vultures, carcasses would rot and spread disease.

The vulture was a scavenger, feeding off the remains of the old to make way for the new. Exactly what they would do today. The old ways were no longer working. It was time for something new. Something better.

The turkey vulture was a perfect example of how something considered grotesque could be quite beautiful and necessary.

But first, they had to finish the preparation. Vennor turned from the window and faced the other Seers in the room.

"It's time," she said. "We've waited long enough."

The other Seers settled into their seats around the table.

They turned to Vennor as she spoke. "The Lantern is ready to be released."

There was a murmur of excitement. Vennor continued. "Cas and Vic have finished their Design. This Game is impenetrable to the anomaly. We will seed the Lantern in our players without interference."

Vennor lowered herself into the velvet-covered chair closest to the window. The girl's hard exit had destroyed the virtual antechamber Cas and Nilo created to shield the upgrade, but after further experimentation, they discovered it hadn't been necessary after all. The Lantern would be released directly into the new Game.

The vulture banked and circled again. She could make out each black feather at the tip of its wings as the bird floated skyward.

"Enayat, how will the Seed make the initial transmission?"

Enayat lifted his chin. "By touch. The Seed activates the Lantern code by coming into physical contact with another aspect. The Lantern will achieve infection of every player in the Game—" He checked his Thread. "—within seven minutes after it's released."

Turning to face him, Vennor smiled. "That's good. That's very good. We won't be in this Game for long. Nilo, what do we know about the design parameters?"

Nilo glanced up from the end of the table. "This Game is a turfer. Built for loads of aspects, lots of room for big action, but we'll only be fielding fifty or so. It's a neutral place. An unpopulated rainforest on a pre-industrialized island."

"Tell me about the speed of infection." She turned to Trueno. "What are the chances of causing any damage to the

NEWRRTH's data streams? Or to the people playing the Game?"

Trueno frowned. "The data will proliferate faster than we'd like. But we think the NEWRRTH can handle the influx. We have monitors on the players we've chosen."

The boardroom door opened. Vic entered, flanked by two Peace Officers. His face was drawn but determined as he walked to the head of the table and sat down.

Cas followed close behind, looking just as exhausted. But there was a fire in his eyes that hadn't been there before. He took his seat next to Vic and fixed his gaze on Vennor.

"Welcome," Vennor said from her comfortable chair. "We are all assembled, then."

A bot came in behind them and deposited a tray of tea on the table. Vennor poured a small cup of the steaming brew.

"Cas, report on the players you've recruited."

Cas folded his hands together. "We have twenty-nine players in this Game, recruited through the Task Force. We would have had more, but..." He glanced at Vic, who stared straight ahead.

"Our players are ready. Good." Vennor spoke a few commands into her Thread. Then she addressed the group. "Let's take a moment before we proceed." She took a sip of tea. "This is not the occasion we would have chosen to launch the Lantern, the most significant upgrade to the NEWRRTH's operating system since its inception. But we must remember our goals. Our purpose. We are championing freedom. We are standing up being who we want to be, creating our best lives, without limitation. This is our moment to secure that future."

She set down her cup and stood. "So let us go into this Game with courage, knowing that what we do here today will echo through the ages."

Dipping her head, she continued, "Thank you all for your

quick work. Because of your talents, we will eliminate the anomaly. Dispense with its interference in our Games, our Threads. And the NEWRRTH's upgrade will be underway. Trueno, are you ready?"

His gaze was level. "I'm ready."

"Bring up the Game, Nilo." Vennor lifted the gamescreen to her eyes, and the Seers followed suit. An Officer stepped forward and dropped two gamescreens on the table in front of the Designers. Vic and Cas grabbed them.

A golden glow filled the room as Nilo synched their devices to the Game. The screens flickered. "You should see the summons."

Cas adjusted his gamescreen over his eyes. "It's here."

"Once inside the Game, we will activate the Seed, the person carrying the Lantern." Vennor shifted to a more comfortable position. "Our players will touch the Seed. When a player touches the Seed, the Lantern code will pass into their aspect and begin passing to others."

She pushed the tray of tea away from her, taking a deep breath. "We tried to make the transmission as benign as possible, but... some will have stronger reactions than others. When enough players have picked up the Lantern, they will exit the Game. They can continue spreading it in other Games."

"A final warning," Vennor continued. "No matter what happens in this Game, remember the benefit we will see when the upgrade is completed. Keep that foremost in your mind. You are making history. Do not exit until we have completed our mission."

THE WHIR of insects swallowed her last words. Birds trilled in the surrounding rainforest. With her paddle, Vennor made a stroke in the water. Glancing back, she smiled at Trueno, who sat behind her in the canoe. Like all of them, he wore a long, white traveling tunic. Waves rippled from the wooden vessel as it glided forward. She closed her eyes for a moment. The humid air brushed against her cheeks and forehead.

"Our players will be on the woodland trail," Cas called to the group. "They should come from the other side of the river, through the field there." He pointed to the lush riverbank. A breeze stirred the greenery.

"A peaceful Game," Nilo sighed. "I like these." Vines wove through her sleek dark hair. Her voice carried across the water to the other canoes. "It's like a little piece of paradise."

"We didn't design it to be a respite," Enayat said. "We designed it to keep the anomaly out. We need to be on our guard."

"We are proceeding peacefully." Vennor rested her oar across the canoe's bow and unstuck a piece of fabric clinging to her skin. "We are the peaceful ones. We are staying true to the original intent of the NEWRRTH." She felt quite pleased with herself. Dipping her oar back in the river, she glanced at the boat next to hers and saw Ana smiling. She was pleased with that, too.

A small island in the river loomed ahead. "Steer your canoes to the island," Vennor called. The three canoes turned, as fluid as gossamer cloth in a wind, then glided to a sandy clearing. Cas and Nilo climbed out of one boat. Enayat and Ana from another. Each helped their partner to shore. Trueno threw his legs into the shallow water, reaching to help Vennor rise. With a wobbly step, she climbed out and walked onto the beach.

The first players appeared on the opposite bank. Three of them. They wore colorful loose pants and long-sleeved tops.

They waited as the Seers pulled their canoes up the beach, out of the water.

"Thank you for coming," Vennor called across the water to them. A breeze picked up.

"I'm Tamas," the short one said. Cas stepped forward in greeting, but Tamas didn't notice. "And this is my partner, Corin." Corin's long hair and muscular build reminded her of Trueno. The third player, a woman, raised her hand in a wave. "I'm Samira."

"You have answered the most important call to action in our lifetimes," Vennor said. She smoothed her tunic, which stuck to her skin in the heat. "For that, we are grateful. The world is grateful for your service today." She placed her hand on her heart. "Today, you will connect with a very special aspect. Once you have made contact, we will invite you to join us in a beautiful upgrade to the NEWRRTH."

Corin and Tamas elbowed each other. Tamas spoke up. "We tag the aspect, and that's it? That's all you ask of the Task Force?" Samira shot him a look.

"Yes." Vennor had to raise her voice above the wind, which made the trees sway along the ridge behind the players. "Do not underestimate the significance of this contact. You will activate a critical code. Without activation..." Vennor waved her hand. "All this, the Games, our NEWRRTH—could be gone."

More players arrived in the field behind them. They each wore the colorful tunic of the Task Force Cas had assembled. Vennor gestured to the Seers standing beside her. "We will not be playing with you on the path. It is important that we stay separate for now. We will be here, on this island, and act as guides for you in this Game. You will come to us if you encounter any... complications."

She turned to Ana. "Activate the Seed."

"I activated her when we arrived in the Game," Ana replied.

In the distance, a boom. It sounded like thunder. "What was that?"

"Nothing to worry about," Trueno said. "We only need a few minutes in this Game." He picked out a pair of binoculars from his pack. They fell from his grasp as a rumble vibrated through the ground. They heard several more resounding explosions.

Nilo lost her balance and fell to her knees. Mud splashed the front of her tunic.

"GO!" Vennor shouted to the players across the river. "Get to her now!" The players scattered into the bush.

"Damn it." Cas walked in a tight circle with his hands on his temples. "Damn it. Vic wanted us to be here when—"

"When what?" Vennor said. The wind gusted around them. "Where's Vic?"

The Seers and Cas turned around, confused. Vic was nowhere in sight.

With impatience, Vennor asked again. "Enayat, where's Vic? We need him! Now!"

"He's not here," Enayat said. "Get him!"

Ana flew into action. She emptied her pack and found what she was looking for. A shard of clear quartz. Cradling it, she glanced at Vennor, who gave a brief nod. A moment later, they heard a crackle of electricity, and a blue light raced up the crystal.

"What is that?" Cas pointed at the luminous stone.

Ana put her hand over the crystal, sheltering it with her body. "Quartz crystal fragment. It's a natural conductor."

"Conductor? Of what?" Cas said, approaching the object.

Nilo put her hand on his arm and drew him back.

The blue light grew brighter. "It connects us to the Thread.

While we're inside the Game. I'm trying to find Vic. But... it's chaotic right now. It's hard to make anything out." Ana muttered to herself as she peered into the shard. Then she looked up with a triumphant expression. "I've found him! He's in the Game, but he's not on this island."

"Where is he?" Enayat asked.

Ana frowned and shook her head. "I'm not sure. It's like he's in the middle of a storm or something. There's too much static to get a clear reading."

A dark smudge drifted in front of Vennor's face. A burnt feather? It landed on the front of her tunic. She focused on it, curious, then brushed it away. "Cas," she said. "Tell me how much time we have."

Cas sat down on the spongy dirt. "I don't know."

"Yes, you do. Trueno?"

Trueno turned away from the glowing crystal, his expression resigned. He stooped to pick up his binoculars and scanned the horizon. "Judging by the size and speed of the ash cloud, we have four or five hours until the last piece of the cone blows. The explosions will trigger tsunamis. I think we're out of flooding range." They glanced at the river. The water was still. "But that's only a guess."

The ash fell more thickly now. Vennor brushed at the flakes that fell on her forehead. *The gray snowfall in the rainforest. Palm trees whipping in the wind.* She had seen this Game before.

"Vic gave us a handful of hours before the volcano blows. More than enough time. But we won't delay." She glanced at Cas. "We are well familiar with the devastation to come."

TURFER__

Rayne

RAYNE TOOK a tentative step into the green-gold rainforest. Muggy heat clung to her skin. Water dripped from ferns overhead. A heavy, sweet scent wafted up through the ground. Her boots sank into the moss carpet as she moved ahead, deeper into the forest.

She wiped a sweaty palm on her tunic and took a breath. The humidity was suffocating. She squinted against the sunlight that came through the thick canopy of trees, but saw nothing except more jungle in every direction.

Another few steps forward. Brushing a vine away, she stopped in her tracks. Turning back around, she stared into the greenery, her breath heavy in her ears.

"Cas?" she called out.

No response. She took a step and then stopped again. "Cas?" Her voice was barely a whisper.

A figure stepped out from a dappled green tree trunk. "You came."

Rayne yelped, her hands flying to her chest. "Vic!" She pressed her palms to her lungs to calm her galloping heart. "You scared me."

She looked at him more closely. "Are you...? Is the mind-virus...?" He seemed different. Older. "Are you contagious?"

"No. They haven't released the upgrade yet. I've hidden in this Game. For now. But I don't know what will happen if you get too close."

Rayne took a step back. "And Cas?"

Vic didn't answer. The leaves around them were shaped like beards. Each leaf connected to its neighbor by inter-fingered hairs. When the leaves blew in the breeze, they appeared part of an unbroken carpet.

"And... my mother? Where's she?"

"Follow me." Vic turned toward a path Rayne hadn't noticed. She stepped behind him, keeping her distance.

The path was only a couple of hands wide. It ran alongside a muddy river. Cocoa trees and teak contorted over the river-banks like frozen bridges, or like bannisters long out of daily use. Bright white blossoms dotted the wall of green.

"Vic, you should know. About Jesla. She's... gone."

Vic paused, but did not look back. "Yes. I know."

"Vic, I'm—"

"I don't want to talk about it. She's... she was..." he started walking again. "We can't let this happen to anyone else." His voice was low and angry.

"That's why I'm here."

And to find out what my mother discovered about the NEWRRTH.

"Vic, what is this place? Have you been working with a

group called Freya's Path? They came up in some research we were doing—"

Vic turned around to face her. "There's no time to explain everything. But Freya's Path is... they've been trying to contact us. To warn us. About Vennor's upgrade. They said it'll destroy the NEWRRTH, disable it beyond recognition. They said it would cause..."

He turned and continued along the path.

"... the end of everything."

"Do you trust them?" Rayne kept pace.

Vic made a noise of disgust. "I trust no one. But they've never been wrong. What they predicted, it's all come true."

Birds, little streaks of light, were everywhere, beating their wings through the soupy heat, shattering the air with screeches. Rayne hurried to keep up with Vic. "But who are they?"

Vic shook his head. "They have some serious coding cred. They can make things happen inside a Game I've never seen before. It's like they're almost..."

Part of the NEWRRTH.

Rayne didn't know what to do with that information. She wasn't sure she believed it. Could humans become part of the technology they created? Were the people of Freya's Path still... human?

Rayne tried to get him to talk about it more as they walked, but he refused. She decided to take a different approach. "Vic, your mother is really concerned. She's at the Haven doing her best to keep your name from coming up in the investigation. She doesn't want you to be linked with Jesla's death."

Vic wiped his face with his palm. "There's an investigation. That's good. But my mother can't do much to protect me."

Rayne wondered if she should say something else. Something comforting, maybe? She felt a stab of fear that she would say the wrong thing, that Vic would retreat into his head and never surface again. That was stupid. He had the mind-virus now. He needed all the help he could get.

"We're here."

Rayne lifted her head. A wall of rock appeared out of the trees. A fracture wormed up from the bottom, disappearing into the leaves above. The crack in the stone was wide enough for a single person to pass through. Vic scrambled up a tangled slope at its base. With a glance at Rayne, he wriggled into the fissure and beckoned her to follow. She shuddered. What giant insects were hiding in there? As she hiked up the rise, she took a last look at the green-carpeted slopes below. A flash of color caught her eye. Somebody was moving down there.

There it was again, but in a different spot. She turned and squirmed through the crack as quickly as she could. "Vic! Somebody's following us!"

A light flared, illuminating the inside of the cave. A group of people stood in a perfect semi-circle, staring back at her. Rayne's breath quickened. "Who—who are you—"

She recognized a shining face framed with curly hair. Before Rayne could place her, Kai stepped forward. "Ma—" Rayne's voice left her. How had her mother gotten into this Game? And who were all these other aspects?

The pain exploded like a thousand needles in her skull. She fell to her knees, gasping.

"It's got her," she heard. The ground rocked and lurched. She felt herself being swept off her feet. Her arms and legs went slack, and her eyes rolled back into her head. She went rigid. The world went white.

THERE WAS A SOFTNESS UNDER HER. A bed? She was lying down. She opened her eyes. A woman stood over her. She appeared like how Rayne imagined Freya the goddess would.

Her long, brown hair was loose around her shoulders, and her face was beautiful and strong, the kind of face that could inspire loyalty and courage.

The woman smiled. She held up a vial of clear liquid. "Forgive me," she said.

Rayne tried to reach out to grab the vial, but she couldn't move. She tried to speak, to plead, but she could barely draw a breath.

The woman tipped the vial up. Rayne saw the fluid flow down into a glass funnel connected to a small bag. The bag was connected to a tube. The tube was connected to a line. The line was connected to a needle. The needle was connected to her arm. The woman turned away. "We're keeping her in a state of... well, call it suspended animation. Until we can be sure." She tucked the empty vial under something by the bed. "It's done."

Voices rose and fell. She recognized Vic's. "How long will it hold? We don't know how close they are."

"They're within range," said a woman with a gravelly voice. "She got hit pretty hard. But we should be able to hold them off."

"Will it—will she recover?"

There was no answer.

She lay there, groggy and weak, and listened to the cave's sounds: the drip of water, the sound of people talking and arguing, and her mother's voice. There was a man's voice, too, and he was singing.

> "Sailing, sailing, over the bounding main,
> Over the deep blue sea.
> The white clouds like sheep do keep,

Lamb of gods, to thee we flee—"

Rayne tried to open her eyes, but they were heavy. She was listening to a poem fragment, she was sure of it. Who else knew about her father's poems? And her random Game-poem generator? Cas. Only Cas. She wished she could see who was singing.

"We sail the ship of the sky,
Speed the sapphire sail.
Her keel is the lightning's way,
When winds give over, rain."

Rayne drifted off. She dreamed of a dark, unfriendly place. She was alone and afraid. Then a bright cloud appeared in the sky. Only it wasn't a cloud. It was all of them huddling together. The people of Freya's Path. They drifted toward her, became distinct shapes. Emerged from the fog. Encircled her. The face she almost recognized came into focus. A long arm reached toward her. She woke with a start.

The woman with the long brown hair bent over her. "Who are you?" Rayne wanted to ask. Her voice wouldn't come out.

"Shh." The woman lifted a finger to her lips. "I'm a friend." She put her hand over Rayne's head, as if to brush the hair from her forehead, then stopped herself. Her hand dropped to her side.

"You're in our care," the woman said. "There's been a— we've had a surprise. The group you call the Seers. Their package wasn't what we expected."

The woman continued, "We thought this package came with the one you call Vic. That he contained the... upgrade the Seers developed. We prepared for him. But this package, this upgrade. It's not inside Vic."

Rayne's eyes widened. *Vic's not carrying the mind-virus?*

"I don't want to alarm you, but please try to align your energy with our coding. This... upgrade... sent by the Seers. It altered your aspect. It's entwined with your DNA, your living genetic code. We are working on containing it. But we need you to help us. We need you to help us prevent an unfortunate release."

Rayne tensed. *The mind-virus. It's in me.*

Her mind reached back to the bar Cas had designed. She was Jesla's aspect then. That must have been when Vennor transferred the mind-virus to her. But why her?

She noticed a scattering of twinkling lights hovering just above her chest. They became brighter and more numerous as she concentrated on them.

"A visual representation of your coding." The woman half smiled and made the lights dance. "It helps us to see your aspect's design." The code shifted, glimmering. It was a beautiful thing, a work of art.

The woman waved her hand, and a tree appeared. It was the Oak from her cottage, and it looked just as it always did. Rayne concentrated on the gnarled trunk and realized that the tree was pulsing with light. She tried to relax, but her mind raced. After a few minutes, her tree began to change its shape and form. Its branches took on a new vibrancy, and she began to calm down. She breathed deeply again.

"That's right," the woman said. "That's good. Stay with your Oak." She got up to leave. Rayne tried to call out again. *Was the mind-virus contained?*

"It won't be long now," the woman said. Then she was gone.

CRYSTAL__

Vennor

Cas gazed at the eddying riverbank, shoulders slumped. Wispy flakes of ash blew across his back. "Why would Vic do this? Put us in the middle of a volcano eruption? He knows how important this Game is."

The air was heavy with a metallic scent that reminded Vennor of the battlefield. Pushing the memory away, she said, "He's a smart Designer, that's why. But misguided. He was a bit too eager to save the world. He forgot a very important thing."

"What's that?"

Vennor smiled. "Putting us here, in a Game he designed around the last explosions of what I'm assuming is Krakatoa in late nineteenth century Indonesia—one of the most catastrophic volcanic eruptions in history. He wants to give the anomaly time to dismantle the Seed. He wants to prevent the Lantern from launching."

She turned to Cas again. "Unfortunately for him, his plan won't work."

"Why not? What's stopping him?"

"We are, Cas. The Seers have always looked after the future of humanity." She placed a hand on her heart. "We protect the NEWRRTH at all costs. And that doesn't end now."

Another rumble in the distance. Embers fell from the sky in black flurries. A few paces away, Ana knelt as she worked with the crystal. Enayat and Nilo discussed options in low tones. Their cheeks and foreheads were streaked with gray where they had wiped them.

Leaving Cas, Vennor drew close to Trueno. She felt a cold sweat forming on her brow. "Trueno, I don't like this at all. We're too exposed—" Her words evaporated in a splash of heat. The distant sky became a ball of light. Over the tops of the trees appeared an enormous orange sun. It grew larger and larger. Dread zinged through her.

A towering wave of ash and soot and smoke and debris thundered toward them. The ground shuddered again. Ana, Enayat, and Nilo all ducked. Trueno shielded his face. The trees around them broke apart with deafening cracks. Vennor's legs shook. Heat spread over her skin, and she tasted smoke in her throat.

The sea of ash swirled around them. For a moment, she thought it might have turned her into ash, too. But she felt the ground underneath her. She heard branches snapping and falling. She could no longer see Trueno. He'd been standing right beside her. He'd been shouting at her.

The roaring stopped. And then the earth fell still. The sun had dimmed but was still there. The sky glowed an alarmingly brilliant dusk color. Layers of grit floated to the ground. The air smelled of fire and sulphur.

Vennor stood. The other Seers lay in the charred mud. Trueno picked himself up and brushed his tunic, smearing it.

Cas's mouth hung open as he gazed at the scorched ground. Ana gripped the crystal in both hands. She lay on her side, facing Vennor. "The water," she whispered. "Look."

"What?" Vennor said. She couldn't see beyond the cresting waves. "What's wrong?"

"Over there. It's a—someone's coming onto the island."

There was a splash. A figure rose out of the river and clambered onto the bank. Long umber hair streamed water over a sodden brown tunic with a bright red sash.

Cas scrambled to his feet. "Briz! Is that you?"

"Cas," Briz said, wiping their eyes and giving their hair a squeeze. River water flowed onto the ground. "We've come to help."

Cas shook his head. "Briz, what are you doing here? Is anyone else with you?"

"I believe the question is, what are *you* doing here?" Briz replied.

"Excuse me." Vennor's voice was sharp. Her fingers worked into fists. "Who are you? And how did you get here?" The Seers drew close around her. "I ask because we're rather busy, and it's important that we find out what's going on. Right now."

Briz walked toward them with squelching steps. "Aren't you going to introduce me to your friends?" Their voice sounded musical, with an accent Vennor couldn't place. Cas opened his mouth, then closed it. Briz squeezed the sleeve of their tunic and more river water spilled to the ground. "What a lovely place. What were you planning to do here?"

"I ask you again," Vennor said. "Who are you? There are rules about who can enter this Game." Trueno crossed his arms. Ana hugged the crystal. Enayat narrowed his eyes. Nilo stood on guard, glancing back toward the beach.

"Rules?" said Briz. They stopped about ten paces away. "There are rules for everything under the sun. I'm here to tell you about one of them." They put their hands on their hips, brown tunic clinging soggily to their body. "You're not allowed to delete anyone's aspect. Especially if it causes their death outside of the Game."

Trueno glanced at Vennor. "What does that mean?"

"Cas knows," Briz continued. "Don't you, Cas? You suspected it. She deleted an aspect. An aspect who dropped to the ground. Dead. In a Game. And in life, it turns out. In the bar. In your—what did you call it? Your *waiting room*."

Cas took a step back. "Briz, I had no idea she could do that. Jesla fell—she wasn't—I didn't know."

Vennor shouted, "Enough! Leave us now." Her voice cracked. "Believe me, you don't want to make us angry." She collected herself, and then continued. "We ask that you leave us to our task. Peacefully. You don't know what you're interfering with."

More splashing sounds behind them. Vennor spun as fast as she could, setting off a series of pangs in her lower back. "What—?"

Three more people emerged from the river. Their wet tunics, dark brown and belted with bright sashes, dripped onto the ashy mud. They stood in a line, spaced out along the shore. Waiting.

"Rook." Cas stepped toward the tallest of them. "I don't know how you found out about this. It's not safe. You shouldn't be here. Take Briz and get out of here."

Rook smiled as water streamed off his chin. He tossed his hair behind him, then worked to rearrange the wet strands into a plait, the blond locs snaking down his back. "Cas," he said. "Good to see you, friend."

"Mo." Cas turned to the person to Rook's left. "Mo, please.

All of you. Please, they have a—this isn't something for Designers to mess around with."

The Game Designer called Mo—who was rather baby-faced, Vennor thought—straightened. "We're not here to interfere." His voice was firm. "We're here for Rayne. And Vic. And for you, too, Cas, if you want to come with us."

Vennor pasted a smile onto her lips. "Designers." She elbowed her way free of the Seers. "You're too late. The upgrade has already started."

The three Designers exchanged glances. The one on the far left, a scrawny young woman with frizzy hair, faced Vennor. "We know."

A ripple of surprise ran through Vennor. They knew about the Lantern, then. What did they want?

Briz took one step closer to Vennor. "It's our Game, too." Holding a hand out to Ana, they said, "Give me the crystal."

No one moved. "I'm not giving it to you." Ana held their gaze.

"We know what that crystal is. It holds code—powerful code. Code that can create aspects, maybe even communicate outside of this Game. But it can also erase players. Quietly. Permanently." They took another step closer. "Tell me I'm wrong."

Ana dropped her gaze, cheeks flaming.

Briz continued, "You've made it your life's work to preserve the NEWRRTH. To protect life." They turned to Cas. "And so have we."

"Wait. You're saying that crystal can be used to delete a player?" Cas's eyes bulged in alarm.

Vennor would not let this ragged band of Designers tell her how to play this Game. "Don't be silly. All of us here are in complete agreement. There's no need to squabble." She smiled again, this time more genuinely. She estimated that the Task

Force players had touched the Seed minutes ago. The Lantern's infection was underway and coming back to them now. "So we can drop the heroism. You're all Designers, yes?" The four people who had emerged from the river nodded. "Then you understand. When a change needs to be made—whether it's adjusting Game design or keeping the NEWRRTH functioning at optimum capacity—"

A series of claps came out of the forest. A gust of wind brought clouds of smoke fluttering around their shoulders. All heads turned up to the sky. No balls of light. But the air seemed to thicken, like something was building underneath the heavens.

"You'll understand," Vennor continued. "When a change needs to be made, we do it with minimal disruption. Without threatening a single life or livelihood. That's why I designed this upgrade." She waved her hand in the air. "An upgrade that will happen with no suffering or hardship. Without making—"

"Our players," Enayat said. He pointed across the river. Tamas, Corin, and Samira stood on the far bank. Their bright clothes stood out against the gray-green field. Tamas clutched his side. Samira rested her hands on her knees, her chest heaving. Corin placed his palm on Tamas's shoulder. It was as though they had run very fast and were catching their breath.

"They've returned."

A COMPLEX PROCEDURE__

Rayne

RAYNE CONCENTRATED on her Oak for what seemed like hours. It pulsed and glowed. She tried to align herself with... whatever she was supposed to align herself with. The woman with the brown hair had said something about their coding. But what coding?

Where had Vic gone? And her mother?

After a while, her Oak blurred. She fought to keep her hands on the bark. She could no longer feel the rasp in her fingertips. The branches got fuzzy. The image dissolved. Her mind let go.

She found herself in a dark, frozen place. Wind whipped her hair. A figure stood nearby, silhouetted in the moonlight. They were on the shore of a great black lake, the water moving swiftly past. His long coat flapped. She opened her mouth and called to him. Called again, more urgently. He didn't turn around.

"He's not here."

The cave's stone ceiling hung above her, flickering in the dim light. Other aspects moved nearby, whispering. Her mother's face came into focus.

"Cas would help you if he could. But he's not with us." Kai leaned over Rayne, taking in the display of dancing lights. "These look different to me. Here!" she shouted. "Something's happening over here!"

Rayne's arms and legs throbbed. She couldn't move. Was something wrong with her lights? Her living code?

The brown-haired woman rushed over. "Let me see." She brushed Kai aside. Used her fingers to tap at Rayne's code. The lights scattered, then dipped in a wave. Frowning, she turned and called behind her. "It's advancing. We need to try something else."

Footsteps rang out as several aspects rushed to Rayne's side. A face loomed. The woman with amber eyes and curly hair. Rayne remembered where she had seen her before.

Entra. The leader of Freya's Path.

Entra narrowed her eyes and let loose a rapid stream of jargon Rayne didn't understand. Put her hands in different places through the shimmering code above Rayne.

"I'm so sorry, honey." Kai leaned over her again, eyes wide. "I should have been there for you." The others crowded her out.

Rayne wanted to tell her mother it was all right, there was no need to be sorry, but her tongue was too heavy. She struggled to move her muscles, but her body wouldn't respond. Her lips were dry.

I'm not afraid, she wanted to say. *I can take on this mind-virus and shut it down.*

"... how hard you've been trying," Kai was saying. "But how long can she keep from activating the virus?"

"We're not giving up." Entra's eyes glittered, and her hands flew as she manipulated the code. "But we should prepare ourselves. There's a chance that disabling the virus will interfere with her living code."

"I know my daughter," Kai said. "She will not give up fighting this thing. And neither will I."

"We've been coding with her living tissue for as long as we can," Entra murmured. "The virus isn't coming out. It's embedded too deeply."

"We can remove the virus, you understand," a second voice said. It sounded like the woman who had tended to Rayne. "But it's entwined with her living code, like a vine that has grown into the bark of a tree. To unravel it could kill her."

"Even attempting to unravel it could trigger a life-altering event," a man's voice said. He sounded agitated.

"That's why we need more time," Kai said, pleading. "And I'm going to give it to you."

The ground rumbled. Or was it a sound inside of Rayne's head? No, pieces of rock pinged from somewhere nearby. Her heart fluttered. The surface underneath her shuddered. The ceiling groaned.

Her mother appeared at her side. "Rayne, I'm here." She stopped short of touching Rayne but leaned over so her face was in Rayne's line of sight. "I don't know if you can hear me." The rumbling died away. Several large pieces of rock fell, followed by a cascade of pebbles. Rayne lay still. She longed to reach out and hug her mother. To take her by the hand and run.

"If you're still in there, I want you to know something."

Rayne tried to blink her eyes, move a finger, do anything to let her mother know she was listening. Her mother's expression didn't change. "I love you," Kai said. "I love you so much. And I know—" Her voice caught. "No matter what happens, we will do our best. I promise you that."

The blanket of lights over Rayne grew dazzling for a moment. *I love you, too.*

Entra paused to examine the code, eyes narrowed in concentration.

Kai stepped back, shoulders sagging. She moved into the shadows of the cave. Raised her arm, reaching for something high up. A light. She unhooked it from the wall, shined it this way and that. Rayne tried to take in what she was seeing. The walls of the cave glistened with moss and ferns and ivy, creeping plants covered in tiny green buds. It was like being in a green sanctuary. Her mother picked a spot and set down the lantern so that it cast long shadows on the ground. Pushed her hands deep into the plants, closing her eyes and tipping her head up, as if she were about to receive a blessing.

A great hum started, then stopped. Thunder bellowed outside the cave. It went on for too long. *An explosion? In the rainforest?* The light dimmed. Rayne smelled fire. She sensed the surrounding people again, working with her code. The tube was still in her arm. Fluid ran into it.

Kai wrung her hands, shook them out. Like she was warming up before a performance. She spread her fingers, palms facing down, and closed her eyes. The hum returned. Stronger. It rose and fell, became the buzz of an angry beehive. Soon it drowned out the roaring from outside.

"She's leaving us again," the man said. "Prepare an exit. We may have to remove her aspect."

The hum filled Rayne's chest cavity. It rang in her ears, vibrated her bones, pricking all the way to her fingertips—

"We can't open an exit now. It's too risky."

"Not an exit, then. A rip. What we did before, when—"

The hum became a roar. Rayne gasped for breath. She could hear the others' voices but could no longer understand them.

"... indexing to original documentation..."

"... register the viral coding..."

"... group it *this* way, you aren't..."

"... not compatible with..."

"... leave it in there! She can't..."

SILENCE FELL. She was back in the cold place, at the roiling lake. Ignoring the wind lashing her face, she rushed to the water. Searched for the figure she had seen before, standing alone on the shore. Where had Cas gone? She turned to her left and right but saw no one.

A jagged light flashed in the sky. Then, as if descending from the moon itself, a fog appeared. It crept over the stones and grass, moving swiftly toward her. She wrenched away from the water. Started running. The fog lapped at her back. Enveloped her. The ground, the air, everything became a misty white.

"Rayne!" Like a bell being struck, her head cleared. She stood in a sea of fog. The lake was gone. The bitter wind stilled. It was as if she had been transported into an empty Game. "Rayne!" There was nothing but a void of whiteness. Her heart pounded. She knew that voice.

"It worked." Vic gave a little laugh as he appeared out of the bright fog. Rayne looked at her hands. It was an old Designer trick. If you could see your hands in a Game, you were playing it. In real life, her gamescreen would obscure her sight.

Vic's mouth curled on one side. "You're still in the Game. Your hands are not really here, I assure you."

"Where is... here?" Rayne lowered her hands. Vic's eyes gleamed, his expression serious.

"We're in the living space of the virus. Or part of it, anyway." His gaze lowered. "I'm afraid I can't stay. It's not safe for me. And I can't hold the exit open much longer."

"The exit?" The aspects working on her in the cave had been talking about an exit to the Game. A rip. "You mean the rip? The rip that the... that Freya's Path created?"

"I knew you'd catch on. Yes, that's where we are. But it won't hold for long. It's a way to pause and try out new ideas. But it's only temporary. And I think it's a last resort. Entra— well, she's not optimistic about your chances. That's why you have to get to work."

"I'm still in the Game. I'm still fighting the virus. I can't access my Thread."

"Yes, yes." The fog swirled. "But you're not alone." Vic took her hands. His skin was warm and smooth. "Call up the code you need. There are no rules here. What we're inside of now, it's like a mirror. It'll reflect what needs to stay hidden, so we can code whatever we can conceive of."

He pulled her close, their hands entwining. She looked up at him as he said softly, "I thought you'd also like to know... I'm..."

Her skin heated, sending a flush to her cheeks.

"... your mother has done something extraordinary for us."

"Oh." She coughed. "You mean—"

"She's protecting us from the Seers and their players. It will hold them off for a while. But if her protection comes down, and someone touches you, the virus will activate. And you'll be—"

Rayne pulled her hands away, gathering herself. "I'll be the one who infects everyone else. But my mother doesn't know how to—" She stopped herself. The surprising discovery Kai made after all those experiments with her plants. How had she phrased it? She had pushed into the network of living green things. And *communicated* with them. Was she doing that now from inside the cave?

Vic's jaw set. "We'll talk about it later. Right now, I have to go."

A sense of urgency filled her. "Am I going to get out of here?"

"Of course you are." He opened his arms wide. "When you've disabled the virus and you're ready to leave the rip, just ask. That's all you have to do. Like I said, the people of Freya's Path are talented coders. They'll hear you. And they'll know what to do."

His body became translucent. Rayne reached out. "No…" Her fingers passed through his image. "Wait. Vic!" Like a flame winking out, he vanished.

Her heart stuttered, and she took a shallow breath. She was alone. Another breath, slower and deeper. She was trembling. A third inhale, and her body relaxed.

Call up the code you need.

The fog was oppressive, wreathing her in jagged tendrils of vapor. A shroud of white insulation. She could see nothing but the mist, no colors or shapes, no glint of metal or gleam of glass. It was silent.

There are no rules here.

Closing her eyes, wiggling her fingers, she pictured the patterns of her living code. Remembering how it twinkled, falling like rain under a lamp. Flickering. Silver. She sighed. Calm spread through her chest.

Keeping her eyes shut, she let herself see the mind-virus wrapped around her code. Tangling like the tentacles of a creature around its prey. Yes, she could see it now.

Her eyes opened. Something fluttered in the fog in front of her face. It was small, but it was enough. A row of bottles on a wall. The faint dinging of an arcade game.

She was coding. Without the Thread. She could Design from here, create frequencies that appeared in this blank space, with her mind.

The snippet of Game code she produced blinked once. Twice. Disappeared.

You are not alone.

She started again, with her eyes open this time. Her fingers tapped on her thigh, working out the sequences. The Game built itself before her. It was Cas's bar. She heard it. Caught hints of conversation and whistles from the pinball machine. A woman laughing.

Rayne focused. More pieces of the Game came alive. The ceiling fans spinning on a tilt. The smell of beer and fried food that made her stomach knot. A face appeared behind the bar. But she wouldn't look at it. She couldn't.

She took a tentative step onto the dingy white tile. *Mighty Fine* read the neon sign. This time, she wouldn't stay. Heading straight for the door, she pushed it open and walked into the sunshine. Blinked in the brightness. The air was stifling and heavy with the stink of traffic exhaust. Skyscrapers soared along the street like giant rows of teeth. A river of people streamed by, jostling her as they hurried past.

Then she heard it. Notes of a song wafting through the street noise. A saxophone, maybe. Pushing into the pedestrians, taking amused note of their late twentieth century attire, she turned into the alley behind the bar. It was dark and narrow. Shaded. Rayne waited for her eyes to adjust. Piles of garbage lined the brick walls and spilled onto the cracked pavement.

A figure stood in the shadows, grasping a horn, making the melody she heard from the street. There was something off about the music, but Rayne couldn't put her finger on what. The notes shifted, became a pulsing rhythm. The person noticed Rayne and lowered the instrument. "What is it you're looking for, sweet thing? You lost?"

Rayne didn't realize how far she had entered the alley. She drew close to the figure, then backed away. Its eyes. They were black holes, iced over and cold. *The virus.* She didn't know how she recognized it. But that's what it was. The person-virus cocked its head, approaching. It tossed the horn onto a pile of trash, sending cans and rotten vegetables tumbling. "Don't worry," it growled. "I'll take good care of you." There was something wrong about its voice.

Get ahold of the virus. Obliterate its code, then exit. That's all you need to do.

The virus ambled toward her, eyes rippling. Rayne took another step back, her voice caught in her throat. She turned to run, but her foot caught on a garbage bag. Her hands slapped the gravel, and she cried out. Rolling onto her back, she pushed herself up. Her palms were scraped and bleeding.

The virus lunged, its face full of fury. "Game's over, Rayne. Time to let go."

She flinched. But it wasn't coming for her. It sprung right past, heading out of the alley and into the street.

Rayne squeezed her eyes shut. *HELP. Come here and help me.* Would it work? Calling to her friends with her mind? Vic was right. She wasn't alone. She could sense the others. It might not have been as easy as placing a call, but it was enough. She willed them to come.

Her brave friends. She felt a rush of warmth as she saw their faces in her mind. They had risked everything to come here. To this Game. Not knowing what they would find, only wanting to help. She could trust them with her life.

She would ask them for one last favor. Before their Game ended for good.

THE DESIGNERS DISAPPEAR__

Vennor

VENNOR CHARGED to the edge of the beach, straight into the river. "What did you say?" When the water came up over her calves, she planted her feet in the muddy current. "Repeat yourselves!"

Trueno caught up to her and put a hand on her shoulder. "Vennor..."

"Don't touch me!" Trueno shot his hands in the air, surrendering, and backed away.

The three players stood on the other side of the river. Just a stone's throw away. They looked uncertain. Tamas lifted his chin. "I said, we weren't able to get to the Seed. We could see where the Seed was. Inside a cave?" He tried again. "They were inside a cave. With the Seed. But we couldn't—there was no way to..." He sketched a dome shape in the air. Tamas glanced at his companions. They shrugged.

"There was no way to what?" Vennor prompted.

"We couldn't get through it," Tamas finished. He dropped his hands and fiddled with his sleeve. "It kept us out. Like a barrier."

Tamas was telling the truth. But Vennor had never heard of a shield appearing in a Game. *The Settlers are behind this.* She would quash this effort without question. "You said you weren't able to approach. What about the others? The other players?"

"They ran off." Samira pointed into the forest. "They got spooked or something. We might have scared them." Her voice hardened. "They seemed very jumpy."

A gust of wind blew into Vennor's face. Ashes skittered across her cheeks and lodged in her eyelashes. "I'm jumpy, too." She let out a laugh that sounded more like a cackle. "I don't mean to scare you."

She waited for them to return her laugh, but they didn't make a sound. "It's been a long day for all of us." She gathered up her tunic, wet at the hem, and turned to face the Seers.

As she came out of the water, the sky shimmered. Two balls of light appeared, arching toward them. They passed over the top of the Seers and drifted among the trees on the island. She was about to shout a warning when a high-pitched, crackling sound came from the trees.

They turned toward the sound. A pillar of fire shot up from the forest. Tendrils of red and orange twisted in the air, climbing high above the canopy of leaves. The heat of the fire rushed toward them.

The Seed. They had to get to her. Now.

"The canoes!" Vennor cried. "Get to the canoes!" The Seers, Cas, and the four Designers all scrambled toward the beach.

"Spread out!" Enayat yelled, pointing to the boats they had pulled up the bank. "Three to a canoe!"

Vennor grabbed the first canoe and began sliding it into the water. Trueno pushed from the stern. "Cas!" Vennor called. The Designers were coming up behind him. "Over here! Get in this one!" Vennor pointed to her boat as it bobbed in the current. "Your friends will be fine! There are enough boats to hold all of us."

CAS HESITATED. Rook and Briz caught up with him. He took Rook by the arm. "Do you feel it?" he asked. "There's something calling to us. It's like an incoming, only..."

"Cas!" The current had taken Vennor's boat, and she struggled to keep it close to shore. Trueno knelt in the back, an oar in hand. "You'll have to jump on!" Ana, Nilo, and Enayat launched the second canoe and paddled away from the island.

Smoke rolled around their faces. Briz started coughing. "Yes," Briz said when they caught their breath. "Yes. I felt it. We all decided—" they glanced at the Designers standing with them. "We're going to answer it. We came here to help Rayne, and that's what we're going to do."

The heat became unbearable. The blaze raged through the trees.

"Go then," said Cas. "She needs you." He thrust the third canoe into the water. "But I'm staying with the Seers. There's more I can do with them." He gestured to the two canoes swirling away.

"I hope you can, my friend." Rook gave Cas a half hug. "We are One." To Briz, he said, "Let's do it."

VENNOR WRESTLED WITH HER OAR, splashing its flat end deep into the river and pulling hard. The canoe straightened.

"Pull!" Trueno pushed his oar into the water. They made a turn toward the beach, where Cas ran along the beach. She wouldn't leave him on this burning island. She needed him for what they would do next. She trained her gaze on him, trying to see past the smoke.

Another pull on the oar. When she lifted her head again, the smoke swirled upward, clearing her view. Cas struggled with the last canoe, angling it into the rising waves. The other Designers were nowhere in sight. Burning debris drifted from the sky. Vennor blinked to make sure. Cas was alone. She watched him push the canoe into the water and jump in. He put one end of his oar into the churning river and made a few strokes on each side.

"We have to keep going," Trueno called out from behind her. "Row!"

She put her oar into the water and pulled. They bobbed forward. "Trueno, where did the others go?" she yelled. "I don't see them." She looked over her shoulder again, but there was no sign of the Designers who had climbed onto their island only moments ago. She felt a chill as she watched the island burn.

"What others?" Trueno grunted as he rowed.

"Those Game Designers! They didn't get into the canoe with Cas. They disappeared."

"I'm sure they're fine."

"There's a sound." Vennor strained to hear it. "Like people screaming. Or are they shouting?"

"That's the fire. It's the trees burning."

"No." Vennor turned around in her seat. "It's something else."

Cas was still behind them, rowing hard to get his canoe moving. Waves lashed at the sides. Cas leaned over, took a deep pull on his paddle, and lost his balance. Gripping the sides of his canoe, he righted himself. But his oar swirled away in the murky water, leaving his boat bobbing in the whitecaps.

"We have to turn around!" Vennor paddled hard on her right side. Their canoe caught a current and drifted downriver. "Trueno, help me!"

Trueno fixed his gaze on the opposite shore. He rowed straight ahead. "We're saving ourselves, Vennor."

"What are you doing? We need to help Cas! He lost his oar!"

"He'll catch up. He'll swim if he has to."

The three Task Force players on the other side of the river had jogged downstream to where their canoe was about to land.

Trueno was right. They had to reach the other side. The Seed was the most important thing.

The island was ablaze behind them. Trees exploded as their sap boiled. Limbs crashed to the ground. Smoke rose like a thundercloud. She could no longer see Cas or his canoe.

They were just a few strokes from the shore. "Right in here!" Tamas shouted from a small clearing. "I got you!" The canoe scraped the river bottom. Vennor scrambled onto the muddy bank. Tamas stepped into the shallows, reaching to grab the canoe's bow. He and Trueno pulled it out of the water.

"They're here!" Tamas called to Corin and Samira, who were further up the shore with the other Seers. Tamas ran ahead to join them. Vennor dropped her oar onto the sand.

"Vennor." Trueno's face was unreadable. "I haven't seen that quartz crystal before. What have you programmed it to do?"

"We have to get to the Seed." She ducked and pushed past Trueno. He stopped her.

"What does the crystal do?"

She wanted to run toward the distant smoke. Instead, she turned to face Trueno. "It's a bit of extra insurance. That's all.

It doesn't matter now. The Seed must begin spreading the Lantern, and this crystal gives us the power to ensure that happens."

Trueno's jaw clenched. "We don't have the power to control anyone in this Game, unless—" He stopped. "No, Vennor. That's a breach of the One. You've gone too far."

"There's a task before us, and we need to get to it."

Seconds passed before he responded. "Violence is not an option," he whispered.

Swallowing hard, she raised her head and swept past him. She wished she could make him understand. How it was their duty to activate the Lantern. How they had no choice. Taking a deep breath, she picked up her pace.

Gods damn them all. She'd keep the NEWRRTH safe.

She'd delete everyone in this Game if she had to.

A REPLICATING VIRUS__

Rayne

RAYNE HEARD them before they materialized. They coughed
and whooped. Her heart soared when they emerged from the
fog. She saw Rook's long, plaited hair. Briz and their fierce
brown eyes. Cha and Mo, both looking nervous, followed
behind.

She wanted to hug them all.

"Rayne!" Rook roared. He lifted her in a crushing hug.

Rayne was glad her aspect could feel it.

"Rook!" When she regained her balance, she took them all
in. "You're here. I can't believe that worked. You heard me!"

"Of course we heard you," Cha said with a glint in her eyes.
"You aren't capable of being subtle."

"Not fair!" Rook fake-punched Cha on the arm. "She gets a
pass on being subtle. Hey, where are we?"

"No time to explain," Rayne pointed to the far end of the

alley. "We have to capture the virus. To stop the Seers' upgrade. It went that way."

The group set off at a sprint. The virus was ten yards ahead. It had come to a halt, its head cocked. It heard them coming. Then, with a mad laugh, it turned and ran out of the alley.

They chased it out onto the avenue. The virus bobbed around a line of traffic and disappeared. Rayne's friends slowed to a stop. Several lanes of vehicles moved past them, obscuring their view of the other side of the street.

"Where's Cas?" Rayne asked.

Stepping off the sidewalk, Briz said, "Cas isn't coming. Said he could work better on the outside. With the Seers."

Rayne swallowed her disappointment.

"There!" Mo shouted. He pointed to the virus on the other side of the street. They took off after it.

Rayne ran, desperate to keep up with her friends. They were faster than she was, even in their aspect forms. Rook was nimble as a cat, ducking and weaving between cars. Cha's arms pumped as she ran, her fists swinging at her sides. Briz was behind them, relaxed and calm, their eyes darting left and right. Mo lagged a bit, bumping into people and elbowing them out of his way.

They followed the virus into a park. Rayne was the last to hop the low fence by the sidewalk, her feet landing on clipped grass. The sound of the city retreated as they got further away from the street. She could see the sky again. Wide, open sky. The crowd was thinner here. Mo stood next to her, catching his breath. "What do we do when we catch it, Rayne?"

She paused. "I don't know." She wished Cas was here. He would know what to do.

Call up the code you need.

"Rayne?" Mo's voice was high-pitched with fear. "I don't know if we can get hurt here. But if we can, how do we stop this?" He squinted, still panting. "I've never beaten a mind-virus before."

Rayne turned to Mo. He was so transparent. And that made her smile. She was scared, too. "Don't worry, Mo. We're going to be okay. We make our own rules here." With a reluctant nod, he joined her as they jogged after their friends.

They caught up to Rook, Cha, and Briz next to a small pond. The water was smooth and dark, reflecting a hulking building that was the only other thing in the park. The virus skidded to a halt on the grass and turned to face them.

"You know you can't win this Game," it said. "You're too late."

"We're not here to win," Rook said. "We're here to stop you." He charged. The virus ducked out of the way. Before Rook could recover, it kicked him hard in the stomach. Rook went down.

"Rook!" Rayne called, but the virus was already on top of him. It had a blade out. Pressed it against Rook's neck, pinning him to the ground.

"What the fuck!" Rook shouted. He was on his back, and tried to throw the virus off, but it was stronger and moved faster than he did.

Rayne's vision became hazy. The virus drew the knife up, ready to plunge it into Rook's neck.

"Don't move," the virus barked. Turning to Rayne, it said, "You won't be able to save him."

She didn't have time to sort through the code. There was no way to stop it.

Cha and Briz were already in motion. They flew at the virus, ramming it with their own bodies. With a surprised grunt, it tumbled off Rook. The knife bounced onto the grass. The virus writhed underneath them until it twisted free and sprung to its feet. With a last look at Rayne, it dove into the pond.

Hearing the splash, her friends clambered to their feet.

Rook made ready to jump in.

"No!" Rayne stopped him. "Don't go after it. I will." Rook nodded, chest heaving.

"Stand back!" She made a rapid calculation, then launched herself into the water. The pond was shallow but dark, and she couldn't see anything in the murk. She swam, her hands out in front of her. She could feel the bottom, pegged with pebbles and mud. The virus was flailing. It was close by. She stretched out her hand, reaching for something to grab.

Her palm connected, and she felt a foot. Her fingers closed around an ankle. A lurch in her arm as the cords of its aspect joined to hers. She squeezed her fist and pulled. The virus thrashed, twisting under her grip. It was strong. Her eyes were open, and she could just make out the muddy bottom. There was no time to take a breath. She started the sequence.

The code kicked in. She turned and started swimming back to the shallows, dragging the virus beside her. It had stopped struggling. When her head cleared the surface, she took a long breath. Standing now, she pulled the virus behind her. It was still.

Her friends stood on the shore, ready.

She deposited the virus face up on the edge of the pond, its black eyes clouded and unmoving. They drew closer, circling the thing. Rayne released the last bit of code in the sequence. It pulsed into the virus, making it quiver and sending a shudder down her own spine. Then the body of the virus disintegrated.

"Holy shit," Mo said. "We just killed it."

"Rayne just killed it," Rook said.

"Did you see that?" Cha's eyes were round. "The virus just... dissolved."

"Well, that was exciting," Briz said, wiping a hand over their forehead. "We should do this again sometime."

"Wait." They turned to Rook. He was looking at the pond. "What is that?"

A ripple. A movement under the water. A shape rising. A head coming to the surface, moving swiftly away from them.

Then a figure emerged on the opposite bank, dripping. *It can't be, it's—*

"It's the virus!" Rook shouted.

There are no rules here.

"It's replicated itself!" Cha, Briz, and Rook took off after it.

Rayne stood frozen to the spot, her clothes sodden.

"I thought you were helping us!" she screamed into the sky.

Mo edged away. "Who was helping us?"

"The anomaly! Freya's Path!" She wiped the dripping water from her eyelashes. "They wanted to merge with the NEWRRTH so they could evolve with it. They can predict what's going to happen. They're the ones who met Vic in this Game. They're helping us destroy this virus. To protect our future."

Mo's eyebrows were up near his hairline. "What are you talking about?" He spoke softly. "Who's protecting the future?"

"Freya's Path. They're... I don't know who they are, but they might be inside the NEWRRTH. They want us to stop the mind-virus from activating." It sounded cracked as Rayne said it.

"So that's how the anomaly got in. They were already inside." He nodded to himself.

"They came to warn us."

Mo pulled away. The others were yelling across the park. "We have to go." He turned and loped across the grass.

She put her face in her hands, drained. *It's finished. There's nothing else I can do.*

"It's not over yet," a voice said. The sky was a radiant blue that stretched from one side of the horizon to the other. Rayne blinked. The smell of exhaust was gone. The echo of the city faded into silence. She stood in an ocean of wildflowers, sweet and ripe and vivid with life. A warm breeze rustled the flowers, carrying a sweet scent. No skyscrapers in sight. The sun shone hot and soft on her skin.

The brown-haired woman was there. The one who had stood over her in the cave.

"Who are you?" Rayne asked. "And where am I?" Was her aspect still lying inside the stone cavern? Was she a second aspect now? With an intensity that took her breath away, Rayne wanted to leave this place and go home. To curl up on her own bed. In her cottage. Have a spar with Luci. Remember Jesla. Play one of her Games—one that hadn't been destroyed by hard exiting.

"I'm Avalon," the woman said. "I don't believe I've introduced myself." The air was bright and clear. Rayne heard birds chirping. Squawking blue jays. Trilling cardinals.

Avalon guided Rayne to a large, warm boulder, and invited Rayne to sit on it. "Where—"

"I'll explain later," Avalon said. "Your friends are safe. They've been using their talents well."

"How do you know? Do you know everything that's happening? Or... going to happen?"

Avalon sighed. "We know certain things are likely to

happen. It's not much different from running probabilities on your Thread. Instead of using the Thread as a tool, we live with it much more deeply and completely. Only—"

"Only what?"

"It's more complicated than that. But I can tell you we didn't expect you. We didn't know you would harbor the code. Things might have played out differently if we had been able to plan for your arrival."

"Oh." It was all Rayne could think to say. "What do we do now?"

Avalon sat for a moment. The field glowed in a riot of color. "We agreed that we would never interfere. But our modeling predicted a catastrophe beyond what even we could handle. So, we took a vote. We honor free will here in the NEWRRTH. But we're giving ourselves every chance we've got to keep this going. To keep our world safe." She drew a breath. "You have a choice, Rayne." Her voice was soft and melodic the way it had been in the cave. "You always have a choice."

"What does that mean? Aren't I going to die? Or release the virus?"

"We're doing everything we can to avoid those outcomes." Avalon turned and smiled at her. "But we are up against powerful forces."

"You mean Vennor and her killing crystal?"

No answer.

"Enough of this cryptic shit!" Rayne blurted. "I'm trying my best to get out of here. But I don't know where *here* is. I don't know where my friends went, what Vic is doing, why Cas is working with the Seers, or what my mother is conjuring in that cave. My mother—her real self—is in a coma at the Haven. My friend is—is—dead, and all you can tell me is *I have a choice?*"

"Perhaps this will make it clear."

A butterfly flitted past, yellow as buttercups. Currents swirled under its wings. The air blurred together in waves, like heat swells rising from the ground. Then the waves solidified. As they watched, a shape revealed itself. Its outline shimmered in the sun.

Rayne didn't hesitate. She rose from the boulder and pushed the door open.

INSIDE THE CAVE__

Vennor

THE JUNGLE REEKED of mud and rot, and the sky churned with clouds. Vennor didn't know if they were thunderheads or ash plumes. Perhaps both. The oppressive heat burned her eyes and throat. "How much further?" She tried to keep her tone light.

Tamas, Corin, and Samira walked single file on the path ahead. "Not far," Tamas said. "The cave is on the next rise." All Vennor could see was a wall of leaves, and another wall behind that one, lime green and sword-shaped, undulating like grass skirts. Wisps of mist twisted around their ankles. Further away, smoke curled into the air. Her lungs felt raw.

She tried not to think of Cas in his boat, spinning in the current, oarless.

Ana and Nilo walked ahead. Trueno had held Enayat back after landing on the mainland. Vennor suspected Trueno wanted to tell Enayat about the crystal. Trueno was right to be horrified. It was astonishing. But necessary.

Enayat would understand. The Seers needed the power of the quartz to break through this wall. To reach the Seed. To activate her. Vennor would do it herself if she had to.

She hugged the crystal to her chest and continued on.

THE AREA around the cave was a chaotic mess. The grasses and mosses were trampled where members of the Task Force had scattered into the jungle. Small piles of ash smoldered. Lumpy strands of soot hung tangled in the vines. Tamas, Corin, and Samira hunkered near the base of a large tree.

Ana and Nilo had flattened themselves against a narrow crevice in the towering rock. Nilo shrieked into the darkness. "Come out! We know you're in there. Come to us now!"

"What are you doing?" Samira called. "We already tried that."

Nilo ignored her. "Come out! I want to see you. Show yourself!"

Enayat appeared out of the forest and was already on his way toward Nilo. His tunic, like all of theirs, was caked with mud and dust. "Nilo, come down from there!" He took her by the arm and guided her away.

Vennor approached the entrance to the cave. She held one hand in front of her, fingers splayed, like a person in the dark. Just before she touched the face of the rock, she felt it. An invisible, rubbery film. Surprised, she pulled her hand back. "Is this the shield you spoke of?"

"Yes." Tamas took a step toward her. "We tried pulling it, ramming it with a log, running through it. It won't let us in."

"We don't even know what it is," Corin said. He held onto

Tamas's arm. Whether to prevent Tamas from approaching Vennor or to steady himself, Vennor couldn't tell.

"How far does it extend?"

"Up and over the rock face. There's no way around it."

A gentle rumble echoed through the trees and a flash of lightning illuminated the gray sky.

"Trueno!" Vennor called. He was just emerging from the path and lifted his gaze when she called. "How long do we have until the final explosions?"

His mouth set. "The sun is barely visible through the ash. It's hard to tell the time. I'd say we have about an hour. Two hours, tops."

Plenty of time. They would touch the Seed. They could start the upgrade. The Lantern would spread to wherever their aspects—or their bodies—landed after this Game ended.

Vennor raised the crystal. Pointed it at the invisible shield. "This is your last chance," she called into the dark cave. "I do not want to cause violence. I act in the name of the NEWR-RTH. Choose peace. Let us in."

"The NEWRRTH requires no such thing," a woman said from inside the darkness. Her voice echoed. "The NEWRRTH never requires a sacrifice of life. You know that."

"You engage with me?" Vennor called. The Seers drew closer. A sudden gust of wind threw soot into their faces. Tamas, Corin, and Samira had inched closer to the cave entrance, but scrambled down the hill as a loud crack of thunder sounded.

The rain fell at once. Vennor threw her arm over her head and was immediately soaked through. The rock face offered little protection.

The wind threw great fistfuls of water into the faces of the surrounding hills. Vennor had never seen such a ferocious downpour. The hills seemed to thrash about like a magnificent animal writhing, its giant limbs reaching for the lowest plains and beating at the clouds for the smallest drop of comfort.

"You were the ones who felt it necessary to introduce violence," the woman said from inside the cave. Her voice was low, gravelly. She shouted to be heard above the din. "That was not the NEWRRTH. That was you."

"Let us in!" Vennor said again. She leaned into the invisible shield. "We're the only ones who can save the girl." Raindrops as big as a grown man's heart splattered upon the vegetation. Lightning flashed against the sky. Thunder cracked, reverberating across the tops of the trees and off distant mountains.

The shield did not give. Vennor steadied herself in the mud with her heels and leaned in harder. "Ana! Help me!" Ana scrambled closer. "I'm going to find a weakness. Help me interpret the data." Ana knelt and put her hands on the shield. Vennor touched the crystal to her cheek and pressed herself into the shield at the same time.

Data stories started flying by. *Oh, this is interesting. The trees.* Yes—Vennor watched, wide-eyed—as streams of data shot through the roots and soil. *The Thread is talking to the Earth.* She turned to Ana. "Are you seeing this?"

Ana, swallowing, nodded. "There's a—Thread. In the trees."

The Earth Thread pulsed wetly through the living green things all around them. The Threads from the trees and branches and leaves came together to form the shield they pressed against. This Earth Thread seemed to be connected to —or emanate from—inside the cave.

"What is this?" Ana shouted. "Have you seen anything like this before?"

Vennor shook her head. No, she had never seen this. But she had learned about the communication plants were capable of. Living trees could send all sorts of messages across vast distances. Still, she wasn't aware they could connect to humans. Or to the NEWRRTH.

The rain stopped as quickly as it had started. The wind died and for a moment the forest became still. Then the whir of insects and screeches of birds returned. Vennor stiffened when she heard shouts from the darkness inside the rock. She abruptly pulled the crystal back.

"—won't stand by while you are doing this to her. It's hurting her!" someone yelled.

"If you would just give us more time—"

"I *have* been giving you more time! I've been protecting you while you work. That's all I've been doing! I thought you were going to make it go away. But it's destroying her living cells. She can't survive this. What you're doing to her, it's killing her!"

"Kai, don't—"

"They can help her. The Seers. The ones who made her this way. The ones who made her into the Seed. They are the only ones who can save her—"

"They say that," a woman said with a throaty growl. "But see what violence they have already caused. They've already violated the One and—"

"I don't care anymore!" Kai said. "We have to save her. Don't you see that? Stop. *Stop this right now!*" There was sobbing. Men's voices. Shuffling and murmuring.

And then a person appeared at the entrance, a necklace of thorns at her nape, a gray braid down her back. Blinking, she raised her hand against the brightness. "Come," she said. "Come with me now." The woman's hand reached out to Vennor. Reached right through the shield. *Can it be as simple as this?* Vennor raised her arm, hesitating. *Does Kai control the Earth Thread?* Vennor took a step toward the woman and took her hand.

Vennor grinned and glanced back at Ana. "It's down," she

murmured. "We're going in." Ana beckoned the other Seers. Vennor caught a glance of Trueno's face, crumpled in anxiety.

"Please," the woman said. "Come with me now. She needs you." She pulled Vennor into the rock. Ana followed.

They were inside an enormous cavern. Lamps lined the cavern walls, casting flickering shadows along the uneven rock surfaces. Blankets of plants coated everything. They stepped on soft moss. The woman led them to a table where other aspects stood. Vials and instruments and a pile of tubing lay in a tangled heap. A young woman rested on the tabletop. Her eyes were shut, and she seemed to sleep. Her breathing was shallow.

"The Seed." Vennor felt a great weight lift from her body. This was going to work. It was going to be all right.

The woman—Kai, Vennor realized, Rayne's mother—turned to Vennor. "Please help her. Can you?"

Vennor pulled the quartz crystal out of her sleeve. It glowed blue and crackled.

She raised it and pointed it at Kai. "I'm sorry," she said. Kai blinked at Vennor as if she couldn't see her properly. "But I have to do this first."

LIVING CODE__

Rayne

She stepped through the door. An icy wind scrabbled at her face. Squinting, her eyes adjusted to the dimness. The light from the open passage behind her disappeared. The way back was blocked. She was in the cold, dark place.

The frozen ground crunched beneath her feet. Her eyes could just make out the outline of trees in the distance. The air tasted of rain. Goosebumps raced across her shoulders. She folded her arms across her chest.

She found herself at the top of a hill. The scent of manure and hay and pine drifted toward her. *A farm?* A house perched a little way down the hill, with a silo and—*there it was*—a barn. The fields rolled out beyond toward a dark horizon.

Then she saw him. He waited for her at the bottom of the hill. She recognized his lean form. His long coat. He stood with his back to the water. Only it wasn't a lake after all. It was a fast-moving river.

"Hello, Rayne," Cas called. His eyes shone in the dim light. "You came."

Rayne cleared her throat, trying to get the lump out. "So did you."

"You're cold." He took off his coat and draped it over her shoulders. It was warm and smelled of woodsmoke. "Better?"

"Yes." She huddled inside it.

"I'm sorry you had to come here," Cas said. "I'm sorry about everything."

"You don't have to say anything." She smiled at him. He smiled back and the lump in her throat disappeared. "I'm so glad to see you."

"I want you to know I made a"—his voice caught—"a mistake."

"But you didn't. You care about the NEWRRTH, you care about life, you wanted to do the right thing. And I tried to stop you. Joining the Task Force was—"

"I didn't listen to you. I should have."

"You followed your instincts. You can—you should—make up your own mind. I can't always be telling you what to do."

Cas leaned against the bridge. As dawn lightened the sky, the birdsong increased. It was the chorus of the world waking up.

She smiled. "I'll never give up on you."

"I'm sorry I let it happen." He stared into the water. She thought of Jesla lying on the floor, staring unblinking at the ceiling. "I'm so sorry."

"You didn't know what the Seers were planning."

"I knew. Part of it anyway. The upgrade. I designed that Game, Rayne."

"It's not your fault what happened to Jesla. Vennor did it."

"But I helped Vennor—"

"No!" She stepped closer to him. "No. You did what you thought was right."

"You can't solve every problem, Rayne."

"You can't, either."

The water gurgled as it cascaded over rocks. At the barn down the hill, a lantern swayed in the darkness. A woman's voice called out.

"Is that Goodwife Munroe?" The sun came over the hill, stealing away the last of the night. They watched the figure pacing between the barn and the house, stopping midway with the light held high. Listening for the British Regulars. Readying the scruffy band of early Americans for their Revolution.

Rayne swallowed. "It's my Game. How did you do this?"

"After your hard exit, I used the data stories. The ones we were working with in the shelter. It wasn't that hard to piece it back together again."

Rayne was about to say how grateful she was, but Cas turned away, distracted by a bright leaf floating down the river. It drifted closer until it caught in the reeds near Cas's feet. He knelt at the edge to grasp it. "I didn't know how hard this was going to be."

"How hard what was going to be?" She followed him onto the footbridge.

He didn't look back. "I need to go now."

"Where? Cas—"

"Here." Cas turned and shoved something into her hands. It was damp and soft. She gazed at it. A paper note. The one she had taken from her boot and released into the water. The poem fragment her Game-father had given her.

He watched her read it. "Are you going to cross the river now?"

"I don't know." She looked down at her boots. The sun glinted over the hill, spreading the first ray of golden light across the frozen field. She stepped back from the bridge. "I'm not finished here. I think I need to go back to the cave."

Cas smiled. When she looked up again, he was gone.

"PUT AWAY THAT INSTRUMENT." It was the woman with the gravelly voice. Rayne opened her eyes. She tried to move, but couldn't. She stared at the ceiling of the dark cavern.

"Do not interrupt the work of the Seers." It sounded like Vennor. "Step out of the way."

"Perhaps you misunderstood, Vennor. *Seer*." The last word was a sneer. "I am Entra. We are the people of Freya's Path. You won't be deleting anyone else. We'll see to that. Deron, prepare a rip."

There were scuffling sounds. Then a voice Rayne recognized. "Stop! All of you, stop." Rayne's breath caught.

"Cas!" Vennor cried. "They're trying to trick us. It's the Settlers, trying to make us believe they're Freya's Path. I knew you'd make it across the river. Help me."

"I *am* helping you, Vennor." Wet footsteps slapped across the stone. "Give it to me."

"You don't have to use the quartz. Go to the Seed, you can touch her—"

Grappling sounds. A gasp. Then shouting from all directions.

Cas appeared in front of Rayne's face. Wet hair plastered to his head. Drops of water flung onto her cheeks and nose. His soaked tunic clung to his chest. In one motion, he yanked out the tube in her arm and pushed the equipment off the table. With his other hand, he showed her a milky white object. Vennor's crystal. He pushed it close to her face. Rayne's eyes widened.

She struggled. Without the fluid dripping into her arm, her fingers tingled with returning feeling. Cas shook his head. "Stay still." He brought the crystal to his neck.

Oh, no. She reached for his hand at the same moment he reached for hers. As their fingers touched, Rayne felt a pulse from deep inside of her body. It ran through her arm, into her hand, and slammed into Cas.

It was the mind-virus leaving her. It slid right out of her palm and slithered up Cas's arm. Its bright trail of code lodged in his chest. Had they just released Vennor's upgrade? *Cas touched me. On purpose.*

Cas pressed the stone to his throat, gritting his teeth. Rayne wanted to scream, to lunge at him, to do anything that might stop him from whatever he was doing. He clasped her hand so tightly her bones creaked. He stared right into her eyes.

Rayne held his gaze. The bright tendrils of code that had danced above her chest started to fade. Something was flowing out of her. Black stars exploded in front of her eyes. Her jaw went slack. Her whole body sagged, wanting to be free of the cage keeping it in place. *If he doesn't stop, I'm going to die.*

Cas held her hand, shaking with the force of his grip.

She wobbled her head, so it faced his. What she saw in his eyes nearly stopped her heart. It was a look of loss. "We are One," he was saying. "We are One." It was the loss she had spent her whole life trying to fix. She had tried to guide him, but he always struggled to stand in his own power. To know himself. And he was about to sacrifice everything.

Her tongue was heavy and thick in the back of her mouth.

She tasted metal. She heard her mother cry out.

Her living code fluttered and went black. A deathly chill unfurled through her, yet she still saw Cas. His frail form leaned over her. Looking at her with love.

I know you're trying to save me. But don't you see? You've taken the virus and removed all of my living code along with it.

Even as her living code vanished, she didn't lose sight of him. Her thought processes flickered and failed, but she could still feel his presence. She let the darkness pool around her.

The second code transfer happened then.

Cas dropped to his knees. His eyes rolled back in his head. Still, he pressed the stone to his neck. She felt another pulse. This time, it jolted into her like a current. With a thrum of panic, Rayne widened her eyes.

A bright wave of living code pulsed from Cas's body toward hers. Then she understood. He wasn't taking her life to destroy the virus. He was taking her living code away with the virus bundled inside and replacing her living code with his own.

Cas strained as a trail of code released from his body. His own code. It collected in a rainbow spiral above her.

Don't do this. Please don't do this. She wanted to shout at him with her last shred of consciousness.

Vennor pushed forward. "Cas! What in the name of the NEWRRTH are you doing? Cas!"

As the last blazing fleck of code tunneled out of Cas's neck, it started spinning in a double helix above her chest. She saw him twist, and reach his arm behind his head, fingers squeezing the glowing crystal. With a lurch, he rocketed the crystal toward Vennor with ferocious speed. Vennor's mouth became an O.

Deleted. She's going to be deleted—

A tall man in a dirty tunic stepped in front of Vennor. The crystal crashed into his chest. He stumbled back, gripping the glowing quartz, and hit the ground hard.

Rayne saw blackness.

Her father's hand touched her face. "Rayne." His voice was

soft. She hadn't heard him say her name in so long. The rough-ness of his hand on her cheek, then the pads of his fingers against her forehead, pushing her hair out of her face. She turned her head to look up at him. He leaned over her, his smile warm. She reached for his hand.

"I'm so proud of you, Rayne." Her father's eyes glowed copper.

She blinked. Her father's face unfocused and disappeared.

She closed her eyes and let the darkness come.

Only it wasn't darkness. It was a tunnel, and she was moving through it. She could hear people talking, but couldn't tell if they were far or near. She heard her mother's deep, steady voice. "Stay with us, Rayne. Stay with us."

She opened her eyes. Everyone crowded around her. Her mother, Avalon, Entra, others she didn't recognize, all pushed close. Each had their hand on her. She felt the energy moving inside of her, swarming to get out.

She bolted upright. Jumped off the table. Stumbled to where Cas lay. His body was sprawled out on the floor, motion-less. Rayne collapsed beside him and patted his face. "Cas. Cas?" She grabbed his shoulders and gave him a shake. He didn't wake up. "No, no, no, no, no." The words came in a flood. "Why did you do that, Cas? Why did you do that?" Cas didn't respond. His eyes were open, their black pupils wide, and his mouth pulled back in a grimace. His wet hair made a damp halo around his head. "Cas? Cas."

She felt a hand on her back. "He saved you, Rayne. He saved us all." It was Vic. "He touched you and activated the mind-virus. It went into his own body. But before it could spread, he... deleted himself. And gave you all of his living code. He saved you."

"No." Rayne shook her head. "I didn't want him to do that."

"Rayne. Let him go." It was her mother. "We have to—"

"I can't." She felt something inside of her stir. What was it? She glanced down at her hands. They tingled. Her fingers pulsed with code. The living code that Cas had given her. *His own code.*

She heard the arguing voices all around her from a million miles away. Someone pulled her away from Cas. "We have to exit now." A voice in her ear. "Ready?"

There was another body. She saw it on the floor, near Cas. The large man. He wore a dirty tunic that had maybe once been white. Vennor knelt next to him, shrieking. Her hair was a thundercloud of black. "Trueno! Trueno, don't—I didn't mean for you to—you can't leave me! You can't go. Don't leave me, Trueno!"

Rayne watched Vennor's hands move over the man's body, over the quartz crystal lying in his hand, over his face. The roars of despair coming from Vennor's throat became distant, smaller. Rayne felt a rush of air swirl around her. The voices of the others had quieted to a hush. She let herself be pulled away from Cas. She took one more look at him and Vennor. "I'm sorry," she said. "I'm so sorry."

She sensed a pull from the center of her head, like someone unwinding her thoughts.

She exited the Game.

Vennor's scream followed her all the way.

RETURN__

Vennor

VENNOR SAT on the floor under the window of the conference room, bringing herself back to reality. Her knees ached. Her fingers were clenched stiff. Her back was on fire with pain. She swallowed once and willed herself to see what was in front of her.

Trueno's body lay in disarray. He rested on his side. His hair flopped over his face. His eyes were open, seeing nothing. She grabbed his hand, wanting to feel its reassuring warmth, but let it fall when she noticed how cold it was.

"Vennor, get up. Get up!" Rough hands hooked under her shoulders and pulled. She went limp. There was grunting and struggling. Her legs wouldn't work. The hands left her again. She fell beside him. She would stay here. Stay with him.

"She's having some sort of break," she heard Enayat say. "It's going to be a problem if we can't get her to come around."

There was a grunt. The rustle of clothing. Vennor closed

her eyes. She hoped they wouldn't try to make her stand again. She didn't think she could survive this.

She had never failed so spectacularly at doing her duty. She had failed the NEWRRTH. The Seed was destroyed in front of her eyes. The Lantern, too. The Lantern was supposed to restore order, to preserve the future of humanity. She had tried her best, but the Seed had let her down. And Cas. The Designers, too. All of them.

They had ruined everything.

"You're next," Vennor said. Her voice sounded dull. "Oh, you're next. You're next, Enayat." She felt a hard slap across her cheek. Her head rocked sideward.

"Focus. Damn it, focus!"

"There is no need for violence." Her skull felt like it was going to burst. Enayat loomed above her. His face contorted. His eyes were red-rimmed.

"He's dead," she muttered. "Trueno. Is dead." She placed her hand on her cheek. The friction of her fingers sent pain zinging through her skin. She longed for a dab of aloe, for the cool, wet sensation of its leafy interior.

"Vennor, please." Enayat crouched beside her. Took her by the shoulder. "They're coming. Justice is coming for us. They know. They're going to take us for questioning. You have to get up. Now."

"I don't care," she said. "I don't care. I don't care. I don't care." A futile, inane mantra of a woman who had failed. Failed at the one thing that mattered. "Let them come."

"Listen to me," Enayat said. He grabbed her by the collar. "You can still do this." His voice was shaking. "We can still do this. We can."

"No. No, I can't. I can't do this. We've lost."

"You have not lost. Cas is—"

"Cas is dead."

Enayat drew back. "Cas is not dead."

"Oh, he is. He is very much dead. In fact, he—" Vennor stopped. If Trueno's body was here, in the physical location from which he had played the Game, that meant Cas's body would be here too. With Vic. Rage flared in her chest. If she could get to Vic, she could detain him. Punish him for what he had done. It was enough to propel her to a standing position. "Vic. We need to find him."

When she stood, the activity in the room accelerated. There was a great deal of muttering and scurrying. Ana and Nilo huddled in a corner, snapping data stories out of an open Thread.

Enayat pushed aside the chair next to him. She took one step toward him. Two. She carefully skirted Trueno's body on the floor. Enayat seemed almost hopeful. "Come with me," he urged. "Come."

She glanced around the room. Some faces were unfamiliar. There were people wiping the walls and tables with small devices, nearly a dozen of them. "Who are they?"

Enayat glanced at the side door. "Scrubbers. We have to go. Now."

Vennor nodded, propelling herself toward the door. Enayat followed. But she stopped in the doorway. "Take his... body... to the garages." She couldn't look at it. At him. She thrust her hand in the direction of the conference room window. "Trueno. Wrap him. Bring him to Flay. Get him into a transport. Have it readied."

Enayat opened his mouth, then closed it. "Whatever you wish," he said. "I—"

A terrific crash from the corridor interrupted him. Vennor stepped out to see an immense glass panel at the end of the hallway had shattered. A figure stood silhouetted against its ragged edges. Vennor recognized Vic's mop of hair in the moonlight streaming through the broken glass. Vic cradled something large and awkward in his arms. A body. Cas's head lolled. Vic carefully hoisted Cas's limp form over his shoulder. Then he started running toward the window.

"Stop." Vennor said. "You! Stop!" Vic continued to run. She heard the sound of his feet on the floor, the panting of labored breath. She heard the hollow thud of Cas's head against Vic's back. "Enayat, stop them!" Enayat took a few halting steps. He spoke urgent words into his Thread.

With one last stumbling leap, Vic hurtled through the uneven opening and disappeared over the edge. There was a sickening silence. Vennor held her breath. They were on the second floor. He wouldn't have far to fall, but he was carrying a heavy load. She started to run after him. He would not get away. *He will not.* She would jump after him and wring his neck with her bare hands. She gained speed, nearing the jagged hole in the wall.

The lights in the corridor blinked once, then went out. Darkness. The ghostly outline of the broken window loomed in front of her. She skidded to a stop. Enayat was a dark shadow behind her. Vennor felt the rage leave her like the air out of a pricked balloon. The despair she had felt sitting next to Trueno's body came back in a rush. She groped for the wall.

"Why are the lights off?" Her voice sounded loud. She thought she could hear Enayat's breath behind her. She felt her way, slowly, carefully.

"They've cut our power. They're almost here. They might even be in the building—"

"Who?"

"I've been trying to tell you, Vennor. Justice knows what you've done. They've sent Peace Officers."

Voices spilled into the corridor. By the light of the moon, Vennor saw Ana and Nilo exit the conference room, followed by several disoriented Scrubbers. A cold wind rushed into the hall from the broken window.

"This way!" Enayat called. "Follow me!" He grabbed Vennor and half-pushed, half-pulled her along.

The corridor was long, and it ended with a flight of stairs. They went down, one blind step at a time. Vennor lost her orientation when the staircase ended. They had reached the bottom floor. It was only a matter of finding the entrance to the garages.

People jostled and cursed softly as they groped their way after her. "I can't see," someone whispered in her ear. "They've taken out the lights on the ground floor, too."

"I know," Vennor whispered back. "But the moon's full tonight. We'll be fine." She thought she could hear a low rumble outside. A crowd? Maybe.

"This way," she murmured, leading them on. She felt the warmth of Enayat's hand on her back. His touch reassured her.

She saw a faint light ahead. "There!" she said. "There!" The light was coming from the end of the corridor. A faint, yellowish pool of light, moving like a wave. "It's the garages! We're nearly there."

"I'm trying," Enayat said to someone behind them. "I'm going as quickly as I can."

"We'll make it in time." Vennor's words were clipped and urgent. "Get Flay," she told her Thread. "We need him ready with the transport. Maybe two transports." There was no answer. Where was he?

"Stop!" It was Ana. "Stop! All of you! Wait!"

"What?" Vennor spun in the direction of her voice. "We have to keep going—"

"It's a dead end. We have to go back."

Vennor stopped. She cocked her head. "It's a dead end," Ana repeated. "We have to go *this* way."

Vennor listened to the rustling of the people around her. "Quiet!" The Seers and Scrubbers froze. Faintly, from outside the building, there was another rumble. This time, Vennor felt a tremor shimmy up her ankles. It wasn't the sound of a crowd. It was the sound of a transport lumbering out of the garages.

The light at the end of the corridor wavered. It sputtered. Vennor saw the men's shadows before she heard them. They wore headlamps. The shadows of their sniffing dogs—at least four—twined around the men's legs, noses to the ground. They tumbled ahead and doubled back to their handlers.

Ana was right. They had reached the end of the corridor. Soon, the Peace Officers would round the corner. The Seers would be taken in. The only way out was the way they had come. Vennor felt her stomach heave. She pressed her forehead to the wall. She couldn't breathe.

"We're trapped," said Enayat. "What do we do?"

A volley of barking echoed in the dark. Huffing and yipping, the dogs rounded the corner. Vennor was close enough to hear the Peace Officers uttering encouragement as they closed the distance to their prizes.

"Find 'em, girl."

"Good job. Take us there."

"That's right, get it."

The animals' shadows grew large. There was only one thing to do. "This way," she hissed. "Hurry."

She pulled Enayat behind her and ran full tilt into the blackness.

VIOLATION__

Rayne

Coldness ran through her limbs, as if her blood was retreating. Pain sawed at her lungs. She felt certain she was dying. Or was already dead. And they were bringing her back.

"She's coming around," someone said. "Rayne, can you hear me?" She turned her head and instantly regretted it. Pain reverberated down her spine. She raised her hands. They weren't there. *I can't see my hands.* Heart pounding, she felt her eyes. Then nearly cried in relief. Her gamescreen covered them. She wasn't dead.

And she was out of the Game.

She removed the screen from her face. It dropped to her side. Blinking in the bright light, she saw a figure in a charcoal-colored jacket standing next to her.

"H. Lynn?"

"She's awake," a man said.

A gentle hand smoothed her hair, while another tucked a

blanket behind her shoulder. "There, there, hon. You're all right now," H. Lynn said. She tapped a few commands into the pod.

The pain receded. After a moment, Rayne tried to sit up. The world went fuzzy. H. Lynn put her hand on Rayne's shoulder. "Not yet," she whispered. "Lie back. You're still weak."

Rayne stuck her elbow beneath her back. Propped her head enough so she could see H. Lynn's face. "Who came out?" Her voice was raspy. She blinked several times to clear her vision. "Who came out of the Game?"

"We don't know. You're only just coming back," the man said. He was on the other side of her pod. "I found you coding out in here. The pod scooped you up, but you weren't responsive—"

"Healor Maddock, please return to your patients now," H. Lynn said to the man. "We can take it from here." H. Maddock nodded and left.

"Was Vic there?" H. Lynn smoothed Rayne's blanket. "In your Game? You've been playing for several hours. Your vitals —" She looked away. "I haven't been able to reach him."

"Several hours?" Rayne tried to clear her thoughts and remember what had happened. Something terrible enough that she nearly lost her life. Maybe that was why she felt like someone had scooped her guts out. "Yes. Vic was there. It was his Game." She focused on H. Lynn's face. "Cas was there, too." She took several deep breaths.

"It was Vic's Game?" H. Lynn narrowed her eyes. "How did he manage that? I thought the Seers disconnected his Thread."

"They did. But they reconnected it so he could help them. But it didn't go the way they planned." Her mouth felt like she had eaten a handful of sand.

Where was Vic now? And Cas? She retraced their movements in her mind. When they entered the Game, both Vic and Cas had been together at the Center for Future Guidance. With the Seers. That's where they would be now.

H. Lynn looked at her, waiting for more.

Cas. In the cave. *What happened?* She felt his hand gripping hers, as if life itself passed between them.

Was it possible? She consulted with her Thread. Yes, there was a possibility Cas had transferred the virus out of her body, and his living code into her body—

"I washed you." Luci placed a broom against the wall. "Looked like you had a fun sleep."

"Fun." Rayne stared at the wall, her mind working. "That's an interesting word."

"Filthy, dirty, disgusting. A bath would be good for you sometime." Luci rolled to its makeshift docking station. It backed in without being asked.

"I'll take that under advisement." Rayne struggled to push herself up. H. Lynn grasped her arm. "Steady."

The two of them got her to a sitting position. "Cas," Rayne said. "I need to find Cas."

"You're not in any condition to leave," H. Lynn said. "Your readings were all over the place. Healor Maddock says—well, your vitals stopped and restarted several times. You need to rest."

"I have to find Cas. He's with Vic." Rayne's voice was a little louder than she intended.

"Okay, okay. You don't have to yell. I'll get you some clothes. But you need to stay here until you've stabilized." She slipped into the hall.

Rayne looked down. Her wool suit was flattened and ripped. It would do. She swung her legs over the edge of her cot. Her head spun. When it cleared, she stood on wobbly legs.

A curtain blocked the view outside. She flung it aside. Winter sunshine streamed in. And there, positioned underneath the window, was another cot. A limp form lay covered to the chin in blankets.

Her mother. Rayne's knees buckled. She took a step, then two more, toward her mother's side. "Ma. Ma. Wake up!"

"I was hoping you could tell us more about her condition," H. Lynn said from the doorway. She dropped an armful of folded clothes on the end of Rayne's cot. "She hasn't regained consciousness. There's still no sign of neurotrauma." H. Lynn's expression was apologetic. "But we haven't been able to extract any meaningful diagnostic information from her pod." She walked over to Rayne. "You look like you could use a little help." She guided Rayne back to the side of her cot.

Rayne gazed at her mother's face. Kai's lips were colorless and her cheeks hollow. But her hair was clean, brushed and braided. "She's sleeping?"

"We don't think so," H. Lynn said. Her arm was around Rayne, helping her change clothes. "There's been a lot of damage to her reticular activating system. That's why she hasn't regained consciousness. But no sign of Thread deactivation. It's just..." She stopped. "We're hopeful she'll come back to us when she's ready. I'll leave you now." She gathered Rayne's dirty suit and tossed it into a basket in the hall. "You should rest. Send for a hot meal." Over her shoulder, she said, "I'll check back in a little while."

Rayne sat on the edge of her cot. Her mother's eyes were closed, but they moved under her eyelids. As if she were dreaming. Rayne reached over and touched her mother's hand. She felt the smallest of movements. Maybe just the beating of her mother's heart. She squeezed. "I love you, Ma. I wish I knew... I wish you'd wake up. I have so many questions. But I can't stay here with you. I have to find Cas. He did something really, really... stupid." Her breath hitched.

She bowed her head and squeezed her eyes shut. She wanted her mother to wake up now so Kai could explain how she had protected them in the Game-cave. Rayne wanted her mother to hold her when Rayne explained that she should have been the one to die, not Cas.

No. She wouldn't think of that. Not yet.

From the docking station, Luci said, "Your friend has been trying to contact you." The words gave Rayne a start. She had forgotten about Luci. "He wants to speak with you."

"Luci, you're not equipped to receive incomings—" She raised her head as someone walked into the room. The words died in her throat. "Vic." She struggled to her feet.

Vic came to her. He gripped her around the waist and helped her stand. She leaned against him, and his arms came around her in a hug. Jagged sobs tore through her. When they passed, he gently pushed her away and lifted her chin. There was a light in his eyes that hadn't been there before.

"Rayne." He tenderly disentangled himself. "Look at you." Shards of glass twinkled in his hair. "You came out of this in one piece. I'm glad."

Blood rushed to Rayne's cheeks. She dropped her head, unable to hold his gaze, wiped a string of snot from her nose. "What happened? Where's Cas?"

Vic sat on the edge of her cot. Bloody cuts crisscrossed his forearms. "Cas and I exited the Game at the Center for Future Guidance. I had to get out quickly. Flay brought us. We got into his skidder just as the Seers—the Peace Officers arrived and wanted to question them—"

"Wait. You *escaped* from the Center? Are the Seers after you now? How—" She sank to her cot beside him.

Vic pressed his hands together. "It's a lot. I know. But I had to get here to warn you."

"What do you mean 'I'? I thought Cas was with you?"

"Rayne. I am so sorry to have to tell you this." He rested his hands on his knees.

"No." She sucked in a mouthful of air. "No, don't say it. I don't want to hear it. Don't!" Rayne stood abruptly and stumbled to the doorway. She clapped her hands over her ears. "I don't want to hear that Cas is dead!" Her knees gave way, and she slid down the doorframe. Hot tears spilled down her cheeks.

Vic let her cry for a moment. Then he stood beside her. "Hey. You'll be okay. I know what you're feeling right now. It's... I lost someone, too."

"I know. I know you did. It's just... it's different, okay? It's different." She wiped her nose with the back of her sleeve. With her palms, she scrubbed the wetness from her eyes. "He was my best friend. I don't know how I'm going to live without him." The tears came again. She caught them with the inside of her elbow.

Luci powered up. "The filth of your face—"

Rayne cut it off. "I don't care!"

Vic glanced at the bot in the corner. "Rayne, we have to go. There are Peace Officers here, and they—"

"Peace Officers? Here?"

"There was a violation of the Principle. Vennor's crystal..."

"Yes, the crystal." Rayne steeled herself against the memory of Cas pressing the quartz to his neck. "But why are they here?"

"They're here for you."

Rayne's eyes widened.

"I told them you had nothing to do with the violation. I told them I could provide all the information they needed. That it was my volcano Game, and I alone designed it."

"You volunteered to speak with them? Why?"

"There's no need for you to offer any details."

H. Lynn's voice rang down the hall like a brisk gale. "Why would Vic have anything to do with a violation? Don't you see he's come here to—"

Several Officers burst into the room, their faces stern and unyielding. "No!" Rayne sprang to her feet. Some instinct made her spread her arms wide, shielding Vic behind her. "No, you don't need him. It's me you want—"

Vic shoved her out of the way. "You don't understand," he said under his breath. "You aren't getting it." The words stung. "You see," he addressed the Officers, "it was my volcano Game. It was my design. I was responsible for every single thing that happened—"

H. Lynn's jaw tensed. "Stop talking, Vic. You didn't do this. You didn't do anything wrong."

Vic squared his shoulders and faced the Officers. "I'm ready." One of them stepped forward.

"Excuse me." The Officer brushed past Vic and went to the window, straight to Kai's pod. The Officer put her hand on Kai's limp arm. She recited the Principle of One and gave the order for the arrest. Rayne heard her say "violation" several times, and "threat" and "new Earth Thread."

Two additional Officers positioned themselves at the head and foot of Kai's pod. They entered a few commands and a translucent shell closed over Kai's body. The pod began to roll toward the door.

Rayne watched the spectacle unfold, unable to blink.

"Is that really necessary?" H. Lynn reached for Vic, as if to steady herself. "She's not even conscious."

Rayne's fingertips brushed the pod as it rolled past. "You can't take her. She's my mother. Ma. Can you hear me? Ma!"

The Officer who recited the One pushed Rayne's hand

from the pod. "No contact until we approve her Thread for communication."

H. Lynn's eyes flashed. "She is under intensive medical care. This is an unacceptable intrusion into patient care—"

Kai's pod rolled out of the room. Vic's face was iced in shock. "Rayne, I'm sorry—"

Rayne shoved past him and out into the hall. The scene felt sickeningly familiar. Rayne remembered Jesla falling to her knees as the Officers pushed Vic down the tunnel of their storm shelter. Now they were taking her mother.

Kai's pod, escorted by the Peace Officers, retreated down the corridor. Rayne leaned against the wall to steady herself. She was shaking now. It was all she could do to keep from screaming.

So this is it. This is how I lose the rest of my family.

She stood in silence, watching the cylinder float down the hall until it disappeared from sight.

FUNERAL__

Rayne

THE SERVICE HAD GONE BETTER than she expected. There were tears, people said nice things, they lowered the baskets. Rayne kept it together by focusing on the surrounding trees.

Cas and Jesla had been loved. They had lived good lives.

But too short. They would be missed.

It had been two weeks since they exited the Game. Vic was still keeping his distance. He hadn't attended Rayne's debriefing session with the Designers and hadn't yet responded to her suggestion that they meet up to discuss the future of the Games. It was best to focus on her own healing right now, anyway. She couldn't spend all her energy worrying about what Vic was doing.

Vic had tried to catch her eye before the service, giving her a tentative wave. He stood in the front, flanked by a Healor who spoke often and loudly, and H. Lynn, who was silent and stone-faced.

Rayne hadn't met his gaze. He said he would be there for her, and he wasn't. He didn't appear to be concerned that Kai was still unconscious and under arrest, and Cas was dead. He didn't even seem to care that Jesla was gone. Vic had returned to his life, and she was still in a haze of grief.

Rayne was so tired. There was no energy to cry anymore. The skidder sat idle next to the two holes in the ground, raw gashes in the snow. From where she sat on the hill, Rayne stared down at them. It felt surreal. Her friends were gone.

A breeze carried hints of melting ice and dirt. Near her feet, blades of grass curled above a patch of snow. There wasn't much time before spring growth would replace the cold snow.

The cycles of life continued.

She pulled the familiar coat around her shoulders. It was big for her, but she would wear it always. It smelled of Cas. *What are you still doing here?* She imagined him saying. *It's freezing. Go inside. You can stop being the sad friend now.*

Birds flitted and sang in the trees. She logged each species into her Thread. "Female cardinal. Two blue jays. Red-bellied woodpecker." She wrapped her arms around her knees. She would stay for a while. She could picture Cas nodding along with each correct bird identification. Smiling.

An incoming trilled in her ear. "Dammit," she breathed.

With a sigh, she accepted. She couldn't put it off any longer.

"Rayne! We've been waiting for you." It was Mo. He was back at her cottage with the other Designers.

"Hi, Mo." She glimpsed Luci streaking past behind him, cleaning pad extended.

"I swear we haven't started the food yet," Mo said. Then, "Hey, stop it! I told her we hadn't started yet!"

Rook came into view. His mouth full, he said, "R-two, you

gotta taste this. Summer jam inside a sweet roll, and there's real butter—"

Mo shoved him aside. "There's a lot of food here. And it keeps coming. People haven't stopped bringing stuff over since the—" He snapped his mouth shut.

"You can say it. It's not a bad word." Two chickadees landed on a wobbly stalk next to her. When the breeze picked up, they took off, chittering. "Since the funeral. Two chickadees."

"Yeah, the... anyway, time to get back here."

Rayne stretched her legs on the damp log. One chickadee came back and landed on a twig in her line of sight, tilting its black-and-white head at her. "I want to log a few more bird sightings."

"Oh, look. It's a... hey!" Mo waved his arms. The chickadee flew off. Rayne spun around. The forest behind her was empty. "You just missed it."

"Missed what?"

A wheezing call cut through the air. Rayne dropped from the log in surprise. In the tree behind her, just above eye level, sat a fat, gray-furred rodent with a twitching, bushy tail. It clung with clawed fingers to a piece of fungus that grew on the bark.

"It's a gray squirrel!" Rayne said. "I saw one last year. I wasn't sure I'd ever see one again!"

The squirrel turned its black eyes upon them. Its belly convulsed as it made several high-pitched barks. Was it calling to someone? Did this squirrel have a mate nearby? Hope flared in Rayne's chest.

A crash from behind Mo startled them both. The squirrel jumped to a higher place on the trunk and scrambled out of view. "Well, it's gone now," Mo said. "Thanks, Rook! That moron tripped over the—oh boy, better go. Get here soon, all right?"

Luci practically fell over getting to whatever mess lay in wait. Mo clicked away.

Rayne took a last look at the thousands of branches swaying around her. Then she rose and stepped through the forest toward home, her eyes on the ground.

She wished her mother had been at the service today. She would have wanted to shovel the earth over Jesla and Cas. Sing the rites with family and friends. Cry with them.

***

"Hey." Vic was sitting on the front steps of her cottage. "I know you don't want to see me right now." He lifted his swollen eyes to hers. His hair was shorn to his scalp. Without the halo of black curls, his face was severe and angular. He looked like a stranger. "I just... I can't..." He rubbed his face. "I'm sorry."

Rayne sat next to him on the step. She looked down at her hands. "I don't think you are. Sorry. Not really."

"But I am. I don't know how to... I was..."

She turned to him. His eyes welled. "So tell me."

"Okay. I know I've been... not around for you. I just can't... every time I try to talk to you, I get so fucking sad. Like I can't breathe."

Rayne nodded. "Yeah. I know the feeling."

"I had this entire plan in my mind. I was going to be your friend. Help you through this. But when it came down to it, I couldn't." He brushed his hands across his scalp. "I'm sorry. I've been letting you do this all on your own."

Rayne said nothing. It was gratifying to hear his apology. He wasn't a total idiot.

Vic leaned on his elbows. "I guess I was... scared."

"Of what?"

He pointed to the edge of the forest. "That maybe all of this wasn't real." He turned to her. "Please. Don't be angry with me."

"I want you to understand something, too." Rayne leaned toward him. "About Jesla. When we were searching for you, Jesla never gave up. She cared for you, Vic. She loved you."

He looked away. She reached for his arm. "It's okay to miss her."

He turned to face her. His eyes searched hers. "It hurts so much."

Rayne slid her hand into his. She knew that people grieved in different ways. She had wrung herself out with emotion. Now, she couldn't think of anything but the way his fingers intertwined with hers. The wind blew her hair into her eyes. Vic brushed it away and tucked it behind her ear. Her heart beat wildly as he inched closer.

"I want them to come back," she whispered.

"Me too."

His eyes reflected the sky. There were tiny furrows around the corners. She didn't know what made her lean in and kiss him. But she did.

Their lips met, and the warm tingle in her mouth spread to her whole body. Vic's hand cupped her cheek, pulling her closer.

"Dirty. Filthy." Luci barreled out of the door holding a dripping mess of fabric.

Rayne jerked away from Vic, her cheeks burning. "Luci!"

Luci wheeled to a stop before it tripped over them. "Excuse me."

Vic shot to standing, shoving his hands into his pockets. "Sorry. I should be going."

"No!" Rayne said. "I mean, don't leave. Not yet. Come inside, have something to eat."

Luci picked its way around them, down the steps, and squeezed red juice out of the cloth. "Disgusting."

Vic hesitated, almost smiling. "All right. I'll come in. Just for a little while." He turned and held the door open for Rayne. Voices spilled out from the living room.

Rayne smiled back. "Go ahead. I'm going to help Luci. I'll just be a minute." With a dip of his chin, Vic stepped inside, the door closing behind him.

"Don't need your help."

"Okay, Luci. But sometimes it's nice to have company." Rayne sat back down on the top step. Lights from the living room painted shadows on the melting snow. She asked her Thread to pull up the poem from her Revolution Game. The one her Game-father had given her. The one Cas retrieved after rebuilding her Game.

The Thread recited it. As she listened, she wondered about the old poet who stopped to watch the woods fill up with snow and considered the distance he had yet to travel.

At the last stanza, she lowered her head and wept. It felt true in her bones, what the poet described. There were so many things she had to do. The Seers had been conducting sweeps of the NEWRRTH, but hadn't turned up any trace of the anomaly. It was like it had disappeared without a trace, and Freya's Path along with it. The Designers needed to rebuild the Games. She thought about the outbreak that was spreading through the Atlantic Ark. Whether she would get her mother back and cleared of all charges. Whether she would ever learn about the extraordinary connection her mother made to the living plants. How she would continue her life without Cas.

And Vic. She wondered if she could ever fix the mess she had just made with him.

Luci finished wringing the cloth and clambered up the stairs. Rayne helped it inside and closed the door.

Vennor

THEY TRAVELED FOR FOUR DAYS. The Peace Officers tracked her but hadn't caught up yet. Vennor would disable her own Thread once she got where she was going. They wouldn't follow her there, anyway.

Hax drove the skidder at night. It was best if they kept moving in the dark. Too many predators after sundown. During the day, they mounded snow into caves and slipped inside to sleep. Vennor dreamed of towering smoke-clouds, of trees on fire. In the afternoons, they ate cold bread and waited for darkness.

On the fifth evening, they climbed into the cab and settled in for the grinding ride. Vennor checked her Thread again. They would reach the Settlement tonight. Hax inspected the powertrain readings and handed her the last of the dried fruit. "Might as well finish it. I can restock once I get home."

Vennor accepted the cloth-wrapped package and tucked it

into her bag. It might be useful to keep for later. The engine shuddered, and the skidder lurched forward. Vennor peered ahead. She had to admit, Hax was doing a fine job of driving. He had forged a path through the white gloom of the snow-covered wildland.

For hours, the skidder glided over the ice. The only sounds were the crunch of the tires and the rasping of Hax's breath. Finally, they slowed. It surprised Vennor to find they were at the top of a hill. Pinpricks of light rose from the ridge ahead.

"That's the Settlement?" she said.

"Yup." Hax's voice sounded dry and labored. He brought the skidder to a halt. "Are you sure you want to do this?"

"I have no choice. If the Peace Officers find me..."

Hax grunted. "If you need to, you know how to get hold of me." Vennor nodded. "Flay still has some connections among the Settlers. He'll come by to check on you. If he—"

"It's okay, Hax. I know what I'm doing." It was all so diffi-cult. Hax had risked his life to help her escape, and to keep her secret safe. That was why she was here. Because of him.

"Thank you," she added. "I'm grateful for everything."

Hax scratched his nose. "You're welcome. Now go. Get moving."

Vennor smiled. "I will." With a trembling hand, she pressed her temple once, hard, and gave the order for her Thread to shut down. The price she had to pay for her freedom.

She stepped out into the frigid night. A gust of wind knocked her off balance.

"Here." Hax handed over her bag. "You've got extra snow gear in there. Make sure you wear it."

"Thank you," Vennor said again. She clutched the bag to her chest.

Hax nodded. He gave her a long look, then pulled the skidder around and drove away.

She watched the skidder fade into the night. Then there was only the sound of the wind. Her breath fogged under the moonlit branches.

She turned toward the lighted horizon. Sweat broke out along her back. The urge to run away was strong, but she forced herself to walk. She told herself she was doing what had to be done. That no matter how much she missed home, she had to keep going forward.

Picking her way over the icy terrain, she noted with dismay the twinge in her right knee. Gods, would her body betray her now? She was so close.

A loud *squinch* at her feet. Vennor stopped in her tracks. A quivering arrow stuck out of the snow. Startled, she glanced up. Where had it come from? The night was so dark—

Voices shouting. Then Vennor saw them. Four or five people, bundled in black, ran out of the woods from all directions. Their head-lanterns glinted in the dark. Three of them stopped short, knelt, and lifted wooden crossbows to their faces. One of them pulled a short arrow from behind and positioned it on top of the cross. She recognized their stances. They were taking aim.

They were going to hurt her. Her blood turned to ice.

A person appeared in front of her. A woman. Her eyes were hollow, as if she had stared too long into a fire.

"What do you want?" Vennor's fingers wouldn't stop shaking.

The woman held out her hand. "Your bag."

"You want... the bag?"

"Give it to me now."

"But that's my—"

The woman lunged. With one sweep, she struck Vennor across the face. The force knocked her to the ground. Vennor cried out, more in shock than pain. The bag tumbled from her grasp. The woman scooped it up and backed away. Vennor stared in disbelief.

Several others lined up behind the woman. The air seemed to grow thin. Vennor put her hands over her chest. She didn't want to die.

"We'll have to ask you to come with us." The woman gestured to the archers surrounding them. "Or meet your fate."

A man's voice cut through the night. "That's enough." He came up behind the woman. He was also wrapped head to toe in what appeared to be scraps of black wool.

The woman whipped around to face him. "That's not what we discussed—"

He placed a hand in front of her. "Stand down!" The three people holding bows tipped them down.

The man and woman stood facing each other. Thick scarves covered their faces, but their body language was clear. It was a standoff.

Vennor cleared her throat. "There's no need for violence." She raised her hands above her head, palms out, in a sign of peace. "I'll come with you."

The woman made a disgusted sounding noise. "You heard her." She beckoned to the others. "You'll pay for this," she said to the man. With a glower, she turned away.

The man watched the group trail after the woman, disappearing into the night. The woman's threat hung in the air.

"Don't worry about them." The man approached Vennor, gingerly lifted her bag, and held it out to her. "They thought they'd have more fun with you."

"Now," the man said when Vennor had tucked the bag back to her chest. "After all that, I think I deserve an explanation."

"What..."

"And don't skimp on the details. I want to hear all about

your time with the Seers. Everything you saw. What you learned. Is it true you can play any Game you want?"

He took her arm. Helped her get moving again. They walked together. Vennor recovered her voice. "There's... much to talk about."

"That's why I was so pleased to hear from you. We'll celebrate your return."

The man led her up a snow-covered path snaking through the trees. As they crested a hill, the towering spires of the Legacy Settlement appeared before them. It was a riot of lights. Despite her aching feet and her heavy heart, she smiled.

They descended. Passed through a boneyard of cracked steel and concrete, picking their way through the darkness, nodding to a sleepy guard when they reached a leaning shack. Vennor gaped. All around, the buildings were fissured and charred, as if a meteor had hit them. Some stood silent and empty, their lower stories exposed. Mirrored windows reflected a modern underworld.

It hadn't been this bad before. The storms have taken their toll.

Everything echoed in the winter darkness: the crackling of burning wood somewhere nearby, their breathing, the sound of her boots breaking through little puddles of ice.

The city had a low-key stench, a combination of spilled oil and rusting iron. She felt the bitter sting of metal dust in her mouth and nose. And something else. It was the tang of the sea.

It had been so long since she had seen this place.

When they reached a squat brick building, the man fished a card from inside his wrappings and waved it over a dented door. It unlocked with a clack. Inside, the darkness was almost complete. A single flickering lantern hung from the wall, lighting their way up a crumbling staircase.

At the top of the stairs, they pushed open a second door, its hinges protesting. A fire glowed in the room, burned down to coals. A threadbare rug stretched over as much of the pock-marked floor as it could. Vennor glimpsed a bunk tucked into a corner. The man turned to her, but made no move to reveal his face.

"Sister." He extended his hands, as if encompassing all that lay before them. "Welcome home."

THE STORY CONTINUES__

Yesterday, she was a savior. Today, she's an outcast.

Vic and Rayne face a fate worse than death. Can they outsmart the Seers and uncover what's left of the Arks—before it's too late?

Find out in **The One Exiled**, Book Two in the *Game of Paradise* series: Books2Read.com/TheOneExiled

Want more behind the scenes—and a free prequel?

Join my Reader's Club and get:

- The *Game of Paradise* prequel for free
- Behind-the-scenes extras
- A chance to be part of my early reader team

Join here:
www.JenniferLewy.com

PLEASE LEAVE A REVIEW__

Will you help? Reviews help readers discover this series. It doesn't have to be long—just a comment or rating goes a long way.

If you enjoyed the story, I'd be so grateful if you'd leave a quick rating or review on your favorite book platform.

Thank you!

ACKNOWLEDGMENTS_

My deepest gratitude for all the people who brought this book into reality with me:

- Christopher Downing, for early coaching and encouragement
- Heather Cox Richardson, whose daily Letters from an American inspired the premise of this story
- Christine Arylo and the Feminine Wisdom Way community
- Beth Osmer and the Spiritual Warrior sisters
- Boomer the bunny, his humans, and all the people who helped shape certain events in this story
- Steve Parolini, my editor
- The MetroWest Writers' Guild and the Littleton Critique Group for writing support and camaraderie
- My rock star beta reader team for making this book better
- My Book Squad for early reviews

- My friends and family, for always being there
- You, dear readers, for picking up this book and joining me on this journey

Jennifer Lewy writes stories about fierce characters, evolving AIs, and the fragile thread that connects us to each other—and to the Earth. Before becoming an author, she worked as a medical assistant, social worker, and voiceover artist, then launched her own healthcare writing business in 2005.

The idea for her young adult science fiction series came to her during the early days of the 2020 pandemic. *The One Game*, the first novel in the *Game of Paradise* series, was published in 2022, followed by *The One Exiled* and *The One Reborn*. The prequel, *When the Light Came*, is available free to newsletter subscribers.

Jennifer was born in the Northeast Kingdom of Vermont, grew up just outside New York City, and now lives in New England with her husband, two teens, and two very opinionated cats.

Join her Reader's Club for free extras, behind-the-scenes updates, and early access to new books:

www.JenniferLewy.com
@JenniferLewyAuthor

www.ingramcontent.com/pod-product-compliance
Lightning Source LLC
Chambersburg PA
CBHW071218210726
48293CB00002B/475